Into the Sky With You

The Ladies Alpine Society
Book 4

Edie Cay

Dragonblade Publishing, Inc. is an imprint of Kathryn Le Veque Novels, Inc.
P.O. Box 23
Moreno Valley, CA 92556
ceo@dragonbladepublishing.com

Produced in the United States of America

First Edition May 2025
Trade Paperback Edition

ARE YOU SIGNED UP FOR DRAGONBLADE'S BLOG?

You'll get the latest news and information on exclusive giveaways, exclusive excerpts, coming releases, sales, free books, cover reveals and more.

Check out our complete list of authors, too!

No spam, no junk. That's a promise!

Sign Up Here

www.dragonbladepublishing.com

Dearest Reader;

Thank you for your support of a small press. At Dragonblade Publishing, we strive to bring you the highest quality Historical Romance from some of the best authors in the business. Without your support, there is no 'us', so we sincerely hope you adore these stories and find some new favorite authors along the way.

Happy Reading!

CEO, Dragonblade Publishing

Additional Dragonblade books by Author Edie Cay

The Ladies Alpine Society
In Knots Over You (Book 1)
In the Money With You (Book 2)
Into the Breach With You (Book 3)
Into the Sky With You (Book 4)

Chapter One

London, 1871

"SIR JULIAN DUNSTAN?" a man called out in the cold downpour.

Julian startled at the honorific. Even at hearing his entire proper name. He'd been *Julio* to the miners, *El Cabro* and sometimes its variations to the men he smuggled for across the Serra do Mar, the Mantiqueiras, and the Andes. For a decade, he'd crawled across the South American continent, nothing more than a sunburnt goat in a hat to the people he came across. And here was a man giving him a "sir" as if he were more than the dirt-slinging low life he knew himself to be.

And yet, to be in cold, bitter, dear-God-what-is-that-smell London was good. He couldn't wait to show his maps to Rascomb, the only man in existence who would share his pure joy at a compiled topographical map. Well, the fellows at the Royal Geography Society would also be curious to see it, but he didn't think they would appreciate that Julian took the data and collated it himself. He sent his numbers and calculations back in dispatches, as he was obligated to do, but it was Rascomb who told him to draw the map himself. Only he could verify if the measurements and math were correct in the end.

Julian waved at the porter who'd called his name, taking his time on the slippery gangplank. His maps were safely tucked in the long cylindrical case on his back. He'd replaced the strap a number of times, but he'd carried it thousands of miles just as he did now, slung over his shoulder.

The woman in front of him slipped, and he caught her elbow as she over-corrected.

"Thank you, kind sir," she said, looking back at him with foggy blue eyes.

Cataracts, he thought immediately, as the shock of hearing English spoken so freely hit him. Still, he smiled broadly at her, wondering how much of his face she could make out. How much of the dark, disorganized stubble across his face looked a proper beard. "My pleasure, madame."

Her elderly husband took that long to twist his own body around and see the predicament. "Strong young men means a strong country!"

Julian smiled at the compliment and tipped his hat, a gesture he barely remembered to make. He was practically feral. He knew he smelled, so he hoped whatever odor he added to the fumes of the Thames would be not accredited to him.

If he wasn't covered in dirt, he couldn't find it in himself to bathe. It was a waste of time that could be spent on compiling more of his data, more maps, finer details. Since he was only stopping in to see Rascomb, he wouldn't bother cleaning up. The man would understand.

Pushing through the crowd of disembarked passengers, Julian made his way to the porter. Even staking his claim of space near the luggage, the crowd still surged and pushed into him. This would be something else to get used to again.

He arranged for his trunks to be sent to the rooms he had leased via correspondence, and set off in the general direction of the Rascomb townhouse. He knew the address after a decade of regular dispatches, but London felt changed and overflowing with people.

The traffic was obscene. Some of the main thoroughfares seemed an ocean of all manner of vehicles: broughams, hansom cabs, omnibuses, and wagons. Pedestrians streamed by on both sides of the street, ignoring the rain, their faces snugged down in their mufflers and hats.

Julian was proud he only got turned around once, but it did take him quite out of the way. Fortunately, despite the long sea journey, he was more than accustomed to a long walk. He wasn't sure how he would manage city life, not trekking every day as he had.

But this metropolitan sojourn was to re-establish himself as an explorer and cartographer. He would write articles, give lectures, and then hopefully take on another commission from the Royal Geographical Society to some other part of the world. Rascomb had been unwavering in his support and enthusiasm for Julian's career, and so like a schoolboy running back to his favorite teacher, Julian would not even detour to shave before presenting his work.

The rain thickened, nothing compared to the tropical afternoon storms he'd experienced in the jungles, although much more uncomfortable and quite cold. By the time he reached his friend's home, the butler let him in out of pity.

Julian stood dripping wet in the marble foyer. He checked the map case—safe and dry. He pulled off his sodden cap to identify himself when he saw a woman descending the wide staircase. Her golden hair was loosely pinned, and it shone like lamplight. The nostalgia of his boyhood fancy for Rascomb's wife hit him so hard he nearly staggered at the sight of her.

He swept into a gallant bow. "Lady Rascomb!" He watched the water drip from his hair down onto the floor. He kept speaking as he rose. "You likely do not remember me, though I remember you. Sir Julian Dunstan, here to see his lordship. I apologize for my appearance, I did not think I would encounter any ladies as I . . ."

The look on the woman's face could be described only as pained. Julian stopped talking, glancing to the butler, who glared at him. There was something very clearly amiss. And that was when he noticed the woman's black collar and dress.

"You wear black, my lady. Tell me, who has died?" His heart

thudded hard in his chest.

And then another lady descended the stairs, this one with a clear limp and a cane in one hand. She too, wore black.

"Sir Dunstan," the new woman called to him. "You mistake my daughter for me, but I thank you for the compliment."

He bowed again, feeling foolish and heavy and bull-headed. "My apologies. I have been away for some time. I forget the world soldiered on without me."

"We are in mourning for my husband. I regret to inform you so callously, but the previous Lord Rascomb passed away last summer, following an injury while attempting the Matterhorn."

The breath swept out of him. His mentor was gone. The man who guided him, steered him, advised him, cheered him on, had died. But Julian had maps to show him. How could he have died without seeing the maps?

"I beg your pardon." Julian felt the cold seeping into his bones and his teeth threatened to chatter. But it wasn't just the cold rain. It was the shock of the news. The blow to how Julian saw the world. "My sincere condolences. I did not know." He glanced around blindly, unsure of what to do. "I must go. Please, may I call on you tomorrow, when I am presentable?"

"At your convenience." Perhaps she smiled or offered some other graceful gesture, but Julian couldn't see it, blinded by panic and loss. He mumbled his goodbyes and stumbled back into the street. His chest felt as if it were caving in, and so he walked. He walked without direction, without seeing, without caring, sodden and cold.

Eventually, his inner compass took him to his rooms, the top half of a quaint townhome. The landlady, Mrs. Talbert, lived in the bottom half, and greeted him. She was a ruddy-faced pleasant-looking woman who promised him a bowl of stew with bread and butter and a pot of tea to be sent up right away.

Julian nodded, but didn't care. Even when Nicholas, the erstwhile combination footman, valet, and man of all work, arrived sometime later with a tray, Julian found himself just standing in the middle of his new flat, dripping a puddle, unable to move.

Without Rascomb, how would he gain those introductions he'd hoped for? Without Rascomb, who would tell him his work was good? He would be stuck with the fellows at the Royal Geography Society without the only decent man he'd ever known. It was like losing a father all over again.

OPHELIA'S MAID, LUCIA, set out a gray and lavender gown again, as she had been doing for the last months. It had been over a year since her father passed, since Arthur became the new viscount Rascomb, since everything in her life turned away from her.

As she had done every morning that a gray or lavender gown had been set out, she went into her closet to find a black one. This time, every black crepe gown had been replaced. Ophelia narrowed her eyes. Fine. She rang for Lucia, who helped her dress in silence, and then had the audacity to suggest some smoky topaz earbobs.

"Why?" Ophelia asked, ending her silent standoff.

"Because you will have a caller this morning, miss. Your lady mother bid me to help you feel better." Lucia had the washed-out complexion of many city dwellers. Her skin was tinged a sallow color and her light brown hair already showed streaks of gray. The woman was younger than Ophelia's mother, but older than Ophelia. She was competent, stalwart, and took Ophelia's oddities in stride, but she'd been hired after her father's death. Ophelia's previous lady's maid had been poached by another young lady about to debut, and Ophelia wished her nothing but the best. It was a far more interesting household than theirs.

"Earbobs are supposed to make me feel better?" Ophelia flicked her fingernails against each other. Thumb, forefinger, middle finger, ring finger, pinkie, then back to thumb. Three times through her sequence and she felt calmer.

"My apologies, miss. I mean to say what your lady mother said: that is, to make you feel more like yourself."

Ophelia stared at them. They had been a gift from her father. A collection of stones from a friend in South America, that he'd had made into jewelry for the women in his family. And the smoky topaz was an opaque gray, suitable for mourning.

Guilt washed over her. Not only for her father, but also her mother who had been managing the household upheaval and all of her children while she grieved a man she had loved. Ophelia clipped on the earbobs. Obedience was the least she could do.

She was the youngest and only unmarried child in the family. And now that Arthur had moved into the Rascomb London townhouse with his bride, Lady Emily, everything had changed. Ophelia's mother was now the dowager Lady Rascomb, no longer in charge of the daily upkeep of the household, and while Lady Emily was gracious in the transition, she knew it must smart to lose control.

While Ophelia was unmarried and there were no little Arthur and Emilys running around, Lady Rascomb was bid to stay on. But when Ophelia married or Arthur started his line of progeny, the dowager would be expected to move on to a different, smaller household. Ophelia might be compelled to go with her. After all, she was twenty-eight. No man married a twenty-eight-year-old.

Ophelia joined her mother in the drawing room. The light was cheerful, and the fire danced a low flame. Her mother was darning one of Arthur's shirts.

"Shouldn't Lady Emily be doing that?" Ophelia asked.

"Good morning," her mother said, ignoring Ophelia's blunt question.

When her life was perfect and happy, Ophelia struggled with her blunt opinions and queries. Now that she struggled with the depths of her own grief, it had somehow worsened.

"Lady Emily is abed for the day. She says that she can smell her megrim."

Ophelia made a face. "Does it smell like that fish sauce she makes us eat on Fridays? If so, I pity her."

Her mother chuckled, but didn't acknowledge Ophelia's complaint. Lady Emily had brought her own cook in, and none of the Bridewells had taken to the cuisine. Dinners were bland when they ought to have been savory, cloying when the pudding was meant to be sweet, and positively maritime when it was fish.

And while typically Ophelia welcomed routine, she found she preferred her mother's subtle three-week rotation of dishes, rather than Lady Emily's weekly habit.

"I suppose I will—" Ophelia peered into the mending basket only to find it empty. There were three women to do the darning, and only one man in the house to mend for. "Embroider some linens for a dowry I will never use."

Lady Rascomb paused her efforts. "Would you like to have another go at a Season?"

"Mama!" Ophelia chided. "I'm twenty-eight! They'll laugh at me."

"We don't have to go on the marriage mart, fuss with those sorts of parties and balls. We could be subtler about it. Find a matchmaker."

No. The answer was no. But Ophelia saw hope in her mother's eyes, and felt the earbobs sway as she lifted her head. If it would make her mother happy, she would do it. "But I will only go through with it if it is a love match. I must *like* my husband, if I am to have one."

"That's a reasonable request, I think. And you aren't too old to bear children, no matter what anyone says. I had you when I was your age." She picked up her mending and hummed.

Ophelia found her embroidery hoop. She felt ridiculous. It wasn't that her embroidery wasn't good—it was very good, in fact. She'd created scenes from her favorite stories, illustrated whole gardens across pillows, and had even started learning effective portraiture and shadowing through the medium of embroidery. It was what Justine had always called Ophelia's "maddening brilliance." But just now, Ophelia felt so at a loss for what she should say or do or feel, that embroidery was pointless.

Ferris appeared in the doorway. "A caller, my lady."

"As I expected," Lady Rascomb said, her voice suddenly subdued. "Is it Sir Julian?"

"Indeed. And he is now dry." Ferris kept his expression neutral, but Ophelia knew he was teasing. At least Lady Emily had let them keep their butler of all these years.

"Show him in, and refresh our tea and add some of that plum cake, please. I would wager Sir Julian has not had good English cake in some time."

"Who is Sir Julian?" Ophelia asked as Ferris left to retrieve the man. When he appeared on their doorstep the day before, he hadn't seemed like anything more than a wretch, soaked to the bone, with unseemly scruff obscuring his face. He'd mistaken her for her mother, which was a compliment. Her mother had many admirers throughout the years, and Ophelia was sure he had been one of them by the way he'd spoken. Ophelia was not as good with recognizing emotions as she was embroidery, but given Justine's proclivity for suitors, she'd trained herself to notice the symptoms of that sort of male admiration.

"His father was a friend of your father's, and then after he died, Sir Julian also became a friend. They've corresponded for years. Your father helped him get the commission to map the South American mountains for a collection of mining interests. Of course, your father convinced him to conduct topographical surveys as well."

The idea of her father encouraging someone to do more, create more, lit a candle in Ophelia's heart. A small remembrance that she hadn't previously known. Of course he'd pushed someone to think more broadly than was expected.

"He was of a younger crowd and idolized your father. As many did." Ophelia's mother put down the mending and stood, wincing as she put weight on her foot. "All this sitting is doing me no favors."

"We can walk more." Ophelia stood and smoothed out her

gray and lavender gown. "Since we are officially out of mourning."

By rights, they were, and Lady Rascomb could remarry if she wished. But instead, Lady Rascomb wore black, even though she prodded Ophelia to go to half-mourning.

"Sir Julian Dunstan," Ferris announced.

The man who entered the drawing room looked wholly unlike the man from yesterday. His face was smooth, his clothes were well-tailored and tidy, and his bearing was upright and polished. "Lady Rascomb, Miss Ophelia Bridewell, I am at your service." He gave a gallant bow.

He had been striking yesterday, but he was handsome now, with dark hair, almost black, that accentuated the darkness of his coal-black eyes. He was thin at the waist but broad at the shoulders, and moved with the same practiced purpose as her father. His skin was tanned in a way Englishmen were not supposed to be, but she supposed the South American sun had something to do with it.

"Sir Julian, thank you for calling. I was profoundly upset to deliver such horrid news to you while standing in our doorway yesterday." Lady Rascomb gestured to the chair opposite her.

He unslung a wide strap connected to a leather tube that he'd carried across his body. "My sincere condolences to your entire family. I am much aggrieved to hear such news. I had wondered why I hadn't heard from him in so long, but I knew of the Matterhorn attempt and hoped it had been all the traveling that kept him from responding to me."

The mention of their failed attempt to scale the Matterhorn made Ophelia burn with shame. She wanted to look down, but she forced herself to meet his eye. It was her failure. Her responsibility as expedition leader included being blamed for the death of her father, even if it had been his loose footing on an ice wall that had caused his injury. They'd done everything they could, and even the physician from Zurich had said that the cold conditions had helped keep him alive.

Despite the months he had lingered, and few moments of consciousness, he had died of pneumonia the winter after the climb. Tristan, Ophelia's other brother, had tried to make her feel better, as he'd blamed himself for years for the accident that injured their mother. But their mother lived. There was no penance she could make for her father's death. And she had to suffer the humiliation whenever someone mentioned her hubris.

But Sir Julian didn't seem to want to mock or shame her. "I thought you'd like to see the maps I've made. Lord Rascomb was the one who got me interested in the science of topographical mapping. It's terribly challenging and requires a great deal of maths, but it is extremely useful. Integrating the data is even more difficult and painstaking. It took me far longer than I'd anticipated, but it was Lord Rascomb who helped me persevere."

Ophelia loved a map. She scooted to the very edge of her chair. Topographical maps were a new way to visualize every peak and valley. While initially difficult to read, the more accustomed one became with seeing elevation charted, the quicker one understood it. If only every mountain had a topographical map made, life would be so much more interesting.

"Please," Lady Rascomb said.

He uncapped the leather tube and pulled out rolls of paper. They were unwieldy, but eventually through much awkward wrestling and paper crinkling, they were spread flat, held down by a teacup, a teapot, and his hands.

And his hands were nice. There was something about their decidedly ungentlemanly ruggedness that seemed correct. Proper, in the way her family was unusual and valued such physical competence. Sir Julian's hands weren't English proper, but rather mountain proper. As if declaring his ability to pitch a tent or make a fire, or haul a person up a rope.

"These are surprisingly beautiful, Sir Julian. I commend you." Lady Rascomb leaned over the table, looking closer at the drawing.

Ophelia took an opportunity to look as well, noting all the

red, razor-thin lines that denoted an elevation change. "This must have taken ages."

Sir Julian looked up at her with pride evident in his almost-too-perfectly proportioned face. "Indeed. Thank you for noticing, Miss Ophelia."

"I have not seen many topographical maps, but I understand the theory of them," Ophelia said.

"I sent my data and measurements back over the years to the Royal Geographical Society, so they may make their own maps, but it was your father who insisted I draw my own, in order to double check the accuracy of my numbers. Fortunately for him, I've always been good with numbers."

She felt as if she were looking down on the three of them, peering over this map. As if she were outside her own body, not wanting to feel that new wave of grief, encountering her father's influence over this man.

"I am by no means an expert, but this looks excellently drawn." Ophelia's mother smiled at him in the way Ophelia recognized as maternal doting.

Sir Julian beamed, as any child would. It made Ophelia wonder where his parents were.

"I should get these off to the Royal Geographical Society. Not that I'm looking forward to showing them to anyone there. They won't be near as kind as you two."

"They should at least recognize your hard work," Ophelia said, doing her best to be as sisterly as she could. But when he looked back at her, he didn't have a brotherly look on his face. Nor anything else. Not the warmth he showed to her mother, but as if she were a stranger. Which, she supposed, she was.

They helped him roll up the map and tuck it safely away in its leather case. "The last time I saw you, Miss Ophelia, I believe you were ten years old."

Her eyebrows went up of their own volition. "I'm very sorry to say I don't recall the event."

"I daresay you wouldn't. I was a young man, very much

trying to gain the attention and respect of your father. I believe you were lecturing your brothers on some matter. You'd all been allowed to dine with us."

"Once the children became interested in the outdoor pursuits, we would allow them out of the nursery when we dined with future explorers. We thought it would take the spark out of them when they heard how physically rigorous it was." Ophelia's mother looked to her affectionately.

"That worked on Arthur, but I'm afraid it only whetted my appetite," Ophelia said.

Sir Julian looked down. "I know that it is difficult to speak of failed attempts—I can't tell you how many of my own I have had—but I should be very curious about the Matterhorn expedition, Miss Ophelia. If you'd be willing to tell me."

Heat filled her cheeks. "Another time," she said, wondering if she would be brave enough to do so.

"Thank you for your hospitality, my lady. May I call upon you again?" Sir Julian stood, slinging his map case across his body.

Lady Rascomb stood, as did Ophelia. Her mother didn't even bother looking at her when she told he was welcome to visit them anytime. It wasn't that Ophelia minded, but she felt quite at odds with herself. There was something she didn't like about this man, this stranger, having this paternal connection to her father without her knowing about it. As if he somehow was claiming something that belonged to her.

❖

Chapter Two

FORMAL DRESS WAS a costume unto itself. While on his travels, Sir Julian had taken on the garb of a local miner, a gentleman traveler, and finally, his own brand of explorer. But the one thing they all had in common was comfort and durability. This—the tightly tailored white waistcoat, the stiff collar—felt the most absurd. He'd rather smear on the greasy paint that protected his skin on the worst summer days of the high Andes than this.

Nicholas frowned as he stepped back. "Pardon me sir, but something still isn't right, but for the life of me, I can't figure out what it is."

"It's me, Nicholas. I'm the part that isn't right. My God, I feel ridiculous." Julian stood in front of the full-length mirror, grateful for the man's attentions. If it weren't for him, Julian would feel a bigger fool. It was at Lady Rascomb's insistence that he attend tonight. He was the support for her and Miss Ophelia, as it was their first outing since mourning.

He'd been visiting them on the regular for a few weeks, enjoying their chats—and their cake. At first he went because it was comforting to be amongst the women his mentor had loved. London felt more welcoming to him because of their hospitality. Over the weeks that had passed, he visited because they made him smile, and he, in turn, made them smile as well. They seemed to look forward to his regular visits, too, greeting him with plum cake and tea, books and maps. Now it was time for him to do his part to ease their discomfort.

Nicholas snapped his fingers. "It's the details, sir. Have you a pocket watch?"

"Are you sure you aren't trained as a valet?" Julian asked as he pointed to the dressing table in the corner, where his father's pocket watch rested. It had not seen the light of day in ten years, stuffed down at the bottom of his trunks for safekeeping. At one low point, upon arrival by ship to Peru, he had considered selling it for the quick money he could get in order to buy food. But then he found his stories of adventure made him a prized dinner guest, and he dined out on his mountaineering experience for the rest of his time there, when he wasn't nibbling on his provisions in the bush.

"No, sir," Nicholas said, rummaging through the desk until he found the piece. He looked at it critically. "Needs polish. Do you mind so very much if I take a moment?"

Julian waved him off. "Take all the time you need. I am not looking forward to this evening."

Nicholas straightened in surprise before continuing to rummage through a basket of polishes stowed in Julian's dressing area. "I thought this was a much sought-after invitation. It made the gossip sheets."

"It is." Julian sighed. "I know I ought to be grateful. But I'm not accustomed to this type of life anymore. It's been over a decade since I waltzed properly. The parties I've been to lately were raucous, and filled with a pidgin Spanish and English, inappropriate jokes, and inappropriate gestures. There was drinking and dancing, and often a fistfight, or at least those on nights where there wasn't a knife-fight."

Nicholas's eyes grew rounded and he stopped searching for the polish.

"I don't say this to scare or titillate you, Nicholas. I'm only saying that I don't know how to conduct myself. I'm nearly forty, and I've forgotten how to be an English gentleman."

The man found the polish and the rag and went at Sir Robert's pocket watch. His legacy was one that Sir Julian benefitted from, but one he would like to distance himself from all the same. "If I may say, you are famous enough and handsome enough that it won't matter your manners. The ladies will be dazzled all the same."

His heart ached when Nicholas mentioned ladies. There was a Maria-shaped hole in his heart still, after all these years. Maria, which hadn't even been her name, but was what the Spaniards had dubbed her, and that which she insisted he call her. At least, until she left him.

The gossip had named Sir Julian as an eligible bachelor, his baronet title a gilded treat on top of his reputation. But no one seemed to realize that he didn't have a fortune of his own. Very little had come from Sir Robert, and Julian was beholden to the Royal Geographical Society to fund his exploration. He'd stretched his budget with gem-trading, sketch portraiture, and eventually, regaling the public with his adventures.

Whichever woman wanted him would have to have wealth of her own, because he couldn't provide for anyone. Not that he wanted a wife. What would he do, settle down back in London for domesticity? He felt like a dog dressed up in finery.

Nicholas finished polishing the watch, affixed it to his waist-coat, the gold chain drawing a dashing line across Sir Julian's lean abdomen. Then Julian got a cab to Lord Sutherford's party, where he was ushered in amongst a crush of carriages, hansom cabs, and top-hatted dandies. The overpowering smell of ambergris, a dark animal musk used as the basis of most colognes and perfumes, gave Julian a hint of a headache. He'd rather be in the crush with everyone's unwashed servants. They, at least, smelled like people.

Julian rode the wave of polite society like a balsa raft on the whitewater-plagued Amazon river, until he was deposited into the sea of people in the ballroom. Despite the fact that he was dressed as every man here, he still felt like he stuck out, obvious and foolish. But soon, his Royal Geographical fellows surrounded him, welcoming and congratulating him on his triumphs.

"Splendid article," said one man whose name Julian couldn't remember.

"The perfect balance between the scientific numbers and the conversant tale-telling we all long for in an explorer's narrative," said Lord Sutherford.

Sir Julian ducked his head in humble thanks as he was smothered with compliments he wasn't certain were genuine. They probably were, but he'd lost his ability to read the subtle emotional range of the British aristocracy.

He could absolutely tell when a Spaniard was about to draw a knife in a tavern, though. Or when a nonverbal trade with a tribesman was going woefully wrong. And he could read the sky and a mountain and a river far better than any person.

"Ah," Lord Sutherford said, maneuvering himself to a new position in their tight circle of gentlemen. "I would like to present to you Lord Rascomb."

Julian's chest caved in for a moment until he saw the tall man approach. The new Lord Rascomb. Arthur, as Miss Ophelia called him. Julian remembered him from before, when he hadn't yet filled out, and was as gangly as any tall young man could be, with widely spaced eyes that gave him the look of some unfortunate sea creature. In fact, he recalled the younger brother calling him something dreadful but accurate during those dinners.

"Sir Julian, I am so pleased to finally make your acquaintance again after all these years." This new Rascomb inclined his head, to which Julian gave a low bow.

"Your father was an incalculable influence, Lord Rascomb. I give my condolences and my gratitude to your family for sharing him with me. At your service." Julian heard the men around him give hums of approval. At least he was able to perform some of his manners correctly. The words were earnest and from the heart.

"I understand you have been calling upon my mother and sister since your return to London. Please let me extend my gratitude for keeping them company and sharing your relationship with my father with them while I was in the country. I know for my mother particularly, she finds your presence a balm."

Lady Rascomb was only eighteen years his elder, but she treated him like another son. Her maternal affection was unmistakable. At first, it nettled him that he was treated like an adult child rather than an equal or even a potential suitor, but he soon realized that she would never remarry. Her husband had been the love of her life, and she had no intention of finding another man. Indeed, why would she?

He wondered how Miss Ophelia thought of his visits: if she felt his company to be a balm as well. She was still somewhat reserved in his presence, as if she were keeping a secret. But each week she smiled more, welcomed him more. She quizzed him on adventures and locations, mineral deposits and gemstones. Julian had noticed the smoky topaz swinging from Miss Ophelia's ears, no doubt coming from the box of them he'd shipped to Lord Rascomb years ago, as thanks for helping him secure the funding for his adventure. It was gratifying to see them adorning a beautiful woman, but he dared not comment on it. He did not want her to think she owed him anything. As it stood, Julian owed her the stories of her father's wisdom and generosity of spirit.

"Are they here? I should wish to bid them good evening." Julian looked around the crowd, but did not see them.

"Indeed, their first night out since father passed. It's quite the occasion." Rascomb gestured over to the far wall, where the older matrons, spinsters, and wallflowers dwelled.

Julian frowned. "Surely your sister will be dancing."

It was Rascomb's turn to frown. "If someone asks her, but she is quite on the shelf."

"I say!" said the man Julian couldn't remember.

"Uncalled for, Rascomb," said another.

"But she is very beautiful, are you not providing an ample dowry?" Julian asked, ignoring the calls of Rascomb's rudeness at his sister's expense.

Finally, he caught sight of Miss Ophelia, who looked a vision this evening. She was in dark blue silk, trimmed with a contrasting white lace that ran in patterns across the bell of her skirt. Her shining blonde hair was done up with matching silk ribbons, curled and braided in ways he could not track. She was beautiful in her drawing room, a serious crease between her eyebrows, but here, she was dazzling.

"Of course I will provide a reasonable dowry, but if you must know, she is eight-and-twenty now." Rascomb lowered his voice to whisper her age.

When he was a younger man, full of London norms and social cues, he would have likely been just as callous about a woman's age as Rascomb was. But now, it didn't seem to matter. There was the issue of childbirth yes, of course, continuing a family line and whatnot, but he'd seen woman her age and much older dominate the taverns and parties in the new world. Beauty paired with a comely spirit made age irrelevant.

"Why would that affect her prospects?" Julian asked, a question he had not meant to say aloud.

"Excellent point, sir!" the man Julian could not remember exclaimed, and Julian did not care for the spark that seemed to flare in the man's eyes. The reason why Julian could not remember this man was because he was bland. His voice, his features, his bearing, all as forgettable as the fifth gingerbread man. They all looked the same on a tray at a bakery.

"By all means, should you wish to dance with her and break up the monotony of her day, I give my support." Rascomb looked over at his sister.

Julian knew his morals and beliefs had changed due to his years of travel. No longer could he subscribe to the Sunday preacher's ideas of natural order for women—or other men! There was no hierarchy to adhere to that placed him at the top. He'd met the peoples of the Amazon who ventured out to trade—for he was not a big enough fool to venture into that green hell—who spoke of groups led by women, and also ones where women fought side by side with the men. Also of tribes where it was the men who cared for the children once they ceased to nurse at their mothers' breasts.

There was no God-given order to life. And he'd also learned that life was precarious, precious, and chaotic. There was no room for manufactured rules that benefited the few, when the many were ubiquitous. It was why he dreaded returning to the Royal Geographical Society, as it was there that Sir Robert espoused his King James Bible-based ideas that women needed to be servile. Where Sir Robert had listened as others espoused the ideas of finding the elusive men whose faces were in their torsos and possessed the minds of small children, as their forebears had once suspected.

And to men who put ideas first and proof second, there was no explaining nor convincing.

"Then I shall be the first to dance with the maiden," said the bland, forgettable man.

Julian scowled as he watched him weave through the crowd. "Have they been introduced?"

"Fairport? Ages ago. Never thought he was much interested after my other sister married Garrett Preston." Rascomb turned to watch the spectacle of prying a woman out of the wallflower nest.

Given what Julian had seen of Miss Ophelia so far, he expected to see her reject the man's overtures. Fairport, apparently, was his name. Julian repeated it to himself in order to make sure he remembered it. While he didn't like the man, it was still useful to know who belonged where. And Fairport was a member of the RGS. In the coming months, his good favor could be a deciding vote on whether or not Julian obtained another commission. "Your other sister—Miss Portia Bridewell—she married Garrett Preston?"

"Indeed. He is a barrister and will likely become a member of the House of Commons soon. Ambitious fellow. Hardworking."

Julian clucked his appreciation. He remembered Garrett Preston as a timid and whiny child who hated attending his father's lectures at RGS. The other son, the older one, had been the paragon of an earl's son, which was likely why Garrett had rebelled. Not that it mattered. It only made Julian feel old and out of touch. His inner self felt the same as it always had—yearning for adventure, clean air, and a singleness of purpose.

But he'd spotted flashes of silver in his stubble not long ago, and no doubt if he grew out his beard, it would be a speckle of salt and pepper colors. He didn't belong in a ballroom as a bachelor.

"Sir Julian, could I persuade you to meet my family?" another man asked. What was his name? "Fecund" was all he could come up with, but he knew it wasn't correct.

"I should be delighted," Julian answered with as much respect as he could muster. Still, all he could think was "fecund." No, Lund! The man was Frances, Lord Lund. That was it. He shook his head and followed him through the maze of dark trousers and swirls of fabrics. He hoped he was being introduced to a spouse, and not daughters.

⟫⟫⟫✦⟪⟪⟪

OPHELIA BLINKED AT the man asking her to dance. But she could almost feel her mother's glee as she watched from one chair over. It had been ages since she'd danced. They'd been in Zermatt for the Season one year, then her father died, so they'd not been at the next Season, and then here they were, returning. She hadn't expected to dance at all, given her age. Given her strange pursuits.

But here was Lord Fairport, asking for a twirl about the room.

"I hadn't even picked up a dance card," Ophelia said.

"Then may I assume it isn't yet full?" Fairport said, and his little joke made him a touch more interesting than before.

"I daresay it is not. Thank you, Lord Fairport. I believe I shall dance." Ophelia stood, allowing Fairport to take her hand as she did so. It made her feel younger, lighter, to have attentions such as these. Perhaps she wasn't as miserable and alone as she'd felt in the last year, consumed with the guilt of her failure.

It was hard not to notice the look of triumph that he shot to her brother's horde, grouped together like some kind of penguin-related spy ring.

Sliding across the parquet in her dancing slippers, she straightened her shoulders, knowing the perfect posture showed her neck in a lovely and graceful light. "I'm surprised you took the time to ask, Lord Fairport. I thought I would reside in the corner all evening."

"You are too beautiful for that, Miss Ophelia."

Her long gloves kept her from flicking her fingernails, but she still lightly touched her finger pads together, hoping no one would notice. Thumb, forefinger, middle finger, ring finger, pinkie, then back to thumb. Just once.

They took a position amongst the other dancers and began the opening minuet. But these steps had been drilled into her since she was a child, and they could not be unlearned even if she wanted. And Fairport was pleasing enough. He'd set his cap at Portia years earlier, and Ophelia didn't want to be his consolation prize, but enough time had lapsed that it was unlikely.

They didn't speak much during the dance, which was perfectly reasonable. Ophelia didn't have anything much to say, and she was grateful to be able to count her steps, as while they were second nature, she was still a bit out of practice.

After the dance ended, Fairport returned her to the wallflower corner and offered to fetch her a drink.

"Fairport, how lovely to see you," Ophelia's mother said, rising to her feet.

Ophelia could see her mother already matching them up and pushing them to the altar. One dance a wedding did not make.

"You as well, my lady," Fairport said with a gracious bow. They chatted as Ophelia let her mind drift to more interesting things.

She wondered if she might convince Sir Julian to teach her how to take the readings necessary to make a topographical map. If she could not be the mountaineer she wished to be, perhaps she could at least contribute to the world in this way. She didn't mind some tedious tasks, as long as they were done after a strenuous hike up a mountain.

As if she had conjured him, Sir Julian appeared at her side.

"Good evening, sir," she said, surprising even herself with how much pleasure was in her voice at the sight of him. He'd grown to be a fixture in their week, coming to call and bringing news of the Royal Geographical Society, his maps and articles. She'd even taken the time to edit his latest article after noting grammatical deficiencies in the one just published.

"I see you've already christened the dance floor," he said.

Again, how different he looked dressed up in his formal attire. His black hair shone like a raven's wing, and his dark eyes were warm and inviting. Indeed, having him stand next to all the other men here, he looked broader and fitter than most. His bearing was at odds with the rest of the company as well. Some men were ramrod straight from military service or from boarding schools for the aristocracy. But Sir Julian looked almost relaxed as he stood perfectly tall.

"I had not expected to dance this evening, but the minuet was very enjoyable," she said. "This is the first I have been out in society since my father's death. I did not think I would be able to enjoy it."

His dark eyebrows raised. "Which implies that you are, in fact, enjoying yourself."

"Indeed. Especially now that you are here." Her cheeks flared in embarrassment. She sounded as coquettish as Justine! "I did not mean, that is, I am glad you are here, but I mean that—" she stammered.

He smiled broadly and held up his hand. One of his teeth slanted over another, she noticed for the first time. It was only apparent when he smiled that widely, which she hadn't seen him do yet. It was a charming feature. "I understand what you meant. I did not think you meant to be forward."

"When I am with friends, sometimes my mouth speaks ahead of me, and I say things that come out in unintended ways." Although, she usually said things that angered or hurt her loved ones, not pleased them.

"I am flattered you consider me a friend. I would like to consider you one of mine as well."

"Of course," she answered.

Lord Fairport finished his conversation with her mother and caught her attention again. "It has been such a pleasant time with you, Miss Ophelia."

"You as well, Lord Fairport." Ophelia bobbed her courtesy and Fairport left. Her mother gave her an impressed look.

"Would you, my friend, care to take on the quadrille with me?" Sir Julian extended his white gloved hand in a formal manner.

She dropped her own hand into his. "It would be my pleasure, friend."

Chapter Three

HE'D MADE THE papers. Not for his insightful articles, not for his triumph or a topographical map. Not even for his excellent dancing. The scandal sheets loved his *shoulders*. It was embarrassing. Nicholas had brought up the papers specifically to call Julian's attention to it.

"I think it's a rather good thing," Nicholas protested when Julian showed his dismay.

"Of all my accomplishments, it is my shoulders upon which my value sits?" Julian huffed.

"I think it's nice anyone notices you at all," Nicholas said, his face screwed up into a doubtful frown.

"Thank you, Nicholas, for your ringing endorsement." Julian pulled on his waistcoat. He wished he were pulling on his hobnailed boots instead, setting up another isolated slope with his equipment.

"I only meant that some of us never get mentioned at all," Nicholas said, handing him his jacket.

Julian accepted the apology and allowed the man to take a brush to his jacket. Today he was attending a lecture by another explorer about his venture into the Amazon jungle itself. He was curious how the man had fared, given his own experiences dallying around the edges. It was so unlike anywhere else in the world, he couldn't imagine how to accurately prepare for a sojourn such as that.

And given the death toll of the expeditions that disappeared into the green hell, as it was named by adventurers, Julian had no interest in that sort of exploration. After the morning lecture, he would stop by the Rascomb house to convey his impressions to Lady Rascomb and Miss Ophelia. They were not invited to attend these talks, as the RGS did not extend membership to women. Another grievous oversight by the men in charge.

When he first returned to London, his visits to the ladies were purely out of a sense of duty and mourning of his mentor and friend. Now, though, he and the Rascomb set seemed to circulate amongst the same people, and he found himself encountering them at dinners and parties and other sorts of soirees. It was always a great excuse and pleasure to dance with Ophelia or dote on Lady Rascomb. Few debutante mamas were interested in pursuing him given his meager pockets, but a great many widows of all ages were happy to listen to his stories. He'd been summoned to dinners that he thought were parties, only to arrive and find a tete-a-tete was arranged.

If he were a younger man, he might not have minded, but now he found that he didn't care for those, as it made him feel as this whole shoulders business did. As if he were an exotic prize, or a notch on a merry widow's bedpost. He supposed this was how actresses and opera dancers felt. Not that he'd ever engaged with one of those. He slurped down the last bit of tea and stuffed the last bit of crust from his buttered toast in his mouth and headed out. He hated to be late, and yet he was chronically so.

As he was about to enter the lecture hall, he was approached by Lord Fairport. The tall, bland man now only existed in his mind as the one who had first asked Miss Ophelia to dance. It was almost as if even while speaking, the man blended into the background noise of faceless Englishmen.

"You seem to be good friends with Lord Rascomb," the man said after giving a polite and equally forgettable greeting.

"I was," Julian said, thinking of his mentor. "And I visit his family regularly."

Fairport blinked. "Ah yes, the former Lord Rascomb, you mean. Yes, I am more friends with the current one."

Fair point to Fairport, Julian thought. He waited as the other man collected his thoughts. Other RGS members started to gather, passing them as they entered the small lecture hall.

"I suppose I mean to say, do you think Miss Ophelia would be open to being courted? I know she makes no effort on the marriage mart, and I know about her failed expedition that killed her father, which is quite the odd thing. But if I made a suit, would she be receptive, do you think?"

Julian frowned. Fairport seemed to imply that Miss Ophelia was responsible for the death of her father, which could not be correct. She had not yet confided in him the specifics of the mission, but it didn't seem appropriate to press for details. Fairport must be incorrect or have heard the worst of the gossip and believed it.

Aside from his obviously erroneous assumptions, the man seemed far too uninteresting to think of marriage with Ophelia Bridewell. He was only a bit older than Miss Ophelia, surely younger than Julian himself, who would be better suited to courting Lady Rascomb than Miss Ophelia. He'd known her as a child after all, and that didn't sit well with his sense of decorum.

But this man? "I am not certain," Julian confessed. "She has been deep in mourning for her father. If you wish, I could bring up the subject to her, in a gentlemanly manner, of course. I mean to call upon them today after the lecture."

"Should I accompany you?" Fairport asked, his face open in milky hope.

"No," Julian answered sharply. "That is, if she were to decline, it would be most awkward. They have asked me to convey the proceedings of this lecture to them. They are very curious."

"Curious!" Fairport laughed, as if Julian had made a pun, that the women were both of curious minds and possessed of a curious—meaning odd—spirit. "Curious but beautiful."

Damn the English language, that's not what he had meant. A

man like this would never have made it in South America. Never would have made it out of port. He used the filling seats of the lecture hall to make his escape. "Looks to be starting. Shall we?"

"Ah yes, right, right. I'm interested to hear about the cannibals of the deepest jungle." Fairport moved in front of Julian.

This was precisely what he hated about the RGS. Instead of having open curiosity, Fairport had already digested the fictional and sensationalist accounts of the region. And Julian sincerely doubted that these men had reached the deepest jungle, for the Amazon was deep enough to swallow hundreds of Englishmen whole. There were entire expeditions that disappeared without a trace.

"AND THEN?" OPHELIA was so far on the edge of her seat, she might fall off. But Sir Julian's stories were so riveting, it was worth a bruised bum.

He laughed, pleasure so evident in his handsome face. "Then I dug a snow cave on the side of the mountain and hoped I wouldn't freeze to death."

She shook her head in amazement, both impressed and envious. "That sounds incredible. I would love to do that someday."

Her mother embroidered a pillowcase. She didn't bother to look up. "You've had your share of hardships on a mountainside, too."

"Yes, but not like this! I always knew Zermatt was there, just a day's hike away. This is different!" She gestured toward Sir Julian, who looked pleased with himself and comfortable as he snacked on a scone smothered in apricot jam. "Sir Julian was in the middle of a mountain range, abandoned by his team, and uncertain of where the next settlement was, let alone if they were hostile."

"But I had plenty of food, Miss Ophelia. That was the key. I was content to sit in my snow cave overnight, knowing I could eat comfortably."

Ophelia looked at the man she now regarded fondly, slumping back into the sofa. "Someday, I want you to take me out there. I want to see these Andes mountains and their odd rounded peaks."

Her mother chuckled.

"What, do you object?" she asked.

Lady Rascomb shook her head. "It is not my place to object anymore, Ophelia. It is your brother's. Or, should you choose one, your husband's. And I should say, given the talk of Sir Julian in the newspapers, a husband would greatly object to you running off to the Andes with 'London's Most Eligible Explorer.'"

Sir Julian groaned. "You saw that, did you?"

Ophelia clapped her hands and laughed. "What did it say? No one showed me."

Lady Rascomb raised her eyebrows, peering over her needlework. "That Sir Julian's appeal was not in deep pockets but rather his broad shoulders."

Ophelia squealed in delight. "That's *fantastic*." And it was. He absolutely did have very appealing broad shoulders, as if he were able to carry anything—or anyone—where they needed to be.

"Does no one respect me for my intellect?" Sir Julian protested, finishing off his scone.

Ophelia laughed, tossing a sugar cube at him. "Now you know how it feels."

"I'm more than a pretty face. Er, I suppose I mean shoulders." Sir Julian tossed the sugar cube back at her.

"How will you deal with the incoming female horde? Plead your unexciting perseverance? Your dry attention to topographical measurements? Your ability to do complex calculations in your head?"

Sir Julian straightened up and pulled his jacket round himself, puffing out his chest. "Those qualities are all very attractive to my female admirers."

Ophelia pelted him with the sugar cube again, smacking him directly in the broad left shoulder.

"Fine, fine, they aren't. But once they see my unimpressive bank account, they shall depart forthwith."

"Only a very foolish woman would take into account your bank register. What you offer is far better than a flat in a fashionable postal district." Ophelia meant it, too. If only he'd been in London, she would have been after him for her Matterhorn expedition.

"Your flattery does not fall on deaf ears, Miss Ophelia, and I thank you for it. I shall remind the papers to print that, instead." His powerful thighs strained at the tweed trousers, and Ophelia had a sudden wonder that if the gossips rags were so fond of his shoulders, had they not discovered his extraordinary thighs? It seemed remiss of them, if they intended to catalogue his pleasing body parts.

There was an easy silence, and Ophelia took it upon herself to pour more tea for all three of them. Sir Julian took the sugar cube lodged in a crease of his tweed coat and plopped it into his cup, giving her a look of satisfaction as he did so. She laughed.

"Oh, and—" he pulled a folded newspaper from the inside pocket of his coat. "I almost forgot. The latest from the RGS. You'll note the article here on the front page."

Ophelia snatched it from him and scanned it. Julian's narrative style was stunningly straightforward, so unlike the other stories of adventures found in the papers. She'd helped him with it, rearranging paragraphs, asking him to put more sensory details in to help the reader feel immersed in the mountains. As she read, she was thrilled to find he'd taken her suggestions. Not as good as having a published article herself, but still. Her suggestions found their way to print by the RGS.

"Thank you for showing me. May I keep it?" Ophelia asked, hugging it to her chest.

"Of course, that's your copy." Julian stirred the sugar dissolving in the tea. "I would have liked to put your name on there as well, but the RGS has a standing policy to not allow women anywhere near their doors or their printing press."

"May I see?" Lady Rascomb reached out to her.

"Don't I know," Ophelia grumbled, handing the paper to her mother. "I have an article that would be so well suited for RGS, about our Ben Nevis run, and how it prepared us for the Matterhorn. I've sent it everywhere I can think of, but it's too much for the ladies' magazines, and it's written by a woman, about women, so none of the men's magazines will print it either."

Ophelia swished her spoon in her tea, letting the milk swirl in its pleasing patterns. She normally drank her tea black, but she'd found that she enjoyed watching the liquids entwine around one another, until their individual identities dissolved into one.

"Have you thought about removing the gendered pronouns, and not mentioning you happen to be women?" Julian raised his eyebrows at her, looking more mischievous than intrepid.

The thought struck her. She could replace their names with initials, erase any mention of a Miss or a Missus, erase the paragraph about skirts, and the article would remain intact. "That is very possible."

"Give it to me when you are ready, and I'll see if I can get it run. I'll tell them it is from an anonymous friend who doesn't wish to boast."

Ophelia couldn't help the bubble of laughter rising from her. "I wouldn't want your fame. I don't have the shoulders for it."

Julian chuckled. "I wouldn't wish it upon you. The women of London are positively rabid."

"It is a very good article, Julian," Lady Rascomb said.

"Isn't it?" Ophelia said, knowing that she was gushing. "Someday I want to go to South America."

"Perhaps someday I'll take you," he said, beaming under Lady Rascomb's praise. She didn't begrudge him the maternal petting he received. Nor his relationship with her father, not anymore. He clearly was in need of that delightful closeness that developed between parents and children when children became adults. Everything shifted, and while they weren't friends exactly, the nature of the relationship deepened and stretched. The love grew stronger every day. At least, with her parents it did. And she was wise enough to know that not everyone had that. Eleanor, for instance, her sister-in-law, never had that with her parents, and likely never would.

Lost in her own thoughts, she wasn't sure how much time had passed when Julian cleared his throat. It shook her from her reverie, and she frowned when she saw how his posture had changed. He'd been proud and loved, and now he looked pained.

"There is an item of business I must discharge," Sir Julian said, looking down into his cup, as if he must concentrate sincerely on his tea. "Which is why I haven't brought it up until now."

"Sounds so serious," Ophelia said, sipping the lukewarm tea.

"I have been asked, as a friend of your family, if you would be amenable to being courted."

Her mother's spine straightened at that statement. "By whom?"

Sir Julian winced. "I'd rather not say as of yet. I don't wish to make anyone think more of it than what it is on either side."

Ophelia's heart pounded. No one had offered a suit for her hand in ages. But the way Sir Julian acted about it clearly made him uncomfortable. She wondered why, thinking it could only be for two reasons. One, the man in question was not someone Sir Julian respected, or two, it was Sir Julian himself.

The latter idea warmed her. Sir Julian was handsome, and the scandal rags of London were not wrong about his shoulders. She sipped her tea as she considered the idea of marriage. It was a concept she'd put aside for herself, much as Prudence had once, even while receiving missives from Justine on the benefits. But Prudence had changed her mind. And Eleanor had no complaints, and she was married to her brother Tristan. But for Ophelia? It wouldn't be so bad if it were someone like Julian who understood her passions.

"I think that while my daughter can answer for herself, as her mother and adviser in such dealings, it matters greatly who is asking."

Ophelia nodded. "I concur. I would only consider marriage to a man who would encourage my mountaineering and attempts to gain what the male mountaineers enjoy as their due."

Sir Julian met her eye. "I'm glad to hear that. A stifled person, man or woman, cannot survive."

"So who is this potential suitor?" Lady Rascomb pressed.

Sir Julian winced. "Lord Fairport."

Ophelia nodded and fell back into her seat once more. He'd danced with her at every social occasion, but so had a few other gentlemen, Sir Julian included. Would Fairport be as encouraging of her mountaineering as she required him to be? That was an unknown.

And somewhere, a small part of her wondered why it was Lord Fairport who was inquiring. As Portia's former suitor, would he recognize Ophelia as her own person? And if Lord Fairport was interested, why not any of the other men? Why not Sir Julian?

"You make a face, Sir Julian," her mother reprimanded. "What is it about this man you do not wish us to know?"

"When we chatted earlier, he made an allusion to something that I did not care for. About the attempt on the Matterhorn."

Ophelia felt herself collapse inward, as if her muscles cinched her up towards her middle. What had been relaxed and happy in the weeks since Sir Julian first visited them pulled themselves taut and closed. "And what was that insinuation?"

Sir Julian studied her. "I don't wish to say—not as of yet. But I would now like to press you for the details of your experience. Not that I wish to cause you pain, but I need to know how my mentor perished and be able to properly defend and disseminate the facts, as your friend."

Ophelia stopped breathing. It was a moment she hated reliving, yet she did so nightly, sometimes waking from a dream, her father's bloodied head cradled in her hands. The silence in the room was deafening.

Lady Rascomb stowed her embroidery. She cleared her throat and flexed her bad foot. "You should tell him, Ophelia. But I apologize, I cannot hear this again. I will leave the door open."

Ophelia watched as her mother left the room abruptly, abandoning Ophelia to the grief and guilt that had for so long colored her existence. The change from joy and hope to the shuttered pain of the last year was jarring.

"I apologize again," Sir Julian said, a blush creeping over his tanned face. His dark eyes searched hers. "I ask as a friend. As someone who loved your father as well."

Ophelia nodded. If she'd ever worried about crying in front of a stranger, those days were over. The entire affair had made her so numb that she didn't think she could descend back into the days where she thought she'd cry enough to soak her entire wardrobe.

"Of course. You deserve to know." Ophelia took a fortifying sip of tea. "Although could we ring for sherry or brandy? This sort of story seems to demand it."

Thankfully, Sir Julian did not seem scandalized by her request in the least, which she thought he might be. An unmarried woman, asking to drink with him? It was uncouth. But this was an extraordinary time, and required extraordinary measures.

When Ferris arrived and Ophelia requested brandy, he gave her an odd look and departed. But when he returned, he was very much at ease. Likely her mother had informed the butler as to what conversation was pending.

"Well," Ophelia said, cradling the snifter, not even taking a sip as of yet.

It was Sir Julian who posed the toast, raising his own snifter. "To your father, ever the motivator and visionary of extraordinary deeds."

A lump formed in her throat. "To my father." They sipped at

their drinks, the Calvados bringing her back to the evenings in Zermatt, after their long preparatory climbs up other peaks. When they were hopeful and excited.

"We did as Whymper had done, using his successful route as our template. After stashing gear at a small church at Schwarz-see—how much do you know of the geography of the Matterhorn and its surroundings?"

"Very little, I'm afraid. My mind is stuffed full of the mountain ranges on the other side of the Atlantic."

"Then it does not matter much if I refer to the precise locations," Ophelia said, sipping again at the brandy.

"I wouldn't know the difference," he agreed. There was a lull, and his face softened as he searched hers with those coal-black eyes. "I believe you might be stalling, Miss Ophelia."

She smiled at him, pained with his accuracy. "Indeed I am. I was expedition leader. All of these events were my calls to make."

"Yes, but you cannot take responsibility for the weather, nor the mistakes of your team."

"No," Ophelia protested. "I know that. But—" she sighed. "I shall start again."

Sir Julian sat back and crossed his legs, looking very much at his leisure.

"My plan all along was to keep our risks to a minimum. We would not try to reinvent a route or waypoints. Our only innovations were to those items that were peculiar to our group and our weather."

"And what was peculiar to your group?" Sir Julian asked, his brows furrowed.

Ophelia couldn't help but look at him as if he were daft. "We were majority women. We wore our long woolen skirts. Our upper body strength is less developed."

Sir Julian nodded. "But I will wager you had the same experience as others who had attempted this climb."

"Some yes, some no. But by the time we attempted the Matterhorn, we'd climbed most of the mountains in the range, including Mount Rosa and Breithorn, which are difficult treks themselves."

"So you had the preparation, the experience, and the knowledge."

Ophelia squirmed. "Of course we did. I made sure we arrived in Zermatt months earlier than other expeditions, knowing full well that we required the altitude and training that only the Swiss Alps could offer. It was no accident, and I certainly would never purposely endanger the lives of those I love."

Sir Julian nodded, his body relaxed, and that made her relax as well. She sipped her brandy. "Everything seemed to be going rather well. We camped overnight on the Hörnli Ridge, a rocky shoulder that sits directly in front of the Matterhorn. The ridge extends to base of the mountain, and is quite treacherous. We slept there and woke early, hoping to ascend to the top by the early afternoon, but it wasn't to be. We were stopped where Whymper first camped as well. It's most of the elevation needed to make the summit, but it was getting too late in the day to make the peak and return down safely."

"So you took refuge? This sounds deeply pragmatic so far."

Ophelia shook her head. "No, and I'll thank you to not interrupt me."

"My apologies," he murmured, his dark eyes fixed firmly upon her.

"It was the chimneys. The chute was covered in ice, and it had turned Whymper and others around on the mountain before. But, with our ropes and our guide, I thought we could end our day there, as we still had some light. My plan was to camp just above it, hoping to make the summit early the next morning and descend, arriving back at the church where we had cached our change of clothes and food by noon."

Ophelia sipped at her brandy, not wanting to relive this next part, the piece that was so indelibly imprinted in her heart. "The guide, myself, and Justine Brewer had made it to the top of the chimney. Each of us had to negotiate different routes on the icy chute given our different sizes and reach. It was then my father's turn to climb it."

Sir Julian leaned forward in his seat, putting down his brandy snifter. Ophelia felt she had no choice but to mimic him. The moment made her ill. Nausea gripped her, but she pressed on, knowing she must continue to tell the story in order for her sickness to ease.

"We all had these spikes we'd devised on our shoes, in order to aid us in the icy sections. My father used them to drive into the ice sheet, held in the grips of the rope being monitored by our guide. And then, he—slipped." Ophelia shrugged. Something so fallible, easy, and common could kill a man. "He lost his footing and pendulated into the wall of the chimney. The sound—" she choked on the memory, her stomach threatening to rebel. "I can never forget the sound of his head hitting the rock wall. There is nothing like it."

Sir Julian reached across and gripped her hand. The softening callouses comforted her. "And this is where he died?"

"No," she said, almost laughing. "My father could not perish so easily."

Julian returned her appreciative grin. "He was not a man easily defeated."

"He was unconscious, bleeding from the head, it was awful." Ophelia saw it all again in her mind's eye, the chunk of bone that had chipped out of his skull, his hair still attached. It was the stuff of nightmares. "I wrapped his head to the best of my ability, and we were forced to abandon our attempt. It was a long struggle to make our way down the mountain, and by then it was dark."

She gripped Sir Julian's hands as tightly as she'd gripped the rock during that descent, that terror for her father making her cling to the mountain with the bottoms of her feet. "And then as we crossed back over the Hörnli Ridge, it was so narrow that only one person could cross at a time. Being the tallest, our guide and Tristan tied my father in between them to carry across the ridge. It's so rocky and uneven, and it was dark, and we were tired and hungry and cold."

"That fatigue is something I understand. I've felt that myself." He gripped her hand back, lending a support that Ophelia hadn't felt since her father died.

The sensation of his hands warm, strong, and still calloused gave her a burst of courage. "One of us slipped. I think it was Eleanor, I can't be sure. And it took Prudence over the edge, and I heard the rope slithering over the rock, another sound I cannot forget."

"What did you do?"

"Before Prudence could pull me off the ridge, I tried to wedge myself onto one of the rocks. I almost fell. I almost didn't make it. Justine was the other end of our quartet's rope, and she had better terrain for bracing herself without falling. And then Tristan and Karl—Karl was our guide—put down my father and came to help us. Tristan tied me into the rock face and then together we were able to pull up Prudence and Eleanor. They were both injured, but not horribly so. Only Justine and I were unscathed."

"I would not say you are unscathed, Miss Ophelia."

She steadied her breath, wishing she could plead with him to fix it. To go back in time and change what happened. But there was no such magic. "Karl and Tristan took my father to the church ahead of us, while we cleaned up the camp and followed as well as we could, with Prudence and Eleanor's injuries. By morning, a donkey cart arrived to carry my father back to Zermatt, and we did what we could. We were told the cold temperatures kept him from dying immediately, but it was weeks before he was well enough that we could leave Zermatt. And then when we did, it didn't matter. He would only come around for short periods, and often not lucid ones. He died, oddly enough, of pneumonia, not of his injury."

They sat in silence.

Sir Julian nodded. "Thank you for telling me."

"It was the worst mistake of my life." Ophelia choked on the words.

"It wasn't your mistake," he insisted.

"If I hadn't insisted we take on the chimneys before making camp, he would be alive. If I had taken into account how tired everyone was, that it was the end of the day, and it would have been better to take the chimneys after rest, he would still be alive." Ophelia burned with rage at herself, the anger of hindsight.

"If you had taken the chimneys the next morning, you would have been even more fatigued," Sir Julian argued.

"No, we would have had decent rest," Ophelia insisted.

"Did you bring food? Tents?"

"No, they're far too heavy. We'd wanted to complete it in one long day." Ophelia stuck her jaw out. She felt mulish and obstinate. Her stomach churned, feeling acidic.

"So you think that if you attempted the chimneys in the morning, after spending the night in freezing conditions with no shelter and no food, it would have improved the outcome?" Sir Julian challenged her.

His words were as painful as if he'd struck her. "But."

"The human body needs food, Ophelia. We require sustenance. And sitting in cold conditions, I can tell you from experience, saps your energy. It makes you need even more."

Ophelia shook her head. "No, that's—"

Julian gripped her hands even harder, ducking his head to make her look at him. "You did the right thing. Your call was correct. I would have done the same."

"But, he slipped—"

"Your father would have done the same. Did he question you on this?"

"No, he agreed with me." Ophelia started breathing faster, and she didn't understand why.

"You did the right thing."

For the first time in months, her eyes teared up. "But. But he died because of the expedition. My expedition."

"He died doing what he loved. I can't think of a better way to go."

"I can!"

"What, feeble in bed? Losing control of your bowels, or a rotten tooth, infecting you from the inside out?"

"No, of course not!" Ophelia drew back, trying to pull her hands from his grip. He stared her down, not letting go. She squirmed.

"You did the right thing," he said again, boring into her with those dark, dark eyes.

"You keep saying that," she said, shaking her head, pulling again, but he wouldn't let go.

"And I'll keep saying it until you believe me. I know what I'm talking about, Ophelia. I don't need to climb the Matterhorn to know what it's like to run an Alpine expedition. That's what I've been doing for the last ten years of my life."

"You can't understand the Matterhorn until you climb it yourself," she insisted, feeling like she had him at last.

"Then take me."

She frowned. "What do you mean, take you?"

"Take me up the Matterhorn. Let's go. You've already done the research and have the contacts. Let's go. I haven't climbed a mountain in months."

"But."

"Then say you made the right call."

The acid churned in her stomach. "We only have a month until the end of July. We can't put together an expedition so quickly."

"Then July of 1872. You, me and whomever you deem appropriate." His cool gaze was a challenge to her. Was he absolutely serious? He was trying to cow her into saying that her father's death wasn't her fault—which it clearly was—and thought she would balk?

"You cannot be serious."

"Then say it wasn't your fault." Sir Julian wasn't smiling. Wasn't showing her any indicator that he was joking.

The thought of returning to the mountain both filled her with dread and thrilled her in equal measures. Would he really climb the Matterhorn with her?

"Or, you're booked for the month of July in 1872?"

It was easily doable. That gave her plenty of time to return to the health required to climb the mountain. Plenty of time for them both to raise the money needed. She could recruit the original Ladies' Alpine Society. She'd promised them a peak, after all.

"We'll climb the Matterhorn in July 1872. You'd better not be teasing me, Sir Julian."

"I don't tease, Miss Ophelia." Julian finally released her hands, and she felt a shift in the air that she couldn't identify, but one that felt good. A shift that felt like more than relief, more than the lessening of her guilt, though those were present as well. There was an unknown new promise between them that she'd never felt before.

Chapter Four

"SIR JULIAN, THIS was a marvelous talk. Thank you so much for making time in your busy schedule for us," Mrs. McManus said. The excessive gauzy veil that adorned her bonnet waved as she bobbed her head, threatening to be sucked down into his throat as he breathed.

Julian dodged the silk as best as he could in the breeze and thanked her. "The Garden Club is the most attentive audience I believe I've ever had, madame. You have honored me." And the money didn't hurt, either. He'd be happy to make this a regular occurrence.

There was a crowd of ladies surrounding him now. "A word, Sir Julian, if I may." A woman who had beautiful blue eyes and thick white glossy hair tidied away as if the color were a fashion choice and not a sign of aging pushed past Mrs. McManus. "While you spoke at length about flowers, do you think it would be possible to tell me about the viability of thick vines in a climate such as ours here in England? I have a greenhouse that could use some vigor."

There was something in the sparkle of her eyes that made Julian think that perhaps when she spoke of a thick vine's vigor that she was not speaking of plants. But Julian gamely spoke of the flora he encountered, and even withdrew his sketchpad from his valise to show her.

More encounters continued, and someone served him tea and

then alternated slices of lemon cake and plum cake as he socialized. It was fun to discuss his adventures. And while most of the women were upwards of sixty, some were decidedly not, and almost to a person, they placed a soft, gloved hand on his forearm.

After most of the clamor subsided, someone snatched his empty cup and plate from his hands. He sighed, coming down from the fervor of the afternoon.

"Quite the accomplishment, Shoulders," a woman purred from behind him.

He turned toward the low voice and saw a woman dressed in a dark green day gown embroidered with beads and black lace. Her dark brown hair was dressed in curls and pinned artfully around. Her bonnet was barely a head covering and more an adornment made of feathers and lace and beads to match her dress.

"I beg your pardon?" Julian asked. She was stunning, likely in her forties, he judged, and with a dress like that, perfectly wealthy on her own terms. Her movements, from the shift of her hips to the languid gesture of her hand, were silky and confident, like the water of the Amazon just before the rapids.

"You had both Mrs. Breton and Mrs. Rielgud vying for your attentions. Those two rarely agree on anything." She walked toward him and became lovelier still. It was the sort of dark beauty that was not objective, rather factual. Her comeliness partly came from her manner of dress, posture, and overall style, but her features were well formed and even.

"They did not need to agree, nor did they seem to talk to each other. They both spoke with me directly," he protested, pushing papers back into his valise. It was time to leave, and something told him this woman would insist on walking out with him.

"They both liked you. An exceedingly rare event. Their tastes in men are typically opposite. Breton favors the fine, well-spoken gentleman, whereas Rielgud prefers the strapping sort of ruffian who could toss her over his shoulder. Of which, you do meld both types exceedingly well." She came to stand next to him but refrained from touching him.

"I know there is a compliment somewhere, but strangely, I don't feel complimented."

She smiled. "Then you have the unique experience of a man pursued as a woman is pursued. The difference being that if we get you in a room alone, you'll be able to fend us off."

"Us? Do you include yourself in the ranks of these would-be wooers?"

She met his eye, and there was a spark between them. "I could be persuaded to throw my hat into the ring. However, I have one rule for competitions."

Julian gestured to the door, but she didn't budge.

"I don't enter contests that I can't win." She sashayed in front of him, and whether it was a move of dominance or one of coquettishness, Julian couldn't say. But he was intrigued and flattered, and suddenly all those polite hand touches from the other women evaporated from his skin, replaced by the searing words of this one.

⫸⫷

OPHELIA THREW THE letter down and did her best to not curl up in a ball like a child.

"What is it?" her mother asked, picking up the letter.

"Read it," Ophelia said, desperate to not cry.

Her mother scanned the beautiful feminine calligraphy of Lucy Walker's penmanship. "*And I hope that with this hasty band, I shall best my rival and arrive to the summit first of my sex.* Oh." Her mother sighed, putting down the letter.

"It's over," Ophelia said. "My dream is done."

"They might not summit," her mother said, a tone as hopeful and as disbelieving as she was.

"It's Lucy Walker, Mama. And she's up against Marguerite Brevoort, that's why she had to be hasty. She found out Mrs. Brevoort was in Zermatt to hire guides."

"But even Miss Walker has been turned around before," her mother pointed out.

Ophelia raised her head and looked at her. "Mama. If both of them will attempt, the conditions are good. And Lucy Walker got Melchior Anderegg as one of her party. He has more summits than most have fingers."

Her mother smiled and that irritated Ophelia. "Are you saying more summits than most, or that most people have fewer than ten fingers?"

"Don't try to make me smile, I'm not going to do it."

"Not going to do what?" Arthur asked, strolling into the drawing room.

"Smile," Ophelia said, already feeling the twitch to do so.

"Both Lucy Walker and Meta Brevoort are attempting the Matterhorn," her mother explained.

"Ah," Arthur said. He did not share the love of the mountains with Ophelia and Tristan, but he'd been on plenty of enjoyable climbs with them as a family. His sense of duty was extreme, and he insisted that as the heir, he could not risk his life for a bit of rock.

"What brings you to the drawing room in the middle of the day, darling?" Lady Rascomb asked.

"A question for Ophelia. I've already checked with my wife, and she is happy to oblige—"

"Is she feeling better?" Ophelia asked.

Arthur's mouth cracked wide. "Somewhat. She's still having the, er, you know, illness. But the doctor is coming next week to confirm our suspicions."

"That it's not the flu?" Ophelia asked, hoping to lighten her own spirits.

"Precisely. That we will be starting our own family." His chest puffed out, the picture of paternal pride.

The swell of warmth in her brother made her own heart ease. It did mean that in nine months or so, she and her mother would have to find a new place to live, but Arthur having children felt correct. He had always dreamed of his own family, and wanted the life promised by his station.

How wonderful that must be, Ophelia thought. *To fit so well and precisely into one's own life.*

Her mother was up hugging him—an unusual event, but this would be her first grandchild from someone besides Portia. She'd gotten the earliest start, after all.

"I'll have to begin making baby clothes. Oh, this is quite exciting."

His news was welcome, but it was only a brief respite from the crushing blow of the letter from Lucy Walker. It wasn't that they competed—except that they did—as they encouraged one another in climbing and adapting to a world that might not be so accepting of them. Lucy managed it by living with her brother, and being the perfect hostess at their home in Liverpool, so no one could criticize her time in the Alps.

But what would Ophelia do?

"Thank you, Mama, but that is not why I came in." Arthur cleared his throat.

"Yes, your business. I apologize for distracting you." Her mother returned to her seat and her embroidery hoop.

"I was speaking with Lord Fairport," Arthur said, turning now to look down at Ophelia.

"Please sit, Arthur. When you speak to me from your great height, it feels like you are purposely trying to lord over me."

"Well, I am the lord," he quipped, taking his seat.

"Yes, well, no one will forget if you sit." Ophelia tried to get her mind around Lord Fairport. He was perfectly respectable, as far as she knew. There was nothing about the man to excite her or anyone else, for that matter. He was unseasoned porridge. It would do when one was hungry, but unappetizing still.

"Lord Fairport has asked to see more of you. I thought we

ought to invite him to dinner." Arthur's expression was one of hope.

So many people with their hope. Her mother, Arthur, Lord Fairport. "May we also invite Sir Julian?"

Arthur blinked. "Of course. May I ask why?"

"He is in the Royal Geographical Society with Lord Fairport and has socialized with him on a number of occasions. I would like to see how he speaks with him. I consider Sir Julian a friend who would have my best interests at heart. It would be nice to hear his opinions on the matter."

"We will have to find another woman to balance out the numbers."

"Why? The numbers are exactly even with Sir Julian in attendance."

Arthur shook his head. "While Lady Emily would adore hostessing such a prestigious dinner, she is not capable of being in a room with, er . . ."

"Food?" Ophelia suggested.

"Odors." Arthur winced.

Lady Rascomb chuckled.

"Is this normal, mama?" Ophelia asked.

"Oh yes, for a woman who is with child, the first few months are unpredictable and fraught. Odors, in particular, can be a challenge."

"Would it be an imposition to wait a week or so, in order to allow Lady Emily to recover herself?" Ophelia asked. "I wouldn't mind a postponement either."

Arthur looked at her with concern. "Why?"

Ophelia squirmed. She had the answer—this whole Lucy Walker situation—but it didn't feel like the truth. What the truth was, she wasn't sure, and therefore couldn't say. "I'm afraid that having my dreams dashed makes me not want company."

Arthur slapped his knees. "Then we shall wait until a more fortuitous time. Lord Fairport waited this long to pay his attentions to you. He can wait a bit longer."

"Thank you, Arthur, er—I mean—" Ophelia still couldn't manage to address him by his title.

Arthur put his hand on her shoulder. "Quite all right. You can always call me Arthur. I know it doesn't seem right the other way."

Ophelia swallowed the lump that formed in her throat and nodded, giving a faint, pained smile as recognition of his generosity. The shades of her father were everywhere.

⫸⫷

"I MUST ADMIT, I do not know who that is," Julian said, not daring to rest his teacup on the table, for fear that Ophelia's wild gesticulations might upend it. He'd never seen her like this, and it was amusing.

"Melchior Anderegg?" she repeated, looking at him with such huge blue eyes that he wondered if they were smaller or bigger than the circumference of a chicken egg.

He shook his head again, trying very hard to hide the smile that was about to break out upon his face.

"Not only is he a vastly experienced guide, he has done first ascents on a number of the more treacherous peaks—" She held up a finger, as if he might dare interrupt her. "—Which are not necessarily the famous ones."

"He sounds like an excellent man to know," Julian said.

Ophelia leafed through a notebook that was stuffed with copious notes in her precise handwriting. There were illustrations for ideas on how to improve gear, instructions on challenging knots, notes on certain snow conditions, all things she had noted during both the Ben Nevis and the Matterhorn expeditions. All notes she had shown and discussed with her father, no doubt. He wondered if she could separate her father from her ambition.

"There are a few other men I might consider, but Anderegg is typically in the Alps for the summer climbing season."

"Would you consider a woman guide?" Julian asked, just to see what she would say.

She dropped her book. "You know of one?"

"You sound so hopeful."

"Of course I do! An all-woman expedition?" She sighed and leaned back on the sofa, as another woman might do when describing her wedding day or perfect husband.

"I thought you might be too jealous to entertain the thought," he said, looking at her sideways, so they both faced the same way.

"Julian," she said, dropping the formal honorific. What a relief to not have that hang between them. He hated the sound of that *sir* on her lips. "I want *all* women to be able to climb a mountain. To have access to the kind of physical freedom my parents have encouraged me to have. We are restricted in so many ways, this gilded cage of frippery, when the feeling of running in cool air, sliding down a snowy hill, jumping to climb a tree, all bring a visceral joy. Why should that be beaten out of us? Do we not deserve a happiness that does not come with the price of pain?"

Julian frowned, not following. "What joy carries the price of pain?"

"Childbirth," she said simply.

Her answer threw him. It was not an answer he expected from a young lady, but then again, Ophelia Bridewell surprised him at every turn. "There are other happinesses in the world besides a child. I know, for I have had many."

"Name one," she said, smoothing out the map of the Matterhorn. There were four sides of the mountain, and she'd already attempted one. Would it be more logical to try a different route? He could suggest it, but knowing her, she'd already thought through the idea and discarded it.

He cast his eyes about the room, his brain suddenly unhelpful in this endeavor. "Music," he said.

She thought about it. "Do you think music creates the same joy as the love of a child?"

"Well," he said, drawing out the word as he thought. "I have only listened to music. I've never had a child. Given birth, or otherwise."

She grinned at him. It dazzled him when she did that. She was beautiful not smiling, but when she allowed her earnest joy to surface on her face, the transformation to goddess was instantaneous. It stopped his breath.

"I suppose the scientific inquiry is limited to those who have had children, and given the existence of a person whose feelings could be hurt, the answer must always be no. It seems this line of reasoning is not going to solve anything."

Julian nodded, putting down his teacup. But it covered the north side of the mountain—rather the most treacherous-looking approach—and Ophelia shoved it aside.

"Children, how are we doing?" Lady Rascomb returned to the room, escorting a footman, carrying the late Lord Rascomb's expedition journals.

It was his turn to grin. "It's been a long while since anyone called me a child."

"That is the inequity that shocks me the most," Ophelia said, straightening up again. "Well, one of many, I suppose."

Her mind whirred and clicked at dizzying speeds. It was fascinating to watch as she spoke and thought simultaneously. "Yes?"

"I am an unmarried woman, and despite being eight-and-twenty, am still considered almost a girl, though most call me a spinster. But you, as an unmarried man, have been considered adult since . . . since when would you say?"

He thought. "I suppose since my father died and I inherited at age fifteen?"

Ophelia threw her hand at him, as if his experience was the exact proof she had been looking for her entire life. "There. Mama. We should be equals."

"Yes," her mother said, gesturing to the footman to put the stack of books on the chair, nearest to Julian. "As you are planning another death-defying expedition that pushes people to their absolute limits, calling you children, as if you were in here playing with blocks, is funny."

Ophelia gave her mother a sly smile.

"Sir Julian, feel free to look through my husband's papers. I don't know if you'll find anything you need, but I trust you to keep his works safe." Lady Rascomb rounded the edge of the sofa with her cane and sat next to Ophelia. Looking at her daughter, she asked, "How are things looking?"

"I can't decide if we should go the same route or try the Italian route."

Julian had opinions, but he didn't dare voice them, and he was pleased to hear that he wasn't an idiot for thinking about a different route. He enjoyed Ophelia's clear revelry in all the minutiae of the planning. They would obviously be staying in the inn they'd gone to before, as her best chum had married into that family. But there were debates about guides and routes, equipment and timing.

Technically, Julian didn't have to be there for any of this. He'd told her to take him, and thus put all responsibility in her hands, and it was a year off, besides. There was no reason to be having bi-weekly meetings, but it thrilled him to see her like this, her glossy blonde hair falling out of its pins as she peered over yet another map.

The resemblance to her mother was palpable, but he no longer thought of her as a younger version. Ophelia possessed a tenacity more like her father.

The grandfather clock in the corner dinged, and Julian checked his own pocket watch against it. "I fear I've overstayed my welcome."

Ophelia scrunched up her nose. "Must you go?"

"Sadly, I must." He looked forward to meeting Lady DeMarius at the opera, the hint of musky perfume and heightened banter luring him in. It was very different from the scene he'd been enjoying all afternoon with Ophelia. He told himself it was because Ophelia was but a girl to him, despite her protestations of being eight-and-twenty, and Lady DeMarius was an age-appropriate woman for him. Was it also that as a widowed aristocrat, Lady DeMarius held the promise of sexual favors, while Ophelia was a wide-eyed virgin?

He cursed himself for even entertaining such a lewd thought. His mentor's daughter deserved more respect than his crude evaluations. Lady DeMarius offered scintillating company, and they would be at the opera, in her private box. It was an opportunity for him to luxuriate in the wealth he himself did not possess, but could appreciate.

Well, wealth in London banknotes. He had other wealth, but not the sort that was so easily converted into goods and services here. Not without finding a jeweler he could trust. In the places he'd ventured, far from the European-style towns that had sprung up all over the South American continent, rubber was quickly outpacing any other resource. He'd been given jewels in exchange for a week's worth of labor in some places. But in others, he'd witnessed horrific acts against the indigenous people of the Amazon. From the first time he encountered them to the last, some tribes were almost wholly wiped out from the growing rubber plantations.

He'd written letters of complaints, but they were falling on unwilling readers. How could one protest the injustice when there were vast amounts of money to be made? He was but one man. And not a powerful one, at that. It made him wish that his mentor was still alive to throw his influence behind Julian's account. That might have had an effect. But this new Rascomb didn't have the same reach as his father. He was a fine fellow, but Julian could already see the difference in institutions like RGS when they lacked members with the moral backbone of a man like his friend.

Once out of the Rascomb townhouse, he had the distinct displeasure of a blustery summer day. He gripped the brim of his hat as a gust of wind blew by. He could already feel the difference in his legs and back in this new, cushioned life. He was getting softer by the day. At least, unless Ophelia Bridewell started up his training regime as she had already threatened to do. He smiled at the thought. She was an extraordinary person. With her exterior beauty, he did not understand how she'd not been snapped up by some lord or another already.

Her unusual passion, while unconventional, was certainly not scandalous. And her status as the daughter of a viscount gave her a respectability that would allow her mildly odd behavior to be overlooked. His thoughts brought him to Lord Fairport, and that quickly dampened his spirits. The man was not worthy of her. Not even close. He would ignore her passion, convince her to stay home, and she would dwindle in his house, become a shadow of the phenomenal creature she was.

Since her father had been his mentor, would it not be his duty to become her mentor in return? He would protect her as best as he could, given his lower status and lack of pound notes. But he had access and influence unique to his role as an explorer. The trouble was, how could he persuade anyone that a match with Fairport wasn't a brilliant idea? A wealthy, titled man who appeared respectable and did not indulge in the vices of many other Peers: he had no known mistress, did not overindulge in drink or gambling. Though, just because it wasn't widely known did not mean the man didn't indulge. Yet, telling somebody the man was boring was not news, and certainly not a reason to reject a suit from him.

Strange how his conversations with Miss Ophelia made him feel more the important explorer of the world than all the speeches and articles he'd so far done. Like the ten years of gathering data and mapping the smaller ranges of the South American continent was a real contribution, and not a way for him to just escape London.

He arrived at his flat, signaling Nicholas when he entered that he would require a shave and help dressing that evening. Mrs. Talbert asked about dinner, and he requested a light repast early enough to make the opera on time. Perhaps if things went well with Lady DeMarius, he could enlist the widow's help with Lord Fairport. She appeared to be a very clever woman.

⟫⟫⟩⟨⟨⟨

"BUT DO YOU like him?" Eleanor pushed her teacup around the saucer, creating an excruciating screeching sound.

Ophelia wanted to stop her, but for some reason, felt paralyzed by politeness. How to tell a friend that her behavior was driving one absolutely insane from noise? Finally, Ophelia reached out and put her hand over Eleanor's, stopping that horrific sound of porcelain on porcelain.

"I apologize, Eleanor. I cannot think while that screech is occurring. What are we discussing?"

Eleanor didn't bother looking sheepish, as she might have years ago when they first met. The Eleanor Bridewell of London didn't look at all like the Eleanor Piper of Ben Navis. She was far more stylish, and far more self-assured. She no longer flinched at perceived slights or cowered when attention was brought to her.

Not that she was brash or loud, but the comfortable love that she and Tristan shared was easy and obvious. If Ophelia believed for one moment that she might be able to have something like that, she would have been envious. But she was happy most of all for Tristan, who came into his own when he found Eleanor. He didn't mind not being the heir, didn't mind finding a profession—if one could call a mountaineering outfitter an actual profession.

They sat out in Eleanor's garden, enjoying the late summer afternoon sunshine. "I was asking if you actually liked Lord Fairport."

"Oh. Him." Ophelia looked over at a cluster of purple flowers dotting the rosemary bush. "He's a fine enough dancer."

Eleanor's shrewd expression would not be deterred. Ophelia knew she must continue speaking on the topic or else Eleanor would ask repeatedly.

"He has inoffensive breath."

Eleanor stared her down. "What do you think Justine would say right now? Have you written to her about this?"

No. Because she'd written to Justine of what consumed her: another trip to the Matterhorn. Lucy Walker and Meta Brevoort be damned. It didn't matter if Ophelia's name was in a history book. She wanted that summit. She wanted to stand atop that pile of rock and scream her own name.

When Ophelia didn't verbalize any of this, Eleanor leaned forward. "I'll tell you what she'd say. Something to the effect of 'Having nice breath and not stepping on your toes is hardly marriage material.'"

"I just don't like thinking about it," Ophelia confessed, looking down at her teacup. The dregs swirled in there, and it made her wonder what a fortuneteller would see in the pattern.

Eleanor narrowed her eyes. Sometimes she could be too insightful. Tristan even said so. "What are you thinking about, then?"

"I'm planning another trip. Another expedition." She wasn't ready to tell the world about it, not even Eleanor, but needs must.

"When?" Her voice sounded possibly interested? Definitely not damning, which is what Ophelia had expected.

"Next summer. With Sir Julian."

"Sir Julian?" Eleanor asked.

"Surely Tristan has told you about him," Ophelia said. But, had Tristan met him? She wasn't sure. To Ophelia, his frequent visits to the house permeated every aspect of her life. As if he'd brought with him some of the South American sunshine, the heat and color that the Amazon was known for.

"No, he has not. Tell me about him. And the trip."

There was something in Eleanor's voice that Ophelia didn't understand, but that was fine. She could speak on this topic for a year without stopping to sleep. And so she did. About how Sir Julian was a friend and correspondent of her father's, about his regular social calls, about him asking her to take him up the Matterhorn.

Eleanor sat back in her chair with an unreadable expression. "And who all do you plan to take to the Matterhorn?"

"So far, just Sir Julian and I. Though the idea of engaging the rest of the Ladies' Alpine Society has occurred to me. I am not ready to extend invitations, as the planning is not complete."

Eleanor smiled. "I'd be willing to go again. To finish what we started."

Ophelia inhaled the sweet summer air. "I'm so glad." Another weight lifted from her chest. They didn't hate her. Or blame her for their injuries. They said they didn't, but words were not always truthful. On the way down from the Matterhorn, both Eleanor and Prudence were injured, an additional piece of guilt that laid on Ophelia every time her mind was quiet.

"But in the meantime, there are other issues to contemplate. Like a suit from Lord Fairport."

Ophelia grimaced. "But I hate the idea."

"Of Lord Fairport?" Eleanor's eyebrows shot up.

"No," Ophelia waved her hand, as if she could erase her previous words. "The future in which I am married is much less interesting than the future in which I climb mountains."

Eleanor chewed on her lip. "To me, that sounds very telling."

"Does it?"

"I think it means you do not wish to marry Lord Fairport."

"Or perhaps I do not wish to marry at all." Ophelia rocked back into her chair. "Though I know I ought to. Otherwise, I'll be a drain on my brother for the rest of my life."

Eleanor gave her a sympathetic look. She was older than Ophelia, though not by much. "It isn't fair, is it? To not have the options to care for oneself as well as men can care for us?"

"It's ridiculous, is what it is," Ophelia snapped. She'd thought about becoming a working woman, as if it wouldn't reflect poorly on Arthur, signaling that he either refused to look after her, or was too cheap to do so. But the occupations available to her were severely limited. Governess? Absolutely not. Seamstress? No, thank you. Actress? Hardly. "All I want to do is climb mountains. If I could open an outfitter like Tristan's, or become a guide like other climbers, I would do it. But no one would trust a woman." And what Ophelia left unsaid was, *No one would trust me.*

"Tristan sometimes gets inquiries about outfitting a woman," Eleanor said. "If any of those ever write back, I know he would pass them along to you. I'd make sure he paid you, of course."

Ophelia smiled at her friend, trying so hard to help. "You're very kind, Eleanor."

"I'm not, really. I'm quite selfish. You're my friend, and I believe my friends should all get what makes them happy." Eleanor shrugged. "It's a failing of mine."

"So you'll go with me to the Matterhorn?"

Eleanor reached across the wrought iron table and gripped her hand. "If I am able, I will go."

Ophelia frowned. "What would make you unable? Does your shoulder still pain you?"

Eleanor looked like she were stifling a grin. Oh, she'd misunderstood something again. But what?

"We are discussing adding a child to our family, Ophelia. So that you might be an auntie. If that occurs before next summer, then I will not be able to climb with you."

An image of a ten-year-old child moving into their house occurred to Ophelia, and she momentarily thought, *Why could she not just bring the child along?* But then the reality sank in: this was far enough away that Eleanor could be very pregnant by the time the expedition would begin. Right. And it would be a baby, not a child who was of a speaking and reasoning age.

"Of course," Ophelia said quickly, once her mind had figured out the puzzle of Eleanor's words. Still, she felt embarrassed for not seeing that already. Her friends were all married now, and children were a real threat to their freedom. "Then let's hope for the best."

Eleanor gave her a strange look, as if she weren't sure which way Ophelia meant to be the best. Honestly, Ophelia wasn't sure either.

✦

Chapter Five

"I'M WARNING YOU not to fall in love with me," Delphine purred, tucking her hands around his elbow.

They walked among the museum's exhibition hall, filled to the brim with paintings and people with large hats. He almost stumbled with her bold speech. "I beg your pardon?"

She smirked at his reaction, pleased she'd caught him off guard. This was their fifth outing together, and that seemed to be what she enjoyed doing the most. He had not yet tried to kiss her, not even her hand, for fear of what she might say next.

"Men tend to fall in love with me and then propose marriage, and I must tell you that I won't be marrying anyone. My portion from my late husband stipulates that it lasts only so long as I remain unmarried. But that doesn't dictate what I do in my spare time."

Julian choked. She was most brazenly suggesting that she was available for not just museum strolls.

"I thought we ought to get that out of the way, so we can have a proper look round today. I didn't want you to be distracted."

Julian swallowed after a coughing fit. "Very considerate of you."

She patted his arm. "Don't think I wouldn't look out for your best interests, for they dovetail quite nicely with mine."

Julian wondered what his best interests were, precisely, but his entire mind had gone blank. They stared at paintings in lovely gilded frames, and he couldn't remember a single one. His body buzzed with what she insinuated. The release that she promised wrapped up in the heady smell of vanilla and lilies. The woman was a walking scandal, and he had to admit, he didn't want to leave her side.

Her lips were plump and pink and it was difficult to not think of what they might taste like. She caught him staring and her mouth curved in approval. He shook his head, trying to come out of the intoxication. It had been a long time since he had been with a woman, and he'd never been with a woman like this, so knowing, so confidant, so obvious.

He exhaled with an audible breath, trying to compose himself. It had been a long time since lust had made such a fool of him, too. At least he knew the difference now between lust and love. Lust made you feel a fool, love made you feel a monster. She snuggled deeper into his elbow, seemingly pleased with his discomfort.

They rounded a corner into the next room, only to run directly into the younger Bridewell brother, who looked so much like his father, only sporting his mother's golden hair. The sight knocked the wind—and the lust—out of Julian.

"Sir Julian!" Mr. Bridewell exclaimed, looking thoroughly pleased. "So good to see you here."

"Delightful," Julian managed to say, wishing Delphine would loosen her grip on him.

"I'd like you to meet my wife," Bridewell said, angling his elbow forward to bring his wife into Julian's periscoped view.

"A pleasure." Julian bowed.

"She too was on the Matterhorn expedition," Bridewell boasted. Pride showed through his expression, and Julian marked it. There were few men who were so viscerally *proud* of their wives. Or at least, proud of the woman themselves, and not proud that they were the ones to marry her, for whatever reason. In Julian's experience, men were proud of their wives' beauty, not of their climbing skill. And it struck him suddenly that if he were the type to marry, he'd want to follow Mr. Bridewell's example.

Mrs. Bridewell's cheeks pinked, but she made no move to contradict him or belittle her accomplishment. She was pretty, with dark chestnut hair and warm brown eyes. "Quite the adventure," she said instead.

"I can imagine," Julian said, his heart warming for the charm of this couple.

"Miss Bridewell tells me you have an interest in the Matterhorn," Mrs. Bridewell said.

Julian stiffened, but smiled. There was something instinctive about keeping Delphine out of the way of his mountaineering efforts. He simply didn't want to share it with her. Not yet.

"I do. But first, let me introduce Lady DeMarius, the dowager countess."

Delphine gave him a charming smile and fluttered her dark lashes at him. "Oh Julian, you make me sound so ancient."

No one in the group could overlook how familiarly she addressed him. She was staking her claim on him as much as he'd tried to hide his interest in the Matterhorn. They chattered on aimlessly, Julian impatient to move them along the hall.

"Do you have a particular interest in art?" Julian asked the couple, hoping this would steer the conversation away from the speculation on Delphine and how deep his acquaintance with her was.

"I did not, at least, not until the Matterhorn," Mrs. Bridewell confessed. "I had some ah, injuries, from the descent, and while I convalesced in Zermatt, I took art lessons from another lady climber's husband. Oh dear, that does sound convoluted, doesn't it?"

"It really isn't," Mr. Bridewell continued. "At least, not for The Ladies' Alpine Society."

"I beg your pardon?" Delphine asked.

"The Ladies' Alpine Society, ma'am. It consists of myself, Miss Ophelia Bridewell, who is my sister-in-law, Mrs. Leopold

Moon, and Mrs. Karl Vogel."

Delphine looked bored by names she didn't recognize. In response to Mrs. Bridewell's recitation, she only made a hum of acknowledgment.

"Very brave, what they did," Julian said.

"Or you could have stayed home, and you wouldn't have been in danger," Delphine said. "So lovely to meet you both. We absolutely must see the next room. I've been positively aching to be here for weeks."

She pulled him away from the Bridewells so suddenly that he didn't have time to argue. He let out a stunned farewell and let her pull him along. They stood in front of another painting.

"That was rude," Julian commented, his consuming lust from earlier completely evaporated.

Delphine turned on him, her eyebrows drawn together in concern. "My apologies, Julian, I couldn't bear to talk about a topic that everyone else loves and I do not. It makes me feel like my life has been utterly wasted."

Julian softened at this. "But what you said sounded so insulting to Mrs. Bridewell."

"Oh, did it? I certainly didn't mean to make her feel bad, the words slipped out." She turned her attention back to the painting, rather than seeking his forgiveness.

It rankled that she didn't offer an apology, and he understood that she wouldn't, because she said she was embarrassed for her actions. And her rudeness was not that she intended to insult the other woman, but rather suffered an insecurity which rose to the surface in polite company. Lord knew he had plenty of insecurities himself. He decided to let the matter drop. It wouldn't do well to think so poorly of her, and he'd found that most people meant well, overall.

"Would you care for an ice? There's a shop not far from here," he suggested.

"Sounds delightful," she said, as if she could intuit his forgiveness. "And then perhaps you wouldn't mind walking me home?"

"Of course," he said, confused as to why she would think he might abandon her in the middle of London.

"And stay for a bit?" she insisted, her dark eyes searching his.

"Er," he said, before his mind understood the inference. *Oh.* "If you like."

She patted his chest, as if she had fixed his pocket square. "I told you I have your best interests at heart."

FAMILY DINNERS ON Sundays used to be a chore. As children, they were called down from the nursery to have them, all together, so that they might learn from watching their parents. Ophelia recalled her dread of them. Sundays were the worst day of the week, from the cold pews of the church in the morning to the tedious evening meal, she could barely keep herself from throwing herself out a window.

Now that she was older, she enjoyed the dinners. Her sister Portia and her husband came, Eleanor came with Tristan. And now Lady Emily joined their table as well. Well, typically, she did. It was lovely to have all of them together, the original Bridewell siblings and their spouses. Except for her, of course. She looked down at her hands. As the youngest daughter, it was conceivable that she would have married long before Arthur or Tristan, which was typical for the fairer sex. Men could wait until they inherited, or were set in a career so they could provide for their future family. Women, given limited self-reliance, were married off as early as some families could manage, as they were a drain on the household finances.

But she would not think on that now.

"A roast!" Tristan rubbed his hands together. "Finally."

"Lady Emily has not been planning the menus of late," Ophelia said. "Too ill."

Arthur shot her a quelling look.

"Don't look at me like that," Ophelia insisted as her mother failed to chime in around the dinner table. "Lady Emily's menus are boring."

"I like her menus," Arthur protested. When no one else seconded his comment, he scanned the room and found no one to meet his gaze.

Ophelia shrugged. "At least I'm willing to say it."

Eleanor giggled. "Now that Justine isn't here, someone has to take the job."

Tristan snickered.

"And what is the news from Justine Vogel these days?" Lady Rascomb asked as she tasted her soup.

"Smashing, no doubt," Tristan said. While he and Justine had made a sport out of bickering, after their subsequent marriages to other people and the bonding of a harrowing night on the Matterhorn, they'd become quiet champions of one another.

"We're discussing meeting up in Paris sometime after the summer ends," Ophelia said, glancing between Arthur and her mother. Someone had authority over her still—her brother, technically—though she didn't know which one would protest this idea.

Eleanor clapped her hands. "That sounds like so much fun. I can only imagine you and Justine running wild through Paris."

Ophelia wanted to kick her beneath the table. Arthur would protest anything that made her "run wild."

"If you have an appropriate chaperone, I don't see why not," Arthur said, looking at Lady Rascomb.

"I cannot go," Lady Rascomb said quietly. "I—I."

"You don't need to say anything, Mama." Tristan reached over and grasped her hand. "Perhaps we could go. What do you think, Eleanor?"

"We could see what Prudence is up to! It's far enough in advance for them to return to Europe, isn't it?" Eleanor lit up.

"A reunion of the Ladies' Alpine Society?" Ophelia smiled. She liked that idea quite a lot. Perhaps she could invite Julian, so that he might meet Karl Vogel, and understand the Matterhorn from the perspective of the team who'd attempted it. She was about to bring it up, but the subject was already changed.

"How was the art exhibition?" Arthur asked.

"It was lovely, nothing terribly surprising, of course." Tristan glanced at Eleanor with a look that Ophelia found curious. "We ran into Sir Julian Dunstan while there."

"Oh, did you? I didn't know he was a patron of the arts," Lady Rascomb said, the maternal pleasure evident in her voice.

"Perhaps," Eleanor said, her entire posture changing from the confident straight spine of the Paris discussion to a rounded sag.

"What is it?" Arthur asked. He'd cultivated a relationship with Sir Julian as well, outside of the baronet's regular drawing room calls. It had made Ophelia feel good that they were able to so honor a man who'd been a friend of their father's.

"The woman he was with was—" Tristan shook his head. "Beyond rude."

"Very rude," Eleanor echoed.

"Who was she?" Ophelia asked, a cold feeling spreading in her chest.

"Lady DeMarius?" Eleanor said. "I didn't know her."

"Oh," Lady Rascomb said, her voice flat. "I know her. She is a rude person, but she has her charms. For some."

"Lady DeMarius?" Arthur looked thoughtful. "I remember Lord DeMarius. But he died some years back. Old as the Roman baths, he was."

Lady Rascomb nodded. "This would be his fourth wife. His widow."

"Four wives?" Ophelia sputtered.

"The previous three all died in childbirth. He has one surviving child from each wife."

"Very Henry VIII of him," Ophelia muttered.

"Very Catherine Parr of her," Arthur joked, but no one laughed.

"But as his widow, she likely has a comfortable pension," Tristan said drily.

Lady Rascomb gave them all a pinched smile. Ophelia couldn't figure out if it was a way to compare their mother's situation with Lady DeMarius's, or if it was because she had unkind opinions of the woman.

"Whatever her financials," Eleanor said, "I don't care for her."

"It's Sir Julian's business who he spends his time with, not ours," Arthur pronounced as the footman entered with the roast.

Ophelia didn't like the idea of that at all. "She must have some redeeming quality or else he wouldn't spend time with her."

Eleanor looked at her with open curiosity. "And why is that?"

"Because he is a discerning individual," Ophelia said, almost insulted that Eleanor would ask such a thing.

"There are some discernments that men make that can be deemed erroneous in hindsight," Tristan muttered.

"Are you suggesting—" Ophelia almost choked on her sip of wine. "That he is with her because she is a loose woman?" Her voice had raised in pitch so high that she was almost squeaking.

Everyone shifted uncomfortably in their seats. Oh, so it was true. Oh, and they'd all understood that from the beginning of the conversation, and she hadn't. Oh. The idea of eating roast suddenly turned her stomach, but she kept still, refusing to flee the dinner table. Julian cavorting with an older woman. No, she amended, an age-appropriate woman most likely, just older than her. More appropriate than her. Better.

Which, of course, wasn't relevant, because she had Lord Fairport to worry about. Or rather, his suit. And possible proposal. Which made her think of Portia, who was sitting there, completely silent on the matter.

"Portia, what do you think?"

"About what?" her sister asked, as if they had been talking about the weather and not what Sir Julian was doing dallying about with some strange woman.

Ophelia scanned the table, but from their shuttered expressions, she could tell no one wanted to continue the conversation.

"Oh, er, me going to Paris."

Portia gave her a critical and pitying glance. Ophelia hated that look, and it was the one Portia used most frequently on her. Portia seemed to glide through people, understanding them, liking them, getting them to like her, so easily. She could sort expressions and emotions and motivations better than anyone, while Ophelia had gotten none of that particular talent.

"With the proper chaperone, all should go swimmingly," she said, echoing Arthur's previous approval.

Ophelia nodded, and let them figure out conversation without her. She pushed the slices of roast around on her plate, listening to the pattern of clinking silverware as comfort. She stayed quiet through pudding, and then the cheese and port.

"Is all well?" Eleanor asked, as they were standing and moving from the dining room to the drawing room, where Lady Emily was intent on joining them for a chamomile tea.

Ophelia nodded, but Eleanor looked skeptical. Eleanor had met this Lady DeMarius. Ophelia wanted to ask her what she looked like, how she dressed, but Ophelia bit her tongue. It wouldn't do to interrogate anyone over Sir Julian's love interest. Whom he was absolutely free to have. Because he was a bachelor and owed no one his allegiance other than himself.

Eleanor tucked Ophelia's arm in hers as they traipsed over to the drawing room, where Lady Emily already sat with her chamomile. Ophelia didn't often see her, but she was wan and thin. Sickly-looking. None of the robustness than so many people touted motherhood giving to a person.

Arthur rushed to his wife's side and doted upon her, which was somewhat comforting to see. A man who truly loved someone. They all filed in, taking up seats all over the room. Portia sat down at the piano and began to play. Lady Rascomb took the seat closest to the fire. Tristan poured the men a measure of brandy from the sideboard. "Anyone else?" he asked as he distributed the liquor.

Women said no, mostly. Lady Rascomb signaled for a glass.

Sometimes Ophelia would as well, but she didn't feel right. "I'm going to go lie down," Ophelia said to her mother.

"Are you ill?"

"Just out of sorts. Excuse me." Ophelia wandered out of the drawing room, feeling sick to her stomach. First Lucy Walker and now Sir Julian.

Eleanor caught up to her in the hallway. "Do you want to talk?"

The amount of empathy in her friend's voice almost pushed her to tears. Is this how it had felt when they were in Scotland? When Eleanor and Tristan were flirting with one another? Is this how miserable she had felt?

"It's nothing," Ophelia said.

"Are you certain?" Eleanor pressed.

And Ophelia knew what she really meant: *Is this about Sir Julian?* And because the answer was probably yes, Ophelia didn't answer at all. She nodded, and left her in the hallway.

⊱⊰

JULIAN PULLED UP his trousers.

"Is that all?" Delphine asked, her dark hair spilling over her shoulders.

Julian laughed hoarsely. "It's all I can manage. If you want more, you should find a younger man."

"Surely someone as virile as you should have no difficulty with a refractory period." Delphine's silk robe slipped off her shoulder. She looked like the pornographic French postcards that circulated through the ship's crew and male passengers on the voyage home. The curve of her delicate white breast, still high and rosy from her exertion, was visible in the part of her robe. There was no question Delphine was perfectly lovely. Her attentions were flattery, making him feel more appealing than he was.

He chuckled at her flirtation. "I'm not as young as I used to be. And I think my jaw is locked up."

She threw her head back in a throaty laugh. "The first time is all about discovering each other's favorite paths to pleasure."

"I suppose mine was more of a meandering path?" He had spent long enough between her legs that he had doubted his abilities.

Her face softened and she looked at him almost like a teacher looked at a favorite pupil who'd gotten the answer wrong. "You are gentler than what I am accustomed to. It was very nice."

He whistled. "Nice, is it?" The top button of his shirt felt too tight and he pulled at it. "Nice is a good roast or a dry wine."

She laughed again, cutting off his soliloquy. "I stand by what I said. But I'm afraid I won't stroke your ego."

"Stroke other things, though." He shouldn't have said such a thing to a countess, but well, she wasn't the sort of countess that was countess-y about physical intimacy. At least, not now. They'd spent themselves in play, joking and kissing, stroking and licking, but Julian was glad that she had not wanted to let him inside her. Oddly, he didn't feel ready for that. It didn't feel right to go that far, whether it was the risk involved, or the lingering echo of betrayal to be with another woman in that way.

Delphine ignored his comment and sighed, lounging back on her satin pillows. He honestly wondered how she didn't slide right off her bed. "When shall I see you again?"

He finished dressing before answering. When he was finally ready, with the scent of her still all over his face, he said, "Are you sure you want to see me again? After all, I'm merely *nice*."

She rolled her eyes, and Julian wondered if Shakespeare's raven-haired beauty ever rolled her eyes at him.

"For a man who spent a decade in the jungle, I'm astonished your ego is so robust."

Julian frowned. "For one, I spent my time in the mountains, which are not jungles, and two, what does that have to do with my ego?"

"Certainly you haven't been with a woman during that time," she countered, and while her voice was smooth, he could sense her insecurity.

Ungentlemanly behavior, but he let out a burst of laughter to match hers. He did not wish to tell her of Maria, of the life he had thought he was starting there. The home that he'd dreamt of, the children he'd assumed he would have had with her. But that wasn't hers to know, and it was sacred. "Your hubris outstrips mine, Delphine."

A sparkling and toothsome smile appeared on her face, and he could see it as false ease. "Then we are quite the pair, aren't we?"

"Send me a note when you wish to see me," he said, not knowing how to proceed. He was not a man of means that had an opera box or whatever it was that Londoners went to anymore. Besides, he was certain that whatever he chose, she would dismiss it as beneath her. "I'll make myself available."

He left without hearing a response, which felt like he somehow had an upper hand. He didn't like that being with Delphine felt like a competition between them. Who would win? What could they possibly win? He supposed he could feel cheap, for being used like a rent boy, but he had wanted to be with her, and hers was an eager invitation. Still, he was anxious to bathe and remove her scent.

OPHELIA WAS ON her way to Tristan's mountaineering shop—imagine, Tristan as a shopkeeper! It was ridiculous enough to imagine him working, but the idea of him at a shop? With bookkeeping to be done? But Eleanor was insistent they go visit. Ophelia wanted to go in a carriage, but her mother wanted to walk.

It was one of Lady Rascomb's rare ventures out of the house, and Ophelia would do anything to help her mother emerge from the overwhelming grief. Their progress was slow, but the day was warm and sunny. The summer would be at an end soon, which would give way to more rain and more of her mother's complaints about pain in her injured leg.

Ophelia sometimes wondered that perhaps her mother's leg hurt more now than before because her father was not around to pull her outside in the garden, or take her out to the opera. To make her move. Perhaps this fledgling idea of a Paris trip would be good for her mother. She said she didn't want to go, but perhaps she should?

They were resting for a moment at a café, and Eleanor had gone inside to retrieve a bolstering pot of tea.

"Is that Sir Julian?" Lady Rascomb asked, peering across the street.

"It certainly looks that way," Ophelia said, standing. She waved her hand, but he didn't seem to notice. She couldn't very well scream over traffic for him.

But the table next to them chose that moment to leave, screeching chairs and clattering dishes, a commotion which made Sir Julian glance over. Once he spied her, he gave a small, tight smile, and faltered. He clearly had somewhere to be, but good manners dictated he come to greet them.

Eleanor exited the building and stopped suddenly as she saw Sir Julian approaching. Ophelia glanced at her, wondering what made her pause. "Tea shall be out shortly," Eleanor said, taking her seat.

Ophelia was surprised at Eleanor's choice to sit before greeting Sir Julian. Surely she had forgiven him for the faux pas of his friend, Lady DeMarius.

"Good morning, ladies," he said, bowing to them all, even if only her mother deserved the courtesy.

Ophelia bobbed a curtsy back and invited him to sit, not that she expected him to.

He deflected all invitations, and there were murmured responses flying back and forth in a way that Ophelia couldn't quite catch. She listened, marking conversations that were clearly direct quotes from deportment manuals, but there was a current she didn't understand. It was like a secret code she couldn't crack. She knew it was there, knew it existed, but no amount of study ever allowed her to decipher it.

Finally, as a way to send Sir Julian on his way, her mother invited him to dinner. And then through the maneuverings of politeness, invited the countess as well. Ophelia blinked rapidly. None of this made sense. She tapped her fingers together, thumb, pointer, middle, ring finger, pinky, and back again. It calmed her enough that she repeated the gesture.

A waiter brought out their tea and it was yet another cue for Sir Julian to be on his way. Not once did Julian meet her eye, despite the fact that she'd called to him.

She sat back down at the table, and watched as Eleanor and her mother exchanged pointed looks. Ophelia felt very perplexed. But if she couldn't ask the question of these two women, her sister-in-law and her mother, who could she ask?

"I beg your pardons, but will you please tell me what happened here?" Ophelia poured for the both of them, looking up only when she'd completed her task.

Eleanor looked at her with a small amount of pity, not a great amount, but it was still there. Ophelia was very sensitive to pity.

"He was clearly wearing clothes from yesterday," Eleanor said.

Ophelia glanced at her mother. "How would we know what he wore yesterday?"

"They were evening clothes, dear. Not something a man puts on first thing in the morning if he has a choice." Her mother sipped at her tea, looking far off in the distance.

"Oh," Ophelia sank back in her chair a moment, trying to recall what he was wearing. But she was so focused on trying to meet his gaze, trying to capture that elusive attention. She liked that when he called upon them that he turned his inky gaze on her, and she felt like the sun shone only upon her. As if she were special. Not in an *Isn't she odd?* Sort of way. Nor in a *Her father is a viscount*, sort of way. But in a treasured sort of way. But there was something else in his demeanor that she detected but couldn't parse. "There is another clue you aren't telling me."

"Ophelia," Eleanor said in a low voice. "Not here."

"Then where?" Ophelia asked, and she could feel a wildness trying to tear out of her throat. The kind of shrieking frustration she'd felt as a child when she realized how utterly unfair life would be for her and not for her brothers. The kind that Portia didn't seem to mind or care to protest.

Lady Rascomb looked at Eleanor and put her hand on Ophelia's wrist. "Darling. He looked and smelled as if he'd recently bedded a woman."

The news sank in slowly, a lump of sugar sinking and dissolving all at once. "How can you know that?" she insisted.

Eleanor made a strange face.

"Once you are married, you will understand what the signs are. It is—" Lady Rascomb choked on her words.

"The signs are easy to spot when you know them. Like knowing a knot will easily fray, once you've tied enough of them."

Ophelia nodded and drank her tea, suddenly feeling very, very stupid. She was. She was a spinster, no need to hide from that title. And as one, she wouldn't know the signs of physical intimacy. It was an experience outside her own, and one that she would likely never have.

While the thought of never having children didn't pain her, the thought of never knowing that sort of love did. The one that could be expressed physically. The kind that her mother and father had shared. The kind that swept over Tristan and Eleanor, Prudence and Mr. Moon, Justine and Karl Vogel. She was alone in her naivety.

She was a silly fool who would never climb a mountain, never find love, and never bed a man. Full of illusions of grandeur, what was real anymore? What had her life been except a string of humiliations?

⚬◆⚬

Chapter Six

JULIAN FELT MUCH better about visiting the Rascomb residence now that he'd cleaned up. Delphine hadn't sent him a note in the week since he'd last seen her, and that felt right somehow. He was not opposed to accompanying her wherever she wished to go, but it was clear that she had held certain assumptions about him that were patently untrue.

There was the idea of the intrepid explorer permeating popular thought these days, helped along by men like Sir Richard Burton. But Julian was nothing like him. First, his exploration was more akin to surveying rather than the ephemeral idea of "truths" and the metaphysical grandeur men like that sought. They were two for a ha'penny at RGS, and Julian steered clear.

As he entered the drawing room, both of the expected women looked down and ill at ease. He didn't know if he should inquire or not. He decided to pretend as if all was well, at least for the moment, in hopes of finding any clues as to what had them both feeling uncomfortable. Perhaps, and most likely, he assured himself, it had nothing to do with him whatsoever. Certainly not his morning walk home from Delphine's. They would not have noticed his level of dishevelment, surely.

After perfunctory greetings were made, Julian tossed in a gambit. "Have you worked on your article, Miss Ophelia? I am happy to say that I've made friends with one of the editors, and I think he'll trust my judgement if I hand off your work. It's no guarantee, but it's better than sending it in blind."

Ophelia's eyes flashed wide for a moment. "Yes, I do. I'd quite forgotten. Please excuse me for a moment, I'll go fetch it for you."

"Lady Rascomb," he turned his full attention on her. "How do you fare this fine day?"

She glanced at Ophelia's retreating form, and Julian's heart sank. It had been years since his mother had passed, but he knew the signs of a scolding.

"Sir Julian, please take greater care of your reputation. Should you be so bold as to parade about London in your evening clothes every morning, my daughter shan't be able to take you up the Matterhorn. You'll be too great a risk to the reputation of an unmarried woman, and no married man would allow you to take his wife!"

Julian sat back, stunned. "But it—"

Lady Rascomb held her hand up, quieting all his protestations. "It does not matter what you are about to say. This is not about facts or truths. This is about perception, which is all Ophelia has left. Climbing the Matterhorn may be a lark to you, but it is what is keeping her going. I beg you not to ruin it."

"This surely has nothing to do with—"

"This has everything to do with the widow DeMarius. She was scandalous before she married the earl, and even more so now. You are a grown man, and may do as you wish. But know that you have intertwined us with your life, and we will suffer the consequences of your actions. If that occurs, I will shut my doors to you to protect my daughter."

Julian sat back, stunned. The idea that he could lose the regard of Lady Rascomb hurt more deeply than he could have imagined. And ripping Ophelia out of his life—he was the weed in this flowerbed, he realized. He was disposable, an interloper. Heat flared all over his body, embarrassment and shame running fast and deep through his veins. "I assure you that was not my intent."

Ophelia returned, handing him her article. "Here you are. I have noted that it is written by Anonymous, and it should stay that way. If there are any identifying marks, it could be assumed my brother wrote it, and it would be acceptable to put his initials, if needs must. But I'd prefer it to remain as it is."

He took it and folded it over once, sticking it in his pocket.

"Will you not read it?" Ophelia asked, her voice bereft of the confidence with which she normally spoke.

"Of course I will. At home." He stood, unable to withstand that disapproval in Lady Rascomb's expression. "As it is, I must be going."

"But you've just arrived," Ophelia protested. A line between her brows deepened. He'd not noticed it until now, and he had an urge to reach out and press that line with his finger until it smoothed.

This room was suddenly filled with conflicting emotions, and somehow, it felt like the morning he'd realized Maria had left him all over again. Everything felt wrong and strange, and he couldn't breathe.

"Lady Rascomb reminded me of tasks I need to accomplish before the day is out. I shall stop in again soon." He gave a curt bow and left, thundering down the steps as if an avalanche nipped at his heels. At least in an avalanche, he'd know when he would be suffocated.

⟫⟫⟩⟨⟨⟪

"LADY EMILY!" OPHELIA turned in her seat. She was the only occupant of the drawing room this morning, as her mother was not feeling well. Instead of sewing, Ophelia was reading letters. She'd just gotten a lengthy one from Justine, and while she adored her letters, it made her miss her friend even more acutely.

Lady Emily was still wan and terrifyingly thin. She padded in, almost uncertain. Ophelia half-stood, unsure if her sister-in-law would lose her footing. But Lady Emily made it over to the sitting area.

"It's good to see you up and about." Ophelia had the urge to find a blanket to drape over her, as if she were an invalid, but she refrained, not knowing how Lady Emily was feeling.

"It's good to be seen," Lady Emily said, managing a thin smile. "I have been abed far too long."

"Arthur has said it has been awfully difficult for you." Ophelia wanted to save her from the embarrassment of knowing that Arthur had informed them of how many times she'd managed to cast up her accounts in one morning.

Lady Emily nodded, her eyes closed, as if it hurt to move her head. "No one told me carrying a child could be so trying. I knew that it could, but I didn't think it would happen to me."

Ophelia tried to murmur sympathetically, but she felt that her pitch wasn't quite right. She had no intention of performing this particular obligation, but it was polite to empathize nonetheless. "It does seem strange that something so terrible is the norm, isn't it?"

Lady Emily gave her a strange look, so Ophelia opted to change the subject.

"I hope—"

"Darling!" Arthur crashed into the room. "You are up!"

Lady Emily barely had time to stand before Arthur was there swooping her into his arms, kissing her cheeks. Lady Emily squeaked in delight and surprise. Ophelia watched them, feeling a hole opening in her heart. She had acquiesced to being courted by Lord Fairport, but she couldn't imagine him swooping in to gather her in his arms. Or smothering her with kisses. Or being affectionate in any way, really.

"What are you doing home? I thought you had—"

"I'm only home for a moment, but Ferris told me you were in the drawing room. I had to see you." He released her, finally, looking at her with stars in his eyes. Ophelia had never seen her serious, studious, duty-bound brother look so . . . smitten. And to think, Arthur almost didn't marry her.

"I'm much better today," Lady Emily said, puffing out her chest in pride. Ophelia was reminded of a robin, cleaning itself on the stone birdbath in the garden. "I have no doubt this is the beginning of a new era for me and the babe." She touched her stomach, where a protrusion, though small, was now obvious.

Arthur looked as if should night fall, he could be a streetlamp himself, glowing as he was. "Must dash, but I'm so glad, Em." He kissed her. As he turned to leave, he spotted Ophelia in the room. The afterthought. "Oh, hallo."

"Arthur," Ophelia said, greeting him with a polite smile, as if she had not witnessed perhaps the most intimate display of affection she'd ever seen between two people.

He continued to the door of the drawing room, and then turned, snapping his fingers. "That reminds me. I saw our friend, Sir Julian, out the other day. I invited him and his companion to dinner this Friday. Should be smashing. Lord Fairport as well. Invite whoever else you want, Fee, we'll get the man to propose before Christmas!"

And then Arthur was gone.

"Who is proposing?" Lady Emily asked the surprisingly still air in the drawing room, now that Arthur had exited.

"No one, yet," Ophelia said, her heart not quite caught up to her ears.

"Lord Fairport or Sir Julian?" Lady Emily asked, sinking back down into her chair.

"Neither," Ophelia said, pulling the lap desk back onto her lap. The barely started letter to Justine was there, waiting. Did she dare detail the intimacy she'd witnessed? Would Justine know this kind of affection with Karl Vogel? Likely so. The Bavarians were far more obvious in their emotions than the English. Or Germans, now, she supposed. She wondered what the Vogels thought about that, and she longed to have a free-wheeling discussion with Justine about everything from life in a newly minted state of Germany to how she liked living in Augsburg, to watching her do impressions of her mother-in-law.

"Don't you want to be married?" Lady Emily asked.

"I want to go to Paris," Ophelia snapped.

"What's in Paris?" Lady Emily asked, and Ophelia was glad she switched topics.

"I want to meet my dear friend and her husband there. Justine Brewer? She's now Mrs. Karl Vogel, and I miss her."

"Yes, I remember meeting her. She's difficult to forget." Lady Emily's hand settled on her lower belly and she stared into the empty fireplace.

"I miss her," Ophelia said, trying hard to not sound defiant. During her years in the nursery, Nanny had always told her she was defiant. Despite the slaps and the many nights without supper, Ophelia had trouble controlling her tone, sounding "too confident" or "defiant." Yet that same attribute was encouraged in Arthur, and not chided in Tristan in the least.

"I have no doubt you do. What can I do to help you see her?" Lady Emily asked.

Ophelia looked up, grateful that Lady Emily understood. Of course she did. Lady Emily knew a great deal more than she let on, which made her an excellent Lady Rascomb. "Help me get through the dinner and have Lord Fairport still like me at the end?"

Lady Emily smiled. "I will do my best."

"And no fish, please."

Her sister-in-law drew her head back in surprise. "But—"

"The sauce is atrocious, and someone needs to tell you." Ophelia turned her attention back to the letter. There was much to plan, and much to tell Justine.

"YOU KNOW, I didn't think you would be taking me to dinners with titled aristocrats," Delphine purred in the carriage. "I thought it would be the other way 'round."

Julian straightened his collar, which somehow seemed tighter this evening. He wouldn't have taken her if Arthur hadn't spotted them together in Hyde Park. Julian was trying to end things with her politely, charmingly, as per Lady Rascomb's wishes, and then Arthur had charged up and invited them both to a private dinner. He couldn't very well refuse. And then he accepted her invitation to return to her townhome. "These are family friends. I was good friends with the late Lord Rascomb, and upon my return, I renewed my acquaintance with the family."

"Which has nothing to do with Lady Rascomb's status as a widow," Delphine said, piercing him with her onyx gaze.

To suggest he was after Lady Rascomb affronted his very honor. "No!"

Delphine relaxed with a smile. "Good. You know I don't like competition."

"These people are the closest thing I have to family left. We will be dining with an eye toward the compatibility of the young couple." Lord Milquetoast the Bland and Miss Ophelia. He still couldn't figure out why Ophelia would entertain the idea of that man, but a title, security, those must be appealing. He'd not had to consider those factors, being a man, and an heir to a frighteningly small fortune.

"And you play the part of a dutiful uncle?" Delphine slipped next to him in the carriage, pressing herself up against him.

They had not consummated their relationship fully yet. Delphine had managed to turn what he'd meant to be a chaste evening of chess into a different sort of game. But still he hadn't wanted to fully give himself over, as if the hours spent dallying without their clothing were not as consequential. He knew in his mind that this was not true, that their proximity and physicality was still intimacy, but when she'd asked him to be inside her, it felt like too much to him. A commitment that felt wrong. He knew other men didn't feel that way, but dammit, he did.

He'd made excuses, used his hands to bring her to another

climax to distract her. It wasn't well-done of him, but he couldn't parse his embattled emotions yet. There was always something else to think about. The Matterhorn, a trip to Paris, his writings, his next appointment to South America by either the RGS or a private company.

Still, he'd squired her to the art exhibition, the opera, Hyde Park, and a few private concerts. It had been instructive to meet Delphine's friends—more artists and bon vivants than he'd known. They were witty and clever, full of vitality. The kind of vigor he'd felt when he was on a mountain. A feeling that he keenly missed, which pushed him even more towards thinking of the Matterhorn.

Delphine seemed content to kiss him and pet him there in the carriage while his mind was occupied with other things, but he caught her hand when it strayed too close to his hair.

"I don't wish to appear unkempt," he said.

"You mean you don't wish to appear as if you've fooled around in a carriage on the way to dinner," Delphine said, reaching out to unbutton the top button of his shirt.

He caught her hand again. "Precisely. I want to be respectful."

She hummed in disapproval. "Terribly boring of you."

"I told you, this is family."

Delphine crossed back over to her side of the carriage and sulked. Fortunately, they arrived not long after. He descended and helped Delphine down, hoping it wasn't a mistake to accept the invitation from Arthur—er, Rascomb rather. It was hard to call his friend's son by his name, even if Julian and Arthur were more of a similar age than Arthur's father and Julian had been.

He hoped that this dinner would smooth over Delphine's rudeness to Tristan Bridewell and his wife. That it would ease Lady Rascomb's perspective of Julian's involvement with Delphine. Even though he'd been ready to cut Delphine off, the idea of the conflict made his temples throb. It would be far easier if everyone got along tonight.

Besides, Delphine's clever wit might be an interesting match to Ophelia's strong mind. They were intelligent in such different ways. If Delphine could only stop seeing other women as competition.

Ferris ushered them into the townhome, taking their hats and coats. The butler still guided them up to the drawing room as if Julian weren't a frequent visitor. Lord Fairport had already arrived, and he was engaged with Rascomb in the corner, while Mr. and Mrs. Bridewell chatted with Lady Rascomb and Miss Ophelia.

The men wore almost identical black and white suits, but the ladies wore a pleasing array of colors. It was something he had enjoyed about going to Society events, and something he missed about his sojourns in South America—the colors. London was so gray and drab. Staid and somber, as he ought to be as well now that his forties were approaching.

Ferris announced Delphine and himself, and the company turned as one. The ladies curtsied and the men bowed to Delphine, given that she outranked them all, with the exception of Fairport. They entered, but had barely enough time for introductions before the dinner bell rang. Since this was a family dinner, they did not follow a ranked entrance, and made their way as they wished.

At the table, however, Delphine was seated across from him, next to Fairport, while Julian was seated between Lady Rascomb and Mrs. Bridewell. On the other side of Fairport sat Miss Ophelia. Fairport was about to get whiplash from the steady stream of witty banter, no doubt. Julian grinned, and wished he'd been seated there. But then, he suddenly worried, if Delphine perceived Ophelia as a threat, it could be a vicious place indeed.

For a long while, dinner seemed to be going well, with light first courses, crisp wines, and easy chatter. Julian couldn't pinpoint where the turning point was, precisely, as he was deeply ensconced with discussing which knot would have been better when hauling cargo down a snow-covered mountainside with Mrs. Bridewell.

"Don't you think?" Delphine asked loudly, catching everyone's attention.

The table quieted. Fairport's expression was perplexed and Miss Ophelia was staring down into her lap. Something had definitely occurred.

Delphine looked straight at Julian. "What do you think?"

"I beg your pardon," Julian said, buying time to look at everyone's faces, trying to gauge the responses. "I did not hear the conversation."

"Miss Ophelia asked Lord Fairport if he believed a married woman could go on an Alpine expedition with a man who was not her husband. I said that it was another way of cuckolding her husband." The coldness in Delphine's eyes conveyed her earlier thoughts exactly: *I don't like competition.*

"I don't see why, with proper chaperones, it is any different than an unmarried woman going on an expedition with an unmarried man. Something that both myself and Mrs. Bridewell have done." Miss Ophelia kept her voice even, but she didn't lower its volume. If he had closed his eyes, he would not think Miss Ophelia upset in the slightest.

"And look what happened," Delphine said, gesturing to Mrs. Bridewell next to Julian, and Mr. Tristan Bridewell seat on Delphine's right.

Ophelia frowned, and Mr. Bridewell's brow furrowed, no doubt wanting to protest the idea.

"I don't understand why this should come up at all," Lord Fairport said. "What does it matter?"

Miss Ophelia looked at Julian, and while he knew why, it stopped his heart with dread. He knew she would out them, and knew that she needed to in order to prove a point—and to see what kind of husband Lord Fairport would make, but Julian still winced, not wanting to broach a topic that would cause him so much upset.

"Because Sir Julian has asked me to take him up the Matterhorn next year," Ophelia said.

Delphine glared at him, an almost too-satisfied expression on her lovely face. As if she had found him out in some kind of lover's deception.

"Oh," Lord Fairport said, squirming in his seat as he looked at Julian. The man was as interesting as a boiled potato, and resembled one as well.

"If anyone would like to come along, they are more than welcome," Ophelia said, glancing around the table.

Delphine scoffed, earning her glares from almost everyone in the room.

"I shall go, Ophelia," Mrs. Bridewell said. "I would love to have another crack at it."

"And of course I would be happy to help plan as well as climb," Mr. Bridewell added, in solidarity. Julian then remembered that he'd opened an Alpine outfitters shop not long ago.

"Would that not be sufficient chaperones?" Ophelia asked Delphine and Lord Fairport. "Besides, it's only Sir Julian."

He flinched. What was that supposed to mean? As if he couldn't be a threat to a woman's reputation. Wait, that wasn't what he meant. Ophelia's dismissal stung, even though it shouldn't. He was too old for her in some ways, yes, but in others, not at all. She was higher ranking than him, but he still had a title, even if he was not a Peer.

"I think planning another expedition is a fine thing," Lady Rascomb said, glancing around the room, quelling the clear feeling of animosity that floated around the table.

The rest of the evening was stilted and stifled, everyone trying not to trigger the avalanche of bad feelings that threatened to rain down upon them. By the time the ladies were being led to the drawing room by Lady Rascomb, Julian had endured all the social discomfort he could take in this house. He would rather sleep a dozen nights without blankets in the damp winter than do this again.

"Thank you, so much, Lady Rascomb, for your hospitality this evening. I regret that we must take our leave."

Delphine slowly daubed her napkin to her lips and rose. "Yes, thank you for the invitation."

As Delphine stood, the men all stood as well, the shuffle of chair legs across the carpet the only sound in the room. She walked around the table and took his arm as they exited the dining room, everyone watching her languid and slow movements.

Once safely ensconced in the carriage, buttoned up and moving, did Julian dare speak. "You must write an apology. I will as well."

She turned a shocked gaze at him. "*I* should apologize? That girl has designs on you. You took me to a husband vetting, not bothering to tell me that you were a candidate. I *told* you that I wouldn't tolerate competition."

"I was not being vetted," he insisted. "It was for Lord Fairport. Besides, you heard Miss Ophelia, 'It's only Sir Julian.'"

"That will last one afternoon alone between you and that girl."

"That 'girl' is nearly thirty," Julian reminded Delphine, but that only made her laugh.

"Which only makes her more desperate."

"Which explains why she should be wanting Lord Fairport," Julian said. He ticked off the man's virtues on his fingers. "He's wealthy, he's titled, and he doesn't seem the type to run off with another woman."

"Yes, how droll," Delphine shot back. "As opposed to you, an impressive physical specimen who reminds her of her dear departed father. I say, which would she choose?" Delphine put a finger to her lips, miming indecision.

Julian scoffed. "Miss Ophelia is a very pragmatic person. She's not about to throw away her future on a pauper like me."

"What does she care if you are a pauper or not? I have no

doubt her brother will settle a fine dowry on her, just to be rid of her."

He stared at this viper in an expensive dress, all lust and attraction snuffed out at last. "Why must you be so cruel?"

"If you'd had my life, you would be worse," she spit. "How dare some doe-eyed child like her get so coddled that she gets to climb mountains *and* have a love match? Women don't get to have it all, Julian. And some women get no choices to begin with."

"I'm sorry you've had such a terrible go, Lady DeMarius," he said, emphasizing her title, hoping to show her the advantages of her life.

She scoffed. "Oh yes, my husband, that I *ensnared.*" She pulled off her elbow-length black gloves in a fury. "I know what everyone says. That I somehow made him want me. Does no one have eyes? He was a disgusting old man, and I paid for it all with my body, no different than any chorus girl or common whore. He wanted me for *fucking*, Julian. This gown? This necklace? Bought by my exposed flesh, and willingness to let him do what he wanted. I was glad he died. And don't tell me his previous wives would have felt any different."

Julian bit his tongue. Her vitriol was unleashed, and there was no amount of words he could say to make this situation better. "I'm sorry that happened."

Delphine glared out the window, her anger fizzling like a candle in the rain. "I know you can't love me Julian. You're too nice. Too soft. Too idealistic. But her? You could love a girl like her. And that hurts."

"You told me not to fall in love with you," he reminded her. "I thought you didn't want that."

"Of course I want you to love me. I want everyone to love me, because I am incapable of it myself." Her eyes welled up, and for a moment, Julian was terrified she might cry. But Delphine was not a woman who would grace him with a moment of weakness. He didn't deserve that honor. When she spoke again, her voice was soft with no evidence of a tremor. "I won't ask for your company again, Julian. But if you come to me, I'll welcome you back."

The carriage stopped at her townhome, and she got out without another word, or a backward glance.

Chapter Seven

THE HOTEL LOBBY was positively baroque, filled with chandeliers, thick carpets, and young French porters who winked at her if her gaze lingered on them too long. Ophelia had let Eleanor and Tristan make the arrangements, passing them along to Justine and Prudence via letter.

She'd even invited Julian, who said he would come to meet Karl, as he would be their climbing guide. After the awkward dinner a few months ago, Julian had kept himself mostly away, sending notes of apology. Ophelia's mother had come back around to bestowing her motherly smiles upon him the few times he'd visited. But Ophelia missed that familiar friendship they'd developed, swapping stories of their derring-do over tea and biscuits.

She'd hoped that this time in Paris, amongst all of them, would bring him back to her. The way their easy friendship had been.

A jostling at the doors caught Ophelia's attention. When she looked up, she couldn't help but smile. Justine pushed her way past the porters, not allowing Karl to protect her with his elbow. She caught sight of Ophelia and ran—ran!—through the lobby, her long skirts swishing like mad.

"Winter in Paris! Ophelia, you brilliant, beautiful buxom friend of mine!" Justine threw her arms around Ophelia, gushing over her.

Ophelia gripped her friend tightly, not caring if she ought to be embarrassed by how much she missed her friend. She inhaled Justine's unmistakable scent, one that had comforted her since their finishing school days. Justine was different now, of course, her scent different, her body rounder from finally eating enough, but still, completely Justine. Ophelia opened her eyes to see Tristan and Karl Vogel shaking hands and making uncertain eye contact.

Then Eleanor threw her arms around both of the women. "My turn too!"

They stuttered around in circles of missing each other and cries of how lovely each of the others were.

Justine wiped her eyes as she pulled back. "Do we know if Prudence will be here?"

"I had word that she and Mr. Moon will arrive tomorrow." Ophelia looked over Justine's shoulder and smiled at Karl Vogel, their once-Matterhorn guide, and now Justine's patient husband.

"Mr. Vogel," she said, affection in her voice that surprised even her.

"Please, you must call me Karl, for I know you by your first name because Justine won't stop talking about you."

Both Justine and Ophelia giggled, knowing that had been a general complaint about them for years.

"Well, come on then," Eleanor ushered them all. "The porters can take the luggage upstairs. Let's go find us some refreshment."

"Not quite yet, we are missing one of our party." Tristan gazed around the room, and it made Ophelia want to gnaw on her lip, if only she were allowed to do so.

"Ah, there he is!" Eleanor pushed up on her tiptoes, still not matching her husband's height.

Ophelia scanned the crowd from her toes, using Justine's shoulder as a bolster, and spotted Julian entering the building.

"There you are," Tristan called out as Julian approached.

Julian kept his hands in his pockets, a casual man with his

bowler hat on, strolling through a hotel lobby. It should have been utterly normal, but Ophelia was strangely affected by the sight. She slammed down her heels, and Justine looked at her with an expression of curiosity.

"Is there . . . ?" Justine trailed off, examining Ophelia, then looking to Sir Julian. Abruptly, she left Ophelia's side, pushing through their crowd to be the first to greet Julian. Her hand was out, as rude as any American. "I'm Justine Vogel, Miss Ophelia's best friend. And you are?"

He smiled at her, thank heavens; Ophelia was able to breathe again.

"Sir Julian Dunstan, at your service."

Karl Vogel came up behind his wife. "And you are looking to climb the Matterhorn, yes?"

"If you are amenable to helping me do it, then yes." Julian searched the crowd until he saw Ophelia. His shoulders relaxed when their eyes met. Funny, because Ophelia felt less relaxed with him around.

They all circled each other, and Ophelia tried to pay attention to the others and not Julian. But she couldn't help it. The memory of that awful dinner still sprang to life sometimes, bringing with it the imagined thought of Julian kissing the bespangled Lady DeMarius. Of his powerful hands roaming her bespangled hips. Which had been both a revelation and a betrayal. The very idea of it hurt as viscerally as any tumble down a mountainside she'd ever taken.

She again pushed the thought aside. Julian was here, with her, and he had announced to both Ophelia and her mother that he had secured some funding through his connections at the Royal Geographical Society. They wanted a comparative essay from him, about how climbing in the Alps was obviously better than climbing any mountain in South America. Julian could roll his eyes all he wanted, but Ophelia would take the cheque any day.

After all, more than anything, Ophelia wanted to climb the Matterhorn next year, and if going with Sir Julian would allow her to do so, then he needed to meet their guide, Karl. But now they were all here. And Ophelia had to see him.

Their troupe finally organized, Eleanor herded them out the door to a nearby restaurant that she was assured was simply the best. Julian waited and fell into step with Ophelia. Justine watched closely, but when Ophelia gave her the look that showed his company was welcome, Justine abandoned her friend for her husband's arm and kept two paces ahead.

"I'm happy to see you here, Miss Ophelia," Julian said, returning to formality.

Ophelia noted that he didn't offer his arm. She sniffed, pulling her shoulders back. "I'm glad you could make it."

"Are you?" Julian slowed his steps, forcing Ophelia to do the same, giving space between them and the rest of the group ahead.

"Yes," she said, as if this were an answer she knew beyond the shadow of a doubt.

"Because you've hardly spoken to me in two months."

"You called me 'Miss Ophelia,'" she pointed out.

"Because you haven't spoken to me in two months," he repeated. "Please talk to me, Ophelia. I have missed our easy conversation." The look of pleading in his dark eyes, one of those powerful hands outstretched, reaching for her, was more than she could take. Her defenses crumbled.

"As have I," she admitted.

"May we be true friends again?" Julian offered his arm, tentative, his head bowed, as if waiting to see her reaction.

She slid her arm around his, feeling the strength and the warmth of him in the windy Parisian November. He smiled down at her, and she returned the gesture. It was as if the ice wall between them melted. "Although I do ask you to never bring Lady DeMarius to dinner again."

"Not to worry. Our connection is permanently and irrevocably severed," Julian assured her, without a hint of remorse or regret.

Ophelia looked up at him again, stunned. "Truly?"

He chuckled and gave her an earnest grin. "You seem surprised. It was but a small matter. Besides, I need to know: will you still climb the Matterhorn with me?" he asked quietly, in tones that sounded more as if he were proposing marriage.

"I would love nothing more," she said.

"Excellent. Now we must hurry to catch up to the others." Julian pulled her arm in close, and as they hurried, they ended up running across the Place des Vosges, laughing wildly in the pending dark.

THE NEXT FEW days were the happiest Julian could ever remember being. They slept in, drank perfect coffee with *pain au chocolat,* wrapped scarves around their necks to marvel at the multicolored leaves drifting to the ground. The sun shone, and they toured every possible site, from museums to sites of famous uprisings. He talked about climbing with Mr. Vogel, who intermittently accepted correction from his bride.

Julian watched Ophelia blossom and relax around her friends, and seeing her outside of London, outside of the expectations of duty was eye-opening. Her cheeks pinked up, and her large pale blue eyes brightened. She made jokes and bantered in the group, swung her clasped hands with her friends, and squealed with delight when another couple joined their entourage, Mr. and Mrs. Moon.

Sometimes it felt as if the men were merely afterthoughts of their daily routines, as the women chatted amongst themselves, frequently erupting into laughter. Most of the time, Julian had no problem observing, as watching Ophelia live so brightly was his new favorite pastime. Other times, however, he grew unnerved when one of the ladies shot a glance in the men's direction.

He leaned over to Mr. Moon, whom he was still getting to know. "Do you think they are talking about us?"

"No," he said, not bothering to elaborate. He wasn't a rude man, but he wasted no syllables, at least not on Julian. Of them, Tristan was the talker, and he was happy to elaborate.

"When they are together like this, I don't even exist. My lungs don't function, even my body seems to disappear completely. I am invisible." Tristan waved to a garçon to ask for more butter for his bread.

"Isn't that your third helping?" Julian asked him.

Tristan nodded. "The French do many things well, aside from the rioting. And that, my friend, is their bread."

"Don't forget beheading aristocrats," Mr. Moon said drily.

"I don't see any," Tristan said, slurping at the dregs of his coffee.

"Aren't you—" Mr. Vogel began.

"I. Don't. See. Any." Tristan stared the Bavarian down.

"Noted," Mr. Vogel said, picking up his own coffee.

"So Mr. Moon, are you interested in this Matterhorn adventure next summer?" Julian tried his conversational bait.

"God, no." Mr. Moon went back to his newspaper. Tristan had the English version, but Mr. Moon seemed to be getting along just fine with the French version.

Eleanor and Ophelia both spoke flawless French, and Julian's French was accented by his Spanish, causing some misunderstandings. Perhaps his dark hair and eyes made him seem Spanish here, while in London everyone believed him to be Welsh.

"Do you not climb?" Julian pressed.

"No," Mr. Moon repeated. "It's pointless."

"Unusual attitude for a man married to a lady climber," Julian said.

Mr. Moon closed the newspaper and put it down, giving Julian his undivided attention, which was, frankly, unnerving. "I love my wife very much, and she is very much her own person, as am I. She supports me, I support her, that's how it's supposed to work. I gather you've never been married?"

Julian swallowed hard, thinking of his time living with Maria.

The time where he thought they would get married, but she didn't understand the difference between Catholicism and Church of England. Well, ultimately, she didn't care about marriage, because she left the village he stayed in, disappearing into the Amazon, back to her people. "No," he croaked. "Never married."

He didn't mean to, but his eyes drifted toward Ophelia then. Watching her laugh and talk, sipping her tea, as they all lingered over breakfast. Mr. Moon followed his gaze.

"Do you intend to be married?"

The question made his heart stop. He blubbered out meaningless sounds, never less articulate in his life.

Mr. Moon smiled suddenly, which should have been friendly, but somehow came across as condescending and vaguely threatening. "Good luck." And he picked up his newspaper and continued to ignore Julian.

Julian glanced at Tristan, who immediately stuffed a heavily buttered piece of bread in his mouth and looked the other direction. Mr. Vogel likewise looked away.

"I'm not—" Julian protested, but Tristan just held up a hand to make him stop. "But there's nothing—" Tristan waved his raised hand. "I'm too old for her."

Tristan swallowed hard, no doubt regretting it. "Mate. Stop. When you've something to tell me, tell me. 'Til then, none of my business."

Breath whooshed out of him as he sat back hard against his chair, causing the legs to squeak across the café's polished floor. Did they see something he didn't? Yes, men married much younger women all the time, but those were men who were of higher rank. An earl could marry a younger viscount's daughter, but a baronet? Especially a penniless one? It seemed uncouth. But was there a possibility? Did she look at him the way he looked at her? He felt foolish and young and utterly ridiculous. He stood suddenly, snatching the green cloth napkin off his lap and throwing it on the table. "Excuse me," he said. "I'm going to take some air."

⟫⟫⟫⟫⟫⟪⟪⟪⟪⟪

AT DINNER, JULIAN sat next to her, feeding her funny quips and insights as everyone talked loudly across the table. Even Mr. Moon smiled and joked, allowing them to see his prodigious wit. With intelligence like that, it was no wonder that Prudence liked him so much.

Ophelia's cheeks hurt from laughing.

"I meant to tell you earlier, but I forgot," Julian said, leaning in conspiratorially.

He smelled good, like cloves and cinnamon. She'd had enough wine that she could admit that to herself. The evening was the most perfect one she could imagine, full of delicious food and good, plummy wine, and his unwavering attention.

She searched his face, wondering when she would be this close to him again. "Yes?"

"I received a note from the RGS. They plan to publish your article next month."

Ophelia gasped. "My article?"

Julian chuckled as he nodded. "Your article. The one you wrote. I handed it to the editor shortly before I got on the ferry. It's set. Next month, you will be a published authoress."

Ophelia squeezed her eyes shut and kicked her legs to keep from squealing. A dream come true! But questions thrummed through her. "Wait, does he know who the author is?"

Julian shook his head. "I told him the author wanted to protect their identity, and preferred to be published as anonymous."

Ophelia could kiss him, she was so happy. "I wish Papa could see it."

Julian took one of her hands in his. "He would have been so proud of you."

"He would, wouldn't he?"

Justine snapped her fingers at them from across the table. "Share the good news with the class, please."

"My article about us climbing Ben Nevis will be published by The Royal Geographical Society next month!"

Justine thrust both fists in the air. "Yes! Ophelia! You are incredible. I knew you could do it! Karl, be a love and order us some champagne!"

"Don't get—nothing young!" Prudence called after him, but when he didn't turn around, she stood. "I'll go help him order."

Soon they were all toasting to her, and Ophelia felt so warm and loved that she forgot to be embarrassed by the attention.

Later, after the wine glasses were emptied, and eyes were drooping, and even the Parisians were going home, they stood and shuffled about, donning coats and hats and gloves. They sky was beautiful and dark, while the light of the city glowed above the buildings. Ophelia felt giddy and warm and free, like she had everything in the world.

Her arms were linked with Justine and Eleanor, but she glanced over her shoulder at Julian. Dear Julian. Handsome, broad-shouldered, capable Julian who would choose her. She made her most daring decision yet—and it had nothing to do with the Matterhorn.

⇶⟨⟨⟨⟨

JULIAN WASN'T NEARLY as drunk as he ought to be after so much wine. It was as if his feet didn't touch the carpet as they entered the plush lobby of Le Pavillon de la Reine. The hotel was far more luxurious than anything he would have sought for himself, but he was willing to spend the money if it meant being near Ophelia.

A smile grew on his face of its own volition. It was because of Ophelia. The companionship of these other men was nice, especially that of Karl Vogel, a man who had travelled widely and climbed nearly as many mountains as Julian had. But as he picked up his room key from the front desk, he surveyed the other seven members of their party. The three couples, newly married and still very much in love, all draped over one another, roaming hands giving no uncertain ideas of what they would be doing behind their closed doors.

The clock in the lobby struck three, and Tristan laughed. "I won't be seeing any of you before noon tomorrow, no offense meant."

"Let's make no plans for the morning. I don't want to have to make an effort to break them." Mrs. Vogel said as her husband picked up the key from the desk.

Ophelia took her own key. Just as Julian had taken his own key. Did she feel as if she were floating? Had the champagne made her giddy as it had made him? She looked up and smiled at him, and his breath caught. She was so lovely. So perfect. So smart and witty . . . he needed to stop and get a grip on himself.

It hadn't helped that Mrs. Vogel spoke lavishly of Ophelia's talents as well, as if she were half in love with her. But then, the level of quiet trust Ophelia placed in Mrs. Vogel made it clear that the regard was reciprocated.

"Tomorrow, then, at some hour," Julian said, doffing his cap to them. He needed to leave before he began to salivate after Ophelia like some disgusting old wretch.

"We'll slip a note under the door should we make plans before dinner time," Mrs. Bridewell said, giggling as her husband pulled her close.

Julian trudged up the stairs, which were infinitely harder now than they had been pre-dinner. Once in his room, he tossed his cap on the dressing table, not bothering to brush it. He shrugged out of his coat and waistcoat and splashed water on his face. His body felt impossibly light and at ease. He pushed the braces off his shoulders and sat down to take off his shoes. Too bad Nicholas wasn't around to take care of the mud on those, either. It was damned handy to have a valet, that was certain.

He chuckled to himself. Was he becoming a soft Englishman, now that he'd spent close to a year in London? He still missed the bright colors of the flowers and the fruits he'd encountered across the ocean, but spending time with Lady Rascomb and Ophelia and Tristan had helped ease the transition. Not to mention his overwhelming and unexpected success in the RGS. That helped too. He'd forgotten his pride while alone on mountaintops.

There was a light scratching at the door. He frowned. Had he imagined it? Perhaps a laundry service, or a valet service for his hat and shoes? These fancy hotels had all manner of amenities.

He padded over, his feet bare, his socks in a pile in the corner. If it was a valet service, hopefully they'd forgive his sloven bachelor ways. He pulled open the heavy polished brass door handle.

But it was Ophelia. Her shining golden hair cascaded around her shoulders and her neck. She wore her evening gown but had taken off her jewelry and unpinned her hair. He swallowed hard.

"May I come in?" she asked.

"Why?" It was a stupid thing to say. But there was no reason for her to be standing here. A beautiful young woman like her had no earthly reason to appear on his doorstep.

Her blue eyes shone, and she repeated her request. He opened the door wider and made space for her. She walked by and he inhaled a scent of vanilla and citrus and jasmine. He could die a happy man with that aroma in his mind.

"Your room is the mirror of my own," she said, smoothing one hand across the busy print of the bedspread.

"Is it?" he asked, which only showcased how incessantly idiotic he was. Did he really have nothing to say to a woman who came to his room in the wee hours of the morning? He knew what this was. He knew it. But he couldn't believe it could be true.

"Do you know why I'm here?" she asked, as if she could read his mind.

"I doubt it's to go over maps," he quipped, and then felt cruel. "You've been drinking, Ophelia. It isn't right for me to take advantage."

She raised a golden eyebrow, but the smirk on her face told him that she wasn't offended, thank goodness. "I stopped drinking long before anyone else. Too much gives me a headache."

"But you thought to come here?" His heart sped up. He'd tried not to think about this. It wasn't right. He was a friend of her father's.

"I've been thinking about it for many weeks. And I don't make decisions lightly."

"I know." He kept his distance from her, circling around to the opposite side of the room. He pulled up his braces, giving him some sense of being dressed, being without his coat and waistcoat with bare feet. It was the only defense he could give. If he was honest, he'd wanted this so badly. His attraction to her was not because she had reminded him of his juvenile tendre for her mother. It was her own wit and charm, her sense of wonder. The way she made him feel like he was important. That she understood and spoke of his endeavors with respect and excitement. That they were, as one might say, two peas in a pod.

"I hated thinking of you with Lady DeMarius."

"I can't stand Lord Fairport," he confessed. "The idea of you marrying him—he's so *boring*."

She laughed, and it was like the tinkling of silver bells. A sound that he wanted to hear over and over. "He is dreadfully bland."

"It is as if blanc mange became a person."

She shuddered. "I only remember that from when I was ill as a child. My nanny used to spoon feed it to me, but only if my fever was high."

"Same for me," he said. Without understanding how, he was close to her. They were standing so near that he could touch her with little effort, but he didn't dare. And the nagging thought wouldn't go away, of what she'd said earlier. "Why would you think of me with Lady DeMarius?"

"I pictured you kissing her," Ophelia said, her gaze locked to his, pulling him in.

"Why would you do that?" He stared at her lips, the color of a not-quite-ripe plum.

"Because I couldn't picture you kissing me," she said. "I didn't think you would want to."

Somehow she was even closer, the heady scent of her pulling him like a magnet. "I want to," he reassured her, without meaning to even open his mouth. "I shouldn't have said that."

"Why?" she asked, and he noticed that her breath was faster than it ought to be when standing still.

"Because I am too old for you. Because I am a friend of your father's."

"You aren't too old," she said. And now she was gazing at his lips, and it made her near-impossible to resist.

"But I'm poor," he said. "I'm feral."

"Julian," she said, and he melted at the sound of his name on her lips. "I climb mountains. I'm not an English rose."

"You are the most beautiful person I've ever seen," Julian admitted. "Watching you discuss your passion has been a privilege."

"Julian?" Again, his name in her mouth was more than he could take.

"Yes?" Now he realized his breath was coming faster than it ought.

"Please kiss me," Ophelia asked.

He couldn't speak, he couldn't resist any longer. There was no man on earth that could have. He threaded one hand along her jaw and pulled her in close, his mouth at last on hers. The feeling of her soft lips, her elegant neck pulsing beneath his fingers, it was better than he could have imagined.

She was inexperienced, but he didn't care. She tasted wine-sweet and eager, the heat and desire melting any resolve he had. Her hands rested on his chest, and it was more than he could have hoped to have her embrace him as he held her. How could this divine creature want him? It made no sense.

He kissed her harder, and she returned the pressure, angling her head to step closer, eliminating the distance between them. Now he felt her warm body pressed along his, and the stirring in his trousers became insistent. If he didn't stop kissing her now, he didn't have any hope of letting her leave his room before dawn. Her tongue touched his lips, an invitation.

Instead of pulling away, he groaned and opened his mouth. He explored her lips, tangling with her tongue, enjoying the sensations far more than he had any right to. She moaned in pleasure, and it was as potent as any drug. He pushed away from her, stumbling back.

"I'm sorry," he panted. She looked confused, her lips red and chafed from his, her blue eyes wide with shock.

"Sorry?" she repeated.

"I shouldn't take advantage. I know better."

She blinked rapidly. "Better than what?"

"I mean, you've been drinking, and you are an unmarried lady; this is very unseemly." He ran his hand through his hair, shaking his head. He was rock-hard and it was difficult to think. His instincts were howling in a way they hadn't with Delphine. Kissing Ophelia seemed to have triggered something basic in him, some blood-deep need.

She licked her lips, and that made everything worse. And harder.

"I'm here for a reason, Julian."

There was his name in her mouth again. That beautiful, lovely mouth that tasted so sweet. "It isn't right. I don't deserve you."

"This isn't about what someone deserves. This is about desire."

"You can't say that word to me right now, Ophelia. It isn't fair." Before he could understand what was happening, she was standing so close to him again, her beautiful hair glimmering in the low light, smelling like jasmine and vanilla and citrus. She was light and goodness and purity. Oh God, she was a virgin, wasn't she? He was about to deflower an earl's daughter? "I can't do this to you."

Both her eyebrows rose up. "Are you telling me that I don't know what I want?"

"Yes! No," he said, not sure what he meant anymore. He couldn't think when she was so close.

"Because I want you, Julian. You. Not anyone else. And I don't want to wait for a marriage proposal from Lord Fairport. I don't want to be the woman who is exchanged for dowry, as if I'm livestock. Let me be a person. Let me choose my lover. Let me choose you."

"I feel like I must be a bad man, because any excuse that allows me to tear your clothes off sounds like a good one."

She laughed, that silver bell tinkling sound he loved. "Julian. You can tear my clothes off."

"Oh, thank God," he said and rushed forward, pulling her into his arms. He kissed her again, letting his mind go blank, forgetting all the worries and reasons he shouldn't be doing this.

She pushed the braces off his shoulders, and he started unbuttoning her evening gown. The buttons were damnably tiny as he fumbled with them. Finally, he'd undone enough that he could push it down to her waist. In the back of his mind, his conscience warned him off, begged him to stop.

He pulled away then to look at her. The creamy expanse of her shoulders, and her breasts plump and round in her corset. She was perfect, a dream that he couldn't have ever conjured up. He exhaled harshly, trying to bring himself under some semblance of control.

She let him look his fill, watching his face carefully, and he didn't have the awareness to monitor his expression. He couldn't, instead he gaped at her in amazement. But instead of waiting for him to be finished, she undid his collar, letting it fly wide, and unbuttoned his shirt. Her fingers were deft, easily opening the larger buttons.

He stared at the two perfect breasts cupped in her corset. He felt like a young man all over again, thinking that he might get to touch them. Then her tender palms touched his bare chest, lying flat over where his heart thrummed. He looked into her eyes, and she raised her gaze to his.

She was here for *him*. This wasn't like anything he'd experienced before. He wasn't *saving* her, as he'd felt with Maria; and he wasn't a toy, as he'd felt with Delphine. She was his junior, yes, but she was also showing him her entire self, expecting him to do the same. He would not deny her this.

The connection felt deep, moving from him to her and back again, circling around one another, as if they had been two pieces of the same soul, broken apart and flung into time.

"Julian," she whispered.

"Ophelia." He cupped her lovely face again. God, she was beautiful. Those blue eyes swallowed him, redeemed him, made every moment from before he met her irrelevant. He had missed her so much in the past months. Even though he had seen her, that distance she'd kept between them had made him feel desperate. And now, now she was in his room, asking for more. Asking for everything he had to offer her.

"I've never felt this way before," she said.

"Neither have I," he admitted, his thumb stroking her cheek. He leaned down and kissed her lightly, pleasant and soft, which gave her hands time to roam his chest, pulling at his shirt.

She was clearly interested in both of them disrobing, but he didn't want to assume too much. He had to remind the demon in his trousers that she was a virgin and he needed to go slower than it wanted.

"May I help take off your corset?" His fingers itched to touch that smooth, creamy skin. So different than his own. But he kept his hands away, waiting for her permission.

She nodded and turned away, clearing her golden hair over one shoulder and looking back at him. It was a coquette's pose, but she looked deadly serious. He loosened the ribbons, his fingers shaking. Why was he nervous?

"I've got it," she whispered, and she pushed it down, wiggling as she inched it over her hips. It was mesmerizing. He unbuttoned his trousers and whipped his shirt off over his head. She turned and gaped at his bare chest. It made him wonder if she'd ever seen a man at this level of dishabille before, and he enjoyed her assessing gaze. Her chafed red lips parted at the sight of him. If he knew how to show off for her, he would. But as it was, his brain could only think of how she still wore some scraps of fabric, and that was unacceptable.

He swallowed hard, his mouth suddenly dry. She turned, holding her arms close to her chest, covering her breasts, letting blonde locks trail down her shoulders. "And the rest?"

OPHELIA HAD NEVER been this bare before. Not just her clothing, but every part of her ego. Any harsh word from him would destroy her, and she trembled at her vulnerability. That he might find her ridiculous and laugh at her. That he might tell her she was doing this all wrong, and if she were smarter, she would know that.

And he asked her to remove her last bit of clothing, her underskirt and stockings. She'd already removed her bustle and the crinoline before coming to him wearing a dress that did not require those enhancements. But now, stripped of all those defenses, she was left only as herself. As the rest of her clothing dropped to the luxuriously carpeted floor, she heard his harsh intake of breath. Had she done something wrong?

His dark eyes were fastened on her, roving her body. She dropped her hands down. This was her. She took a deep breath, waiting, uncertain what came next.

"You're so beautiful, Ophelia," he murmured.

He was bigger than she expected. Somehow, with clothes, he was unassuming, harmless. But without, the lean expanse of his chest, peppered with dark hair that convened below his navel, seemed more powerful, stronger, wider than before.

She'd once overheard some newly married women talking in a ballroom, saying that the most ridiculous-looking thing in the world was a naked man. But Ophelia would have to disagree. At least with this naked man. Julian was proportional. His upper arms were wide and muscled, just as someone with such capable hands would require. And his thighs were thick, likely from all the mountain climbing he'd done. And the other part . . . it was unlike anything she'd seen before. It waved in the air as Julian stepped closer, bringing them touching.

The cool air in the room should have caused her to shiver, but she felt as if she were on fire. He touched her shoulders, let his hands graze down and one moved over to gently cup her breast. It was surprising, but pleasant.

"We can stop any time you like," Julian reassured her, leaning in and kissing her.

"I don't want to stop," she said, putting her hands on him, letting them roam all over his shoulders and his chest.

He guided her to the bed and they lay down on their sides, touching one another. But her inherent curiosity couldn't be subverted by her desire. "May I . . .?" Her eyes flicked down to that unfamiliar piece of anatomy that pushed insistently at her stomach.

"Of course," he said. "Do with me as you will."

She smiled and he looked almost drunk on his lust. Admittedly, she did as well. She took him in hand, plumping the sac underneath it, which felt like precisely like an overfull coin purse. To her shock, the skin moved as she explored.

"Oh my," she said, alarmed. "Is it supposed to do that?"

"Mmmm?" Julian propped himself up on his elbows. "Move? Yes. Has a mind of its own sometimes."

"How odd," Ophelia said. "How do men get anything done?"

Julian laughed. "It takes effort, but we learn to control it. Most of us, anyway."

Moisture beaded at the tip, which Ophelia touched, feeling the silky liquid and smoothing it around the top of his erection, which was hot to the touch, and nearly purple. Julian began to breathe harder, and occasionally exhaled strongly, as if he were climbing a mountain now.

"Ophelia." his voice sounded strangled. "If you keep that up, I'm going to come, and I want to make sure you have your pleasure before me."

"Oh." She immediately released him, as if his cock were a hot tray. "I'm only curious."

He chuckled again and said, "That's why I'm having trouble controlling it. Your curiosity is very attractive."

She laughed and touched his chest, which seemed to be acceptable.

"May I have my turn to explore you?" he asked, rolling onto his side.

She nodded, much more comfortable now. His hands roved her breasts again, and this time, he slid kisses down her neck, stopping to suck each of her nipples into his mouth. It was a shock of pleasure, and as he continued, she found it more and more enjoyable.

His other hand skirted down her abdomen to the thatch of silky curls between her legs. He gently massaged and kneaded and pulled until Ophelia moved her legs open, falling onto her back. His fingers found the slit there, exploring gently. She expected it to be uncomfortable, but it wasn't. He moved in small circles until she arched her back involuntarily. It felt better than she could have imagined. She had explored on her own before, and had been able to feel this pleasure, but it was nothing compared to the way her body shook tonight. Nothing had prepared her for this. Pressure built in her, as if the gas lamp key was turning past its capability, opening her wider and wider until it broke, and she erupted into light and heat and her head threw back as she panted.

As she came back to herself, she waited to hear him laugh,

but he didn't. He was serious as he climbed on top of her.

"I want to be inside you, Ophelia. Will you let me?" He held his cock in one hand, away from her body, as if it might get away from him and wreak its own havoc.

She nodded, curiosity and desire again winning every argument. "Yes."

He pushed his cock downward, rubbing it along the inside of her. The sensation sparked her all over again, and she knew it wouldn't take nearly as long this time to build that feeling. Then, something was inside her, but it didn't feel like much.

"Is that it?" she asked, lifting her head to look down at where they were touching.

He laughed again. "No, darling. Just a finger. I wanted to try to get you used to having something there."

"Oh," she said, suddenly very glad that at least one of them knew what they were doing. "Will you tell me before you do it?"

"Of course," he said. "I'm slipping two fingers in now."

The sensation increased, and she rocked her hips with it, an instinctive push. It felt better than the first.

"Your body seems ready. Are you, beautiful Ophelia?" Julian looked down at her.

"I think so," she said.

"You can say no, and I'll stop," he said, wearing a very pained expression.

"I'd like to keep going," she said.

"Thank God," he said, and he continued to rub himself against her. "I'm going to push in now."

And he did, and she felt a lovely expanding in her lower belly. It was a completely foreign and shocking feeling. He pulled out, and she could feel it, a dragging sensation, before he entered her again.

Soon, a rhythm emerged, and she couldn't help but mirror it. When she did so, Julian's eyes glazed over and he pulled on her shoulders, making her hit against him harder. Even though each thrust came with more and more power, it didn't hurt. And soon, that gaslamp key turning sensation took over. She threw her head back, concentrating on that feeling because it was so good.

"Come, Ophelia," he panted.

She understood what he meant, and while she couldn't manage it, suddenly his fingers were there, blindly moving as opposed to their deft execution earlier. It didn't matter, the sensation came, and light appeared behind her eyes as she crested, moaning as he pumped harder and harder into her. Then he moaned, pulling out, spilling seed all over her thighs.

Blinking, comprehending that a threshold had been crossed, she looked down at him. He was on his knees, sitting back on his ankles, holding his deflating member.

"Towel," he said breathlessly, and got to his feet. He wound unsteadily until he reached the towels folded in the top drawer and pulled one out. She expected him to hand it to her, but instead, he slid it under her bottom, and then lovingly wiped her and her thighs. He then cleaned himself, discarding it in the corner. He pulled down the top blanket and ushered her underneath.

Before he came to bed, he turned down all of the lights and then slipped in next to her. Sliding over, he fitted his front to her back, wrapping her in a tight embrace. Ophelia was still forming questions and thoughts from the experience, ordering how she might even say them aloud, when light snores drifted up from behind her. He was already asleep. So she must be expected to stay the night.

She wondered if she had acquitted herself well. Considering Julian was already asleep should be an indication that the event had gone well. And being held so tightly in bed was a revelation. She loved it. So warm and protected—it was not a familiar sensation for her. Should she talk about this experience with Justine? Or should she keep it to herself, so as not to let the secret escape? What she was doing was against the moral code of women of her rank. Marriage first. But she knew of so many girls who hadn't married as virgins, and she was almost thirty.

And really, the truth bubbled to the top: she didn't want to marry Lord Fairport. Not one little bit. And once she admitted such a truth to herself, that she had only been allowing the courtship to please her mother, she felt lighter, and clearer. So she snuggled down in Julian's capable embrace and fell asleep faster than she'd ever done before.

❧ ❦ ❧

Chapter Eight

OPHELIA WOKE UP disoriented. Then she felt the heat of another body and looked over to see Julian lying next to her, reading.

"Good morning," he said, as if she were in the dining room having breakfast, and not naked in his bed.

Her body felt light and . . . wonderful. There was a pinching feeling near her sex, but the rest of her felt elated. The sheets slid around her naked skin, a decadent sensation. "Good morning."

"I ordered a tea tray to be delivered to the room, but I didn't want to arouse suspicion, so there will only be one cup."

Ophelia nodded, still groggy. She'd never felt this relaxed in her life. Stretching out and flexing her toes was incredible. Julian closed his book and put it on the nightstand, sliding down in bed and capturing her around her middle. It felt strange that his bare palm could skate across her fleshy abdomen so easily, so close, so warm.

Her body flooded with another overwhelming surge of decadence and lazy desire. She tugged him closer and he obeyed. No wonder Eleanor and Tristan didn't rise until noon. If this was how being in love while married felt, she'd never get a thing done. He fitted himself against her back, and she raised his palm to her mouth and kissed it.

His mouth scraped her shoulder, his stubble zinging along her skin. The sun flooded in the window, despite the curtains. She could feel the chill of the room outside of their blankets, and it somehow made it all the cozier. Her eyes batted shut. Bliss.

She awoke sometime later, Julian dressed but with bare feet, reclining on the bed over the comforter, reading and drinking from the lone teacup. She blinked. "How long did I sleep for?"

"Which time?" Julian asked with a smile.

"I never sleep this long." She yawned, and noted the room was warmer than it had seemed earlier.

"Then you must need it." Julian reached out, touching her hair, pulling a lock away from her shoulder. The expression on his face was one Ophelia had never seen before, but it was so welcome. It was close to how her father had looked at her mother. How Tristan looked at Eleanor. How Karl Vogel looked at Justine. Well, that was not quite right. Sometimes Karl looked at Justine with a perplexed sort of frown, as if he couldn't predict what she would say or do next.

"Would you . . . be interested in trying that again?" he asked.

His question made her toes curl with the anticipation. "I would."

He whipped his shirt off and dove for her, causing her no end of giggling. It was faster this time, more pointed. He figured out what made her open, and again he spilled on her thighs.

The drowsy decadence of the morning caused her eyelids to grow heavy. "I suppose this is why they keep this from unmarried women."

"Keep what?" Julian cleaned her and then himself with a towel before slipping into bed next to her.

"This absolutely sated feeling I have. I've heard so many terrible stories about what to expect on my wedding night. Not one had a story that was remotely similar to this."

"I think there are a thousand reasons for that, but mostly it is considered disrespectful to be so passionate with one's wife. That touching you, making you cry out, watching you as you find your pleasure, that is not for wives."

Ophelia thought her eyes might pop out of her head. "What

do you mean?"

"It is what one does with a lover, or a woman of a lower class."

"Then how did you learn?" Ophelia asked, and as the words came out of her mouth, the possibilities spiraled out in her mind. How many lovers had he already engaged with? Was she adequate in comparison? Would he regret this encounter? Was he thinking of someone else when he was with her?

He gave a tight smile. "Men talk about this sort of thing."

A stab of insecurity pierced her. "How many lovers have you had?"

"Ophelia," he chastised gently, drawing out the last vowel of her name.

"Please tell me," she said. Her mind was clicking through so fast she couldn't keep up. She was full of overwhelming emotion and it unsettled her. Under the covers, she ran her fingers in the familiar pattern, thumb, pointer, middle, ring, pinkie, and back. "I've never been with anyone before, and I want to know if I did it right."

"You did beautifully," he said, cupping her head to smooth down her hair.

"Better than Lady DeMarius?" Ophelia pressed. The woman's name caught in her throat.

He sighed. "Ophelia. I'm going to say this one time, and I mean it with all the gentleness I can muster. What I have done in my past, who I have been with, is not really anything I must tell you."

She pulled herself up, sitting against the pillows and the head-board. "So you're telling me it's none of my business."

He nodded. "I wouldn't say it in that harsh of terms, but essentially, yes."

"So you get to know who I've been with, but I don't get to know yours?"

He shook his head. "If you'd had a partner before me, I would not ask his name. I don't care, and I'd prefer not to know."

"But I haven't, though." Ophelia said, her mind spinning and calculating at an alarming speed. "I volunteered my past. Shouldn't you, as well?"

"I don't want to think of any other woman but you right now. Why is that a bad thing?"

"Because you said you'd never felt this way before," she insisted.

"I haven't," he said, still lying on his side, head propped up by his hand.

"But how do I know that it is true, since you won't tell me about the others?"

He put his free hand on her lap, grasping for one of hers, but she moved them away. She didn't want to hold hands anymore.

"I don't see how what I feel now has anything to do with my past. They are separate. I am not the man I was yesterday, and he is not the man I am today."

"And obviously I am not the woman I was yesterday either. Yesterday I was an odd but eligible young lady. Now I am ruined, even though I don't feel it."

A frown burrowed its way into Julian's forehead. "Your mind hops about so quickly, I'm afraid I'm having trouble keeping up."

Ophelia waved her hand, perturbed now. She'd lost that dreamy, sleepy, sated feeling from earlier. Now she felt troubled. Julian somehow had managed to make her feel alone, even though they were together. For the first time since her father died, tears began welling up in her eyes.

"Oh," Julian sat up, surprised, when he noticed. "Er—"

"I shouldn't have come," Ophelia said, doing her best to keep her tone even and polite. "I do apologize for being so forward." She slipped out of bed, collecting her discarded things. She pulled on her shift and then her corset, pulling it loosely around herself. Oh, she could smell herself, with Julian's scent on her layered on top. She found her stockings, and then her underskirt.

"I thought I was somehow different. Special. The way you looked at me," Ophelia said, ashamed that tears fell out of her eyes as she bent over. Dark circles bloomed on the lush red carpet.

"You are special, Ophelia," Julian said, but he remained in bed. He didn't try to talk her out of it, nor did he stand to beg her to stay.

It was only logical to conclude he didn't care if she stayed or went. So she would go and bathe and rid herself of all these reminders. No longer could she claim a virginal status. No longer eligible. But at twenty-eight, what did people expect from her?

She longed to shed this skin. The skin of expectations, of dashed hopes, of defeat and disappointment.

"Ophelia, I don't want—"

She pulled her dress on over her head, muffling whatever it was that he'd said. She was done listening, because he wasn't willing to tell her what she wanted to know. Why wouldn't he just give her a number? Five? Ten? Fifty? How many women had he purred his loving words to? Exactly how not special was she? One in ten was certainly a different level than one in fifty. That was just mathematics. Slippers on, she swiped her key from the table nearest the door.

"Forget this ever happened," she said. "I will."

And she was glad to make it down the hall without running into anyone else. She fumbled with her key, but finally got it unlocked. She threw herself on the bed and cried.

⯈⯈⯈⯇⯇⯇

Julian stared at the closed door in shock. Then he fell back against the pillows. It smelled of Ophelia everywhere. A heady aroma of sex and jasmine. He rubbed his hands against his face. He'd thought he was doing the right thing. How often had it been drilled into him to not kiss and tell? That it was disrespectful, rude, and potentially life-endangering for the woman?

But Ophelia wanted him to disgorge his past like it was a tidy memory, wrapped up in a bow. It was impossible. And there were some nights he'd purposefully forgotten. Times that made him feel the way Ophelia now felt.

What did he expect when he seduced his friend's daughter? "Oh, that was stupid." He squeezed his eyes shut. In being respectful, he had disrespected her. In being disrespectful to his mentor, he'd respected his own heart. And now, the stupid git he was, he'd ruined a friendship with not just Ophelia, but with Tristan and Rascomb and Lady Rascomb.

He'd blown everything to pieces because Ophelia had come to him. It was a test, and he'd failed. What would his friend say to him if he were still alive? Julian sighed and stared at the ceiling. He didn't know anymore. If it were any other woman, Rascomb would have advised marrying the girl because she was a virgin and high-born and he'd ruined her. But if she weren't, then Rascomb would advise an apology, a gesture, and then to move on and try to never see her again to avoid the embarrassment on both their parts.

But his own daughter? Rascomb would have raged at him. Julian didn't know what the right thing to do would be. Should he ask her to marry him? Him—a broke, wandering baronet without a family or a home. Or should he keep quiet and let Lord Fairport propose and solve everything for him? But the idea of that man's soft hands on her hips, the idea of him kissing her with his dry lips—it was going to make him vomit.

He dressed, bathing so as not to smell like he'd done what he had done. He went out to walk Paris—the salve to any problem. In the lobby he encountered Tristan and his wife, people he really did not want to chat with as he mulled over what to do with Ophelia.

"Looking a bit down there, mate," Tristan said, clapping him on the shoulder. "Too much wine?"

If only it was a hangover making him feel this way. "Must be."

"We are going out for a walk before meeting up with everyone for dinner." Mrs. Bridewell said, pulling on her gloves.

Julian grimaced, trying to think of an excuse he might give that he wouldn't be invited on a walk, but nothing came. "As am I."

"You should join us!" Tristan put his arm around Julian and steered him towards the door.

There was no resisting the man without seeming unpleasant, so he acquiesced, knowing that it would give him no opportunity to think. Would he accidentally blurt out his problem to Ophelia's brother? He didn't think so, as long as he could keep himself partitioned. To keep himself to the man he was two days ago, and not the man he'd become when Ophelia announced her desire for him. Which had changed him completely.

⤜⤛⤜

THERE WAS A knock at the door. Or rather, a rhythm that Justine pounded on every surface and this was no exception. Ophelia lay in her bed, clean but clad only in her underthings. She didn't want to get up and go anywhere. The world was too much, and she was too little.

"Come in," Ophelia called, muffled by an over-stuffed pillow, because moving was impossible.

Justine popped in, and Ophelia could feel her happiness emanate from her. Good for her, but Ophelia couldn't stand it. Not right now.

"Oh. It's this, then." Justine kicked off her slippers and crawled into bed next to Ophelia. Her wide brown eyes stared down the pillow until Ophelia clapped it down to peer at her. How was it that Justine could see through the pillow and Ophelia could still feel her eyes on her?

"It's nothing," Ophelia said into the pillow, letting the fluff rise back up.

"What did he say?"

"Who?"

Justine pushed the pillow down so she could look Ophelia in the face. Justine already knew, so why did Ophelia have to say it aloud? "If this isn't about Sir Julian, you are a terrible best friend and you need to update me right now."

Ophelia sighed. "It is." If she thought about it more, she might start crying, and that was unacceptable. She was angry, wasn't she?

"What happened last night after we all went to bed?" Justine asked, but as soon as she finished speaking her eyes went wide and she gasped. "You hussy! Tell me everything."

Ophelia flipped over onto her back, and gave a pleading look to Justine. "Please don't tell anyone."

"Who am I going to tell?"

"Eleanor, Prudence, Karl, and then they'll tell their husbands, which includes my *brother*—"

Justine shrugged. "Fine. I won't tell. So. What happened? Did you go to him? Oh, I bet you did."

Ophelia groaned. She was so foolish. And Justine knew her too well. "Yes. And he tried to turn me away."

"Good man, he has manners." Justine clucked and rearranged the folds of the blanket around her.

"But then I told him that I wanted him to kiss me, and so he did."

"Good man, he has eyeballs."

"Why does that make him a good man?" Ophelia demanded.

"Because if he hadn't kissed you, you would have been exactly like this but with absolutely nothing to show for it."

"What do I have to show for it now?" Ophelia asked.

Justine waved her hand all around, as if there were an entire swarm of bees on her. "You're different now, are you not?"

"I don't know. I just feel miserable, so I suppose that's different." Ophelia covered her eyes with her hand. "I am so stupid."

"But Sir Julian is, well . . . he's in love with you, isn't he? That's what all the hinting about a marriage proposal was about?"

Ophelia frowned. "What marriage proposal?"

"In your letters! You kept talking about possibly finally receiving a marriage proposal. You never said who, so I assumed it was Sir Julian! He followed you to Paris, after all. And the way he looks at you, it's as if daisies were springing out of your head."

"I wish daisies were springing out of my head," Ophelia grumbled. "Far more interesting than being jilted."

Justine gasped again. "Who could jilt you? Honestly! First, though. Marriage proposal. Who is it if it isn't Sir Julian?"

Ophelia tried very hard to keep a neutral face. "Lord Fairport."

Justine screwed up her face, her tongue sticking out of the corner of her mouth as she reached back into the memories of the ballrooms. "Ugh. Really? Didn't he try to marry your sister?"

"And now me," Ophelia said, raising her arms, and then letting them fall down and hit herself. "Ow."

"I'd prefer Sir Julian," Justine said.

"So would I, but it isn't up to me, is it?" Ophelia said.

Justine poked her in the ribs.

"Ow, what was that for?"

"I wanted to see if you were real. Because Ophelia, when was the last time something you wanted didn't happen?"

"You make me sound like a spoiled child."

"I don't mean it like that and you know it. I mean that you work for what you want. You see it, you want it, you get it, whatever it takes."

"And what you don't understand is that I'm not good enough. Example, I didn't summit the Matterhorn."

"If another woman tells me that she is past her prime after twenty-five, I'm going to scream." Justine threw a pillow across the room. "And being intimate with a man and climbing the most dangerous mountain in Europe are *not* the same."

"Ophelia rolled her eyes. "I'm saying that I can't do what I set out to do. That these challenges are too big, whether it's the

Matterhorn or pursuing Sir Julian. He was absolutely clear about that."

Justine put her hands together had took a steadying breath. "Darling. You are literally perfect. There is no one in the world more perfect than you, and I know that because I've met you and I've met them. And they are terrible."

"That's a very limited sample, Justine." Her friend's loyalty was zealous and biased, but it still made Ophelia feel better.

Justine held her finger up, as if she were making an academic point. "But it doesn't mean I'm wrong."

"I don't know what happened, really. Everything seemed fine. I thought he really liked me, and then when I asked him deeper questions, he wouldn't answer me."

Justine's mouth twisted off to the side and she frowned. "Firstly, I'm absolutely on your side no matter what. I will burn his house down for you if you like."

"Please don't."

"Well, the offer stands. But what did you ask him, exactly?"

The question made Ophelia feel very small. "I don't wish to say," she whispered.

Justine looked at her with pity. "Oh, my darling. Is this your fault?"

"I don't know." Ophelia threw her hands up in the air and sat up, suddenly agitated where she'd been completely lethargic. "He had said I was special, and I believed him. He said he'd never felt this way before. And I wanted to believe him, but you know how I prefer numbers to feelings."

Justine lifted her eyebrows and nodded. "Very aware."

"I wanted a number, so I could make a statistic. Am I special in terms of one in fifty?"

"Fifty?" Justine asked. "Wait, did you ask him how many lovers he'd had? Ophelia. You can't just ask someone something like that. It's private."

"How could it be private, when what we did, what he saw of me is the least private thing one can do?"

Justine sighed and frowned. "It is very private between you, yes. But is that not why he should keep his acts with others also private?"

Ophelia wiped her cheek with the flat of her palm, unsure if there was moisture there or not. "But if I'm the special one, then—"

Justine shook her head and put her hand on Ophelia's arm. "Jealousy is a terrible emotion, Fee. But Julian has a right to keep this to himself. And, I must remind you, he is not your husband. He is nothing to you."

"He's my climbing partner to-be." Ophelia defended.

"That's not enough. You should talk to him if you want to keep him in your life."

"Is it wise to, though? He might force me to marry him. Or Arthur might." Ophelia made a face. Her older brother was quite the stickler for appearances, and if Ophelia had been compromised, it was only right for Julian to marry her. But what if Lord Fairport proposed? Would that not solve the issue as well? But then she'd be married to Lord Fairport. "What if I do not wish to marry?"

Justine shrugged. "Then don't. But you told me that you were open to it, which is why when your mother suggested going back to the Season, you said yes."

"I did, but I didn't think anything would come of it. I'm so old."

"Positively decrepit, yes, but I love you anyway."

Ophelia gripped her hand, feeling better. "So I should speak with him."

"I think that would help." Justine scooched off the bed and began searching through the clothes on the floor. "Now let's get you dressed."

❧

Chapter Nine

JULIAN DIDN'T KNOW what to do with his hands. Dinner was awkward, but Mrs. Vogel fussed over Ophelia so much that Julian wondered if she knew about their indiscretion. Would Ophelia tell anyone?

The conflicting sides of the argument warred as he passed a bread basket down the table. The walk earlier with Tristan and his wife had garnered no accidental insights, but rather reenforced how much Julian enjoyed the entire clan. He fit well with them, as if there had been a dark puzzle piece off in the corner, waiting for him to appear and press into place with a satisfying click.

The party ordered more wine and Julian capitalized Karl Vogel so he wouldn't have to speak with Ophelia. Or look at her. Or remember what she looked like when she said she'd never felt like this before. The softness of her thighs, the sighing from her lovely mouth, the golden tresses he'd fisted as he'd come, wanting so badly to spill into her, but pulling out because the consequences were too great.

He shook his head to focus, clearly not thinking well. Perhaps he should leave Paris early, claim to have a lecture to attend. Anything to get out of here and not think of how horribly he'd sabotaged the only relationships of value in his life. Yes, bow out gracefully. Be gone. Let Ophelia be Ophelia, and have her carry on as she always had. Marry Lord Fairport, climb whichever mountains she could manage. It really was of no concern to him.

He had no claim on her.

Julian mechanically ate his meal, not registering the taste or the texture. The restaurant was filled with diners, and the air was stifling with all the windows and doors shut against the winter chill. Finally they adjourned and walked out into the fresh night air.

Ophelia hung back in the group, as he did, and it made him wonder if she was going to speak to him. He wasn't sure he could manage it. He was eleven years her elder, and he wasn't emotionally capable of going toe-to-toe here.

"May we talk?" Ophelia said in a low voice.

"Of course," he said, slowing his pace.

"Last night was . . ." she trailed off.

He wanted to supply her with words, but they were words that described his experience. Words like, *incredible, decadent, transcendent, beautiful, life-altering,* all came to mind. But those were his ideas, not hers, and his heart thudded with cold dread.

She cleared her throat, and Julian couldn't help but notice she was looking at the ground. He already felt terrible enough about the ramifications, but he couldn't say that he would change anything. Being with her had been more than he'd ever hoped for. He knew that he would pine for her for the rest of his life. He wouldn't be able to watch her marry Lord Fairport. In fact, he'd already written to the RGS requesting another posting. Anything that would take him out of England and Europe at large.

"Last night was better than I imagined," she finally said, wringing her hands and making her plush leather gloves squeak.

That was something, but it didn't alleviate his guilt. How could he feel guilt but not remorse? Because he was not at all sorry for what they'd done, only that the rest of the world would condemn then for it. And that his friend would have condemned him for doing this with his daughter.

"But I'd still very much like it if we could ascend the Matterhorn together."

That was not what he thought she would say next. But then,

Ophelia was always surprising him. "But—"

"It wasn't right of me to ask about your past, I see that now. It was childish of me." Now she looked at him, her blue eyes staring up at him. "I sincerely hope you might forgive me for that intrusion, but also understand the impulse of my curiosity."

He was mesmerized. There was no question he could forgive her anything. He nodded, his mouth slack, unable to come up with any words to convey how relieved he felt. However, it was probably uncouth to ask her if she would come to his bed again tonight. "I absolutely forgive you, Ophelia. It is natural to be curious."

She smiled at him, and his heart could burst from relief.

"And will you forgive me for being obstinate?" he asked, his body surging with a fervor for her that bordered on zealotry. He must control himself. "For not remembering what it was like to be the one asking questions?"

The comment about remembering visibly needled her, but she swallowed the discomfort. "Yes, of course."

He offered his arm, but she ignored it, or didn't see it. Still, this was what he'd hoped for, a reconciliation, even if something felt wrong.

"Will you . . ." He pitched his voice low, so the others wouldn't hear. He was a weak man. The idea of her in his bed again was making him feel drunken.

But she shook her head, a tight, polite smile on her face. "No, it's not a good idea."

"You are right, naturally. Forgive me." He hated not that she had declined him, but the way she had. That impersonal smile created a distance that yawned between them.

She made a high-pitched noise in her throat that she'd never made before. She'd had his contrition. Was it not enough? Perhaps his relief at their reconciliation was not as apparent? Did she require more dramatics from him?

"Perhaps you might meet me down early to break our fast before the others?" That felt at least proper. It was public and easily explained. Perhaps he could get her accustomed to his presence again, and he could find a way to not stare after her like a lovesick puppy.

"Yes, that I can do." She still didn't take his arm, but Julian still considered it a victory.

THEY ARRIVED BACK at the hotel and everyone dispersed up the stairs. Ophelia felt drained, and was glad she didn't have a maid with her to fuss about her clothes and hair. It was a bother to be without one, but still manageable.

As she slipped out of her dress and took the pins out of her hair, she sagged against the weight of her life. She could acknowledge that it was better than most, yes, but what had she done with it? She was a failure, and when she'd tried so hard to prove that women could be as adventurous as men, she had failed more than herself. She'd failed her father, who had believed in her. Believed so hard that he'd died in her attempt to prove it. And it wasn't infrequent for her to receive a letter or suffer the comments of men who hadn't so much as climbed a molehill to tell her how her failure was foreordained on the basis of her body.

And now, she was a failure at trysting. Julian had seemed so right and so perfect, but there was something about their interaction that left her feeling so very bereft. That she had opened up to him in every way possible, and he'd given nothing. She felt like a schoolgirl with a crush on a teacher who had patted her head when she confessed.

But perhaps they could repair this at breakfast. Get back to the familiar space for them: fully clothed conversation. That was better. Easier. She went to bed, but tossed and turned, not falling asleep for hours.

JULIAN SKIPPED DOWN the stairs the next morning. He'd slept well, relieved that Ophelia understood him enough to let him have his privacy. That what they'd shared was special, but that certain things were inviolate. They'd had a very intellectual apology exchange, which was such a relief. He remembered Maria's occasional crying fits that he'd never quite understood, as she never explained them in Spanish or English. He hadn't understood what was happening, and was only relieved when she calmed herself.

What a novel experience to be with such a level-headed woman like Ophelia.

He stopped by the front desk to pick up his post and saw Ophelia already in the morning room, taking tea and toast. She likewise had gotten her post and was reading letters. It would be a lovely, easy morning together. Friends. Even if he'd prefer to be more, despite his guilt.

Had she regretted their intimacy? Had it not been good? He was fairly certain that she had climaxed several times. He wasn't an egotistical person about most things, but he could admit he kept count of his partner's pleasures. It was merely a good way to analyze the situation for improvements. Frankly, he would be shocked if every Englishman didn't do so, given their national propensity for bureaucracy.

"Good morning. May I?" Julian stood beside the chair, waiting for her permission, despite their previous invitation.

She waved her hand, and he sat, notifying the waitstaff with a raised finger to bring another cup for the pot that already steamed in front of Ophelia. "Please. And good morning to you as well."

Her hair was hastily pinned up, and strands were coming loose. It was more than the amount of curled tendrils that was fashionable, but it was tantalizing to see the locks catching the morning light. It made him think of her hair strewn across his bare chest. Across his pillow. Wound between his fingers.

"Did you sleep well?" he asked, pouring his own tea when she made no motion to put her letter down, or even make eye contact with him.

"Thank you for asking," she said, still not bothering to look up.

He let the moment pass, but it was frustrating. He thought they'd repaired the squabble they'd had. "That's not an answer."

"What's not an answer?" she asked, still engrossed. She chewed on her lip as she read.

It was an unladylike habit, but he confessed he found it appealing, giving her lower lip a bee-stung appearance, just as her mouth had looked after he'd kissed her senseless. Was she a coquette? Had she more schooling in the art of drawing a man in? If it were Delphine, he would absolutely believe this to be an act. But with Ophelia, could she be such a flirt? "Are you doing that for me?"

"For who?" she asked, flipping the letter over, continuing to read.

"For me."

"No, the letter is for me," she said, shaking her head. "Obviously."

Julian sighed. "You aren't listening."

"You aren't looking," she said, her eyes finally snapping up to meet his. "I'm busy reading. Stop talking."

Julian blinked, taken aback. "That was uncalled for."

"Was it?" She sighed and put down her letter. "I see you feel that I must adjust my behavior because you have arrived in my sightline."

Julian's mouth fairly gaped open. Who was this harpy? "It is merely polite."

She waved her hand. "Yes, yes, a woman is to serve, I understand. Any activity I engage in is not worth continuing once a man enters the room."

"That is not what I said," Julian protested.

"No, but you implied that me biting my lip is somehow bait for you."

"I thought you weren't listening." Julian narrowed his eyes.

So she was a coquette?

She huffed and set her jaw. "I wasn't at the time. But I spooled it up in my mind and examined it again. So yes, I know what you said now. And no, I was not reading *for you*, I was not drinking tea *for you*, and I certainly was not biting my lip *for you*. Do you know how many times I was paddled for that growing up? Not for you."

Julian flushed at the idea of Ophelia being paddled. Because he didn't picture a little girl, he pictured her as she was now, in her pretty pale blue day dress, with ruffled lace at the collar, bent over a table. Not helpful. "How about we start over? Good morning, Ophelia."

"Good morning, Sir Julian."

He flinched at hearing her say *sir*. They were past that. "You don't need to be so formal."

She blinked her large blue eyes at him, but didn't say anything.

"Right, well. If you would like to spend the morning reading correspondence, I will continue with my own."

"Excellent," she said, picking up her own letter again.

They sat in companionable silence, or at least, it was companionable on his side. He had news from the RGS on the date of Ophelia's article's publication. A letter from Mrs. Talbert asking about his return date and rent. Another letter, forwarded to him by the RGS, smelled of perfume as he opened it.

The scent was strong enough that Ophelia put down her letter and stared at him as he perused the contents. It was innocuous enough. A woman who had attended a short lecture he'd given about South America in a RGS member's parlor a few weeks back wrote to say how much she'd enjoyed hearing about the other side of the world. The paper was of high quality, but he didn't remember the woman by her signature.

"What news?" Ophelia asked.

Julian smiled. Apparently Ophelia could be made jealous, as evidenced by the aroma of his admirer. She could be teased about this, and perhaps that would finally break the tension between them. He put down the scented envelope and held up the others. "Publication date for your article. My landlady concerned I won't return before my next rent is due, and—" He flourished the scented letter. "—A love letter."

Her expression went blank. She didn't take the bait. "I see."

"Ophelia—"

"I must share in kind, as is only polite. I have a lengthy letter from my mother. It seems Lord Fairport has requested that my brother draft a wedding contract. He means to propose to me upon my return. Arthur has assured him he will sign no such contract if I do not consent."

Julian's stomach dropped. That thought of teasing her was gone. No wonder she had been so tight-lipped with him this morning. It was his turn to study his teacup. "And what will you say?"

"To my mother? Thank you for the information, of course." Ophelia was already folding the paper back.

"I mean to Lord Fairport," Julian said gently.

She stared him down, expressionless. "What ought I say?"

He swallowed hard, not trusting his voice. His teasing was utterly forgotten. This sunny day had definitely soured. "I know that I have no claim—"

"Haven't you?" she asked.

He knew it was a challenge. She was asking him if he would do right by her and marry her, but he was not wealthy. Lord Fairport was a higher rank—honestly, Julian couldn't remember if he was a viscount or an earl. Everything regarding the man dropped out of his head as soon as it went in. "No, I don't."

Ophelia nodded. "Not while you have your ardent devotees to attend to."

"That's not what I meant. It was a joke, Ophelia. I was trying to tease you."

Her jaw set. "Because I am so easily mocked."

"No!" He put his hands flat on the table to keep himself trying to grab her hands, to touch her, to try for a connection that he was so clearly unable to establish. "I'm not mocking. Mocking and teasing are different. Besides, you are the one who is marrying someone else."

"Am I?" she asked coolly.

They heard a bustle of noise and saw the rest of their party entering the dining room, ready for their morning repast.

"We must get a table to fit all of us," Eleanor said, looking about at the other white linen-covered tables.

"I'm sorry, I have a headache. Excuse me." Ophelia threw her napkin on the table and gathered up her letters before pushing away from the table.

Julian was left feeling like he would have preferred Maria's crying jags to Ophelia's cold distance. He didn't know what to do. He only knew that he felt like an utter cad.

OPHELIA TAGGED ALONG with Justine and Karl for a walk through the shops. She registered nothing she saw, but at least she didn't have to pretend. Karl cited professional interest in shopping, and Justine kept one eye on Karl and one eye on Ophelia, waiting for Ophelia to crack wide open. But she wouldn't.

The life path that had been so obscured to her now became obvious. Ophelia would marry Lord Fairport. She would become a lady in marriage, and not only by her own birth. There would be dinner parties and charities. Loveless nights of perfunctory attempts at producing heirs. She would likely never climb another mountain. Never run through the woods like a deer. Instead of a wild animal, she would become a pet. Caged and confined.

As a woman ought to be. No voice. No ambition. No gumption. A prop for her husband. And then for her children. An ache opened in her chest again as she wished for her father. He would have looked at Lord Fairport and scoffed. He would have known from the beginning that they would be a poor match, regardless of his wealth and status.

But Arthur was not her papa. And Ophelia was getting on. She was well past the declaration of spinsterhood, and approaching being an eccentric. She should count herself lucky indeed to nab a man like Lord Fairport.

They settled into a café for a cup of chocolate. The drink was rich and thick, adulterated with delicious heavy cream. It warmed her insides and allowed her to look at her best friend. Justine felt her gaze and put her hand out to Ophelia.

"Karl, love?" Justine said, not breaking her gaze with Ophelia.

"Hmm?" her husband said, pulling his attention from the newspaper he was reading.

"Go away." Justine wasn't angry when she said it, rather it was said with all the love she always had in her tone when she spoke to him.

"I'll be gone twenty minutes." Karl folded up his paper without another word and walked off.

"That was extraordinary," Ophelia said.

Justine pulled her hands back and sipped at her cup. "Not really. I told him it might happen, especially when I saw you leave at breakfast."

Ophelia put her hands in her lap. "I'm sorry about that. I couldn't—"

"Don't apologize!" Justine interrupted. "You needed space, you took some. It was exactly the right thing to do. Would you like to talk about it now?"

A lump in her throat formed. "I'm not sure? I think perhaps yes, but it's so messy, I'm not sure I can."

"Fair enough. But do your best?"

Ophelia nodded. "You know of the night I spent with Julian."

Justine nodded, leaning forward, which told Ophelia she'd dropped her voice too low.

"And my apology to him. And then he apologized to me. And then he invited me to his room again—"

"He did what?" Justine shrieked. It was then she noticed all the people staring at her. But she merely waved at them as if they were acquainted already before lowering her voice. "I cannot believe he asked you to his room."

"He suggested it, but I refused. I didn't feel like I could do that again. Not with the way I felt."

"I'm proud of you." Justine folded her arms, outraged on Ophelia's behalf.

Ophelia took no small amount of comfort knowing that Justine would be there for her no matter what. "Thank you. We agreed to meet for tea before everyone came down this morning. But I was reading a letter from my mother as he arrived, and he wanted to talk, but I just couldn't. She was writing to make me aware that Lord Fairport asked to marry me, and that Arthur was drawing up a contract."

Justine withdrew with a gasp. "He wouldn't!"

"Arthur apparently told him that he wouldn't force me into marriage, but everyone believes it to be so obviously my only chance that plans are going ahead without me."

Justine shook her head slowly in shock. "That's forward of them."

Ophelia sighed. "It does make sense, looking at it from their perspective. I'm twenty-eight, Justine. This is my only chance."

"You are perfect and I love you just as you are." Justine stared into her eyes as she declared her love, which always made Ophelia smile. "But I want to know if it makes sense from *your* perspective."

Ophelia had been trained not to shrug. But this felt like a very appropriate time to do it. Even so, she forced herself to answer with words. "From my point of view, it is rather practical. It is what is expected of me. With certain conditions, I think I might be able to marry Lord Fairport."

Justine winced but nodded her assent. Ophelia interpreted that to mean that she was willing to be supportive, but wanted to know what those caveats might entail. "For instance," Ophelia said, gaining some confidence as she thought quickly. "I would be allowed to climb any mountain I wanted, with anyone I deem fit."

"You're thinking of Sir Julian."

"No," Ophelia protested automatically. But wasn't she? "I'm not *not* thinking of Sir Julian, but also perhaps someone else I might meet in the future. Or you and your husband."

Justine's mouth made a flat line, as if she didn't really believe her. Which, Ophelia could see why she wouldn't.

"Any other stipulations?"

Ophelia thought about it. "After an heir is born, I choose if he is allowed to touch me again."

Justine's eyelashes fluttered with how rapidly she blinked. This was clearly unexpected. "Oh."

"I think it would only be right to be the one to control my own person."

"Yes, of course, but I'm not sure he would agree to such a stipulation," Justine said, looking down at her cup of chocolate.

"Why not? It is my body. I should control who has access to it."

"But a husband wants to retain those rights for his own pleasure," Justine said, nearly choking on the last word.

"But if it doesn't please me, then why should I engage in that sort of behavior with him?" Ophelia protested.

"I agree with your sentiment wholeheartedly, Ophelia. However, I'm not sure Lord Fairport would. But it would be a good negotiating point. I've learned a great deal about negotiations from the Vogel family."

Ophelia frowned. "He is not forcing you—"

Justine's laugh cut her off. "No, not that. No, they are merchants, and deal in goods across Europe. Negotiations are critical and can do a great deal of revealing work. So if you put those two things down as your stipulations, and Lord Fairport doesn't like it, you remove one of them to obtain the other, as a compromise."

"But I don't wish to compromise."

"No one does," Justine said, putting her hand on Ophelia's arm. "The question is, do you want to enter this negotiation at all?"

"I think I'd rather walk and talk about this." Ophelia did not wish to talk about this at all, but she couldn't very well say that. It was a betrothal, and she knew she ought to be ecstatic. Even with Justine, who was not ecstatic about the prospect, Ophelia knew she needed to feign interest.

Because how depressing would it be to marry a man she didn't like? On top of everything else?

They finished at the café, rounded up Karl, and returned to the hotel as the others were as well. They stood in the lobby discussing adventures and where they should make reservations for dinner. Tristan finally took charge and went to the desk to ask the concierge to make reservations, and he told the man to hold a table for seven.

"Seven?" Ophelia asked. "But our party numbers eight."

Eleanor took Ophelia's hand and whispered, "Sir Julian left this afternoon. A telegram arrived, and he said he had urgent business in London."

The words burned. Justine looked at her with worry. Prudence detached from Mr. Moon and came over to stand near them. Turning, Prudence announced brightly in her American accent, "I have a brilliant idea. Men, why don't you go out together for dinner, and us four ladies will dine in tonight. We will have all our potions and lotions out to refresh and renew ourselves, and you all can visit some place we would hate."

"Not the Moulin Rouge," Justine said, staring daggers at Tristan. Tristan put his hands up in his own defense.

Ophelia sagged with relief.

"We will not go to the Moulin Rouge," Tristan agreed. "Gentlemen? Where shall we go with our newfound freedom?"

Prudence returned to Ophelia's side. "Let me take care of everything. Would you like Champagne, wine, or sherry?"

"Or gin?" Justine suggested.

"The first two," Ophelia said.

"Why don't you get her a bath sorted, and I'll order up provisions for the evening." Prudence said to Eleanor.

"Can we use my room to gather in?" Ophelia said. "I don't want—"

"Absolutely." Justine said, cutting off Ophelia's lack of explanation. Her best friend knew that Ophelia sometimes wanted to only be in her own space. That she could only truly relax in a space that was for herself.

The emptiness that she had felt after her father's accident yawned wide open, knowing that Julian had left without saying so much as a goodbye. She pulled away from the rest of the Ladies' Alpine Society and went to the desk, asking if there was any note or post for her. The man checked but shook his head in the negative. Nothing.

Julian hadn't even bothered to leave her a note. Could he have received a telegram, requesting his presence? It was possible. But as far as Ophelia knew, the only urgent business was making sure his landlady would get the rent. A task easily fixed from the safety of a Paris hotel. Perhaps it was the love letter that was urgent.

"Come on upstairs, Fee," Justine said, taking her shoulders and guiding her upstairs.

Ophelia knew her brother was looking to the others for an explanation. But Ophelia didn't cry, didn't contort her face in despair or even sniff out of turn. That wasn't her way. No, she was not prone to outbursts. Rather, she retreated. That scared some, how far she could go inside of herself. Thankfully, Justine knew this. And with Justine's help, she could return to London without gossips catching wind of what might look to others like a deeply depressed state.

⌁

Chapter Ten

J ULIAN LOOKED AROUND his flat. He hadn't accrued much in the months he'd been in London. Packing shouldn't be too much of an ordeal. Travel would still be a nightmare, as he had missed the preferred crossing months. He would likely put off travel for a few more anyhow, but he wanted to be prepared.

It was January now, and the view out his windows was bleak. Fog and cold wrestled for dominance, and the wind wormed its way in between his collar and bare neck no matter how carefully he wound a muffler. He had not seen nor spoken to Ophelia in well over a month.

He tried very hard not to count the days, but every so often, the calculation came to him unbidden. She likely understood that their proposed Matterhorn escapade was off, didn't she? They'd not explicitly stated so, but any right-minded person would understand his leaving in the middle of their Paris holiday meant they had severed all ties, including a professional one.

There was the option of dropping by Tristan Bridewell's outfitter, but that made his stomach queasy. The man would ask why he'd run from Paris, and what was he supposed to say? There would be an explanation of an emergency, and given that he had no living family, what was the nature of his supposed urgent return to London? His investments? That was a laugh. Everyone knew he didn't have two shillings to rub together. No, he would have to admit that the RGS has requested an interview to further his application for a grant to return to South America. It wasn't a final interview and likely could have waited. But Julian was a coward, so he did a runner.

There was a knock at his door, the familiar pattern of his valet. As it turned out, Julian had grown fond of having a valet, if not for keeping him turned out looking his best with his subpar fashion, then for the news and conversation. Julian opened his door.

"This just arrived," Nicholas said, thrusting a journal at him.

"What's this?" Julian took it, instantly recognizing the Royal Geographical Society masthead.

"Look there," Nicholas said, excitement evident in his face. "You made front page. Big article. They pay by the word? You must have done well by that one then."

Julian frowned. He hadn't penned in a new article in months. And as he read the first lines, his heart sank. It wasn't his article, even though his name was there on the byline. It was Ophelia's account of her Ben Nevis summit. It should have been printed by Anonymous, and instead was credited to him.

Every curse word he could think of in three languages ran through his mind. This was bad. If it were anyone else, he might consider this a faux pas easily fixed with a bottle of brandy or a night on the town. But not for Ophelia, who faced so many impediments that being printed even anonymously was a challenge.

"This isn't mine," Julian said, wanting to tell everyone that it was Ophelia's work, but not wanting to out her as the author, since the journal didn't allow women. "This should be written by Anonymous."

Nicholas frowned. "You aren't Anonymous?"

Julian shook his head. "I only handed in someone else's work. Someone who didn't want to be credited in print."

Nicholas crowed. "But everyone wants to see their name in print!"

Julian gave the valet a tight smile. "Not everyone has the

luxury of wanting such a thing." He turned and went to the desk, eyes glued on the text. They hadn't editorialized a thing. This was purely Ophelia, and she wrote so convincingly and lively of their travail. She had done well.

He sat to write a strongly worded letter to the editor, but then realized that it wouldn't do. Instead, he would go himself, in person, to make this right. And collect any payment owed to Ophelia. Would he bring it to her himself? Or would he wait and hand it off to someone else because his cowardice was too great?

⇶⫷

"WHAT IS IT? I don't like it when your face looks like that," Ophelia said to Arthur, as he came in holding a handful of newspapers and pamphlets.

"My face looks fine," Arthur said.

Ophelia glanced to her mother to monitor her expression. There was no use looking at Lady Emily. Her face was far rounder than normal, and it was difficult to focus on her head when her belly was so extraordinarily large.

"You have the Royal Geographical—" Ophelia stood to paw through the stack of papers Arthur held.

He pulled them up and over his shoulder, out of reach. "I do, but I have to say something before you get upset."

Ophelia frowned. "Why would I be upset? Did they pull the article?"

"No," Arthur said, dropping his hands once Ophelia withdrew her grasping fingers. "But I received a note today warning me to keep the journal from you until something had been fixed. I don't pretend to know what the something is."

Who would send Arthur a note about the article other than Julian? He was the only one who knew she penned the article. The man couldn't be bothered to reach out to her, but he could send a note to her brother *about* her? The slow-building anger against Julian grew again in size. He abandoned her, left without saying goodbye, made her feel like an absolute wretch, and now something was amiss with her article and he told her *brother* to keep it from her? Would it not have been better to write to her and tell her what was happening? The man was such a coward. "Will you show it to me?"

Arthur handed over the blue-boarded bound journal. "Of course. But I will warn you that something is amiss."

Ophelia snatched the proffered journal, smoothing her hand over the gold embossed seal. She opened it, reveling in the frontispiece, with the insignia of the RGS, stamped with *Ob Terras Reclusas*. "For the discovery of lands," Ophelia whispered, translating the Latin text. She turned the page, and while of course the first article was the opening address, as it always was, the next title below it was hers!

"I got top spot! Mine is first!" she squealed, paging to it, longing to see her words in print. But then she realized it wasn't accredited to Anonymous. It was credited to Sir Julian Dunstan.

Ophelia sank down in her mother's plush chair.

"What's wrong?" her mother demanded, looking from Ophelia to Arthur.

Arthur gently removed the volume from Ophelia's grasp. He tsked. "It looks as if this has been credited to Sir Julian Dunstan."

"He took it," Ophelia said. "I didn't think he would do that. But he did."

Ophelia was hardly the first to pen an academic article and have a man take credit for it. In the small world of academic and unusual women in London, this was a common worry. Some preemptively made arrangements with brothers or friends to take the credit while giving the proceeds to the women behind the work. Others took on male pseudonyms if their families were not well known. And others, like Ophelia, naively believed that the protection of the name Anonymous would be enough.

If she couldn't be the first woman to climb the Matterhorn—indeed, if she could summit this coming summer, she would be the third—she hoped to have an article in the most prestigious journal in the world. And now, Julian had taken it from her. At least on a mountain, it was weather that turned a party around. It was outside forces that thwarted the attempts. But here, it was a man. A man she had trusted.

And a man who had let her down for a second time. That pit yawned inside of her again. Had his month-long silence been his sign that he would not be going with her to Switzerland? That in addition to leaving her in the lurch with his assurances of RGS funding for the expedition, he was also stealing her work? How could he do this? How had things spun out of control so quickly?

"Please excuse me," Ophelia said, standing.

"Do you want—?" Arthur spun around to hand Ophelia the blue Royal Geographical Society journal.

"I want nothing," Ophelia said, leaving the room.

She heard them whispering behind her, but she did not care. Nothing mattered anymore.

⟫⟫⟩✕⟨⟪⟪

"YOU MUST RETRACT this edition," Julian argued with Mr. Murray at the press.

"I'll not retract an entire print run. How did you not catch this when you spoke with Bates?"

"I did, and I insisted that the article be attributed to Anonymous," Julian insisted. He ran his hand through his hair. He couldn't imagine what kind of pain this would cause Ophelia. It made him ill thinking she might believe he did this on purpose. He would never take another's work. Never. Hers especially. He knew how much this meant to her.

"I asked Bates if all was in order, and he assured me it was. If there is anything to be done, take it up with him. Good day, sir." Murray dismissed him.

Julian shrugged on his overcoat and slammed on his hat.

Damn him. He'd walk over to the RGS and hope that Bates was there. As the assistant secretary, he did all of the actual work. The secretary, as the other main positions in the Society, was maintained by only those who were of aristocratic birth and therefore had no actual tasks to complete. The assistants were men of lower birth who did the work that made the Society run.

So fine. Out in the January slog of London he went. At least he'd warned Rascomb, that was something. If the man could keep his inquisitive sister at bay, that would be a small boon. The pain Julian felt was almost visceral. More than anything, he wanted to go to her, hold her and tell her he'd tried. That he was doing his best to rectify the situation, and that he would make it right.

Make it right, make it better. If only he could. He had been a cad of the absolute first order. If he hadn't, she would be entering marital negotiations with him, and not that milquetoast Fairport. At least, that's what the gossips had said when he went in for a round of cards at White's—at a member's invitation, of course. He didn't have the money to belong to a gentleman's club of any stripe. But who was he to say no to free drinks and companionship to occupy his mind?

He'd even grown so desperate as to think Delphine might help him. He didn't want to rekindle their relationship, but he'd thought that she might give him a perspective on what he could have done differently with Ophelia. It hadn't taken him long to realize that was an utterly foolish idea. Delphine couldn't stand competition—she'd said so herself.

The one good thing was that his mind was so obsessed with thoughts of Ophelia that walking in the cold winter of London, he didn't even register the icy wind. When he finally arrived at RGS, he was able to catch Bates.

"We can't retract!" Bates said, after Julian explained the predicament and his solution. "And we can't publish Anonymous. It's not what the Royal Geographical Society does. After all, how can we verify that the account written is fact if we don't have a name?"

"I would be happy to vouch for its veracity," Julian said.

"But that isn't the draw, you see. We need to see the explorer, that's what compels our readers." Bates walked down the hallway, leaving Julian to chase him down.

"I understand, but the way it stands, I'm given credit for something I haven't done. I've never climbed Ben Nevis."

Bates turned and narrowed his eyes. "Do you remember where you stand, sir? There is a great deal of work being done by men whose minds are sharper and quicker than our figureheads. That is the way it is done."

"But—" Julian felt his arguments losing ground, but he couldn't give up yet. Picturing Ophelia's crestfallen expression killed him.

"It is done, sir," Bates said, his tone brooking no more protestations.

Julian sighed and sagged against the wall as Bates left him. There was nothing to do. If he told them Ophelia wrote it, the article would be pulled and he would definitely be blackmarked for knowingly submitting it. He pushed a knuckle into his eye where a headache had been lingering all day.

This was beyond the pale. There was nothing to do but call on Ophelia tomorrow and beg her forgiveness. The very idea made his bowels go watery. He didn't want to face her, but he also longed to see her. How could she evoke both emotions in him?

Because he'd known better than to touch her and yet he had done so gleefully and with abandon. And again. And again the morning after. Had she been amenable to visiting him the next night, he would have just as happily bedded her then. Not because it was a release for himself, but because it was *her*. Because of all the ways he already missed her. That cleverness and unexpected wit. Her teasing charm and easy smile. The way she made him feel that the ten years he spent in South America were not just unique but worthwhile. That she actually *envied* him such an adventure.

He had no doubt that Ophelia would enjoy small excursions like a stroll through the British Museum as he'd done with Delphine, as well as accompanying him on larger ones, like climbing mountains. She was a Londoner, yes, but she was also a person who looked beyond the British Empire. A global citizen as much as a British one. And she didn't seem to possess that air of English superiority that so many of the explorers at the RGS seemed to be harboring. It drove him mad.

How lovely would it be to come home to a woman that he could really talk to? One who was not just a helpmeet, but a partner? Able and funny, beautiful and curious, strong and ambitious. And there was that need inside his aching heart again. Waxing poetic didn't make him want her less. But that telegram from RGS, asking for an interview as soon as possible made it easy to swallow his cowardice.

"Oh, Dunstan, good chap," Lord Fairport said, strolling down the damp hallway. "I am well to bursting with excitement."

The man looked pleased, but no more than the type of expression a man might have than having a good apple tart placed in front of him. "Are you?" Julian inquired, not caring, but unable to snub such a blandly amiable man.

"I am. It's been months, and that Rascomb is a hard negotiator, he is." Fairport put his hands on his hips, as if he were chastising a dog. "But we've finally come to an agreement, and tonight I shall propose to Miss Bridewell formally."

Julian would have much preferred Fairport thrash him. There was an impulse that scratched through him, to tell him he'd already been with Ophelia, and therefore staked his claim. That there was no amount of negotiation that Fairport could do to erase the fact that Julian knew her body better than Fairport ever could. That the sound of Ophelia's ecstasy, her arched back, her mewling gasps as her climax coursed through her haunted his dreams nightly. But he couldn't. He never staked his claim to her heart. That awful breakfast the morning after her apology, where she sniped and taunted him. The disdain for him that made him run. "Do you think she will agree to marry you?"

Fairport blinked at him. "What do you mean?"

It was Julian's turn to blink and frown. "I mean, do you think she will accept your suit?" Because Julian wanted her to say no. Julian wanted her to run away with him to Ecuador or Chile, to the beautiful green Andes, shaped unlike any mountains in Europe. Any place where they could be themselves, and he didn't have to constantly belittle himself for not being a viscount, or not having a fortune.

"Why wouldn't she?" Fairport looked vaguely concerned.

"I don't know, but is that not why you are asking?" Julian countered. In a perverse way, he enjoyed watching Fairport squirm.

"I'm asking as a formality. I've signed contracts with her brother. It's done."

"But it is contingent on her agreement, is it not?"

"Well, yes, but why would we go to all this trouble if it were not certain?" Fairport backed up, as if he needed the support of the opposite wall to keep him upright.

"I don't know," Julian said.

"Well, I don't know either." Fairport held his hand to his head. "Why would you bring up such a difficult conundrum?"

"I did not bring up a conundrum," Julian said slowly. Was the man entirely daft? "I merely asked a question."

"A question designed to utterly undermine my efforts! It was you, after all, who pointed her out. It was under your influence that I set my mind to asking Miss Ophelia Bridewell to dance. What is your game, sir?"

Baffled, Julian raised his hands, as if it could indicate some defense. "I have no game. I was merely being polite in inquiring after your impending nuptials."

Fairport sighed, relief streaming into his wide-set features. "Oh. Oh, I see. I see it now."

"Yes," Julian said, wondering if Fairport was moments away from an entire mental breakdown. How very tedious it would be to deal with this man's temperament. Which Ophelia would have to do for the rest of her life. And apparently, he had orchestrated it all, unknowingly. As if he couldn't ruin her even more than he already had. He let his head fall back against the wall, the impact stinging.

"But thank you for bringing me back to reality, sir." Fairport collected himself and stood fully upright again and shook a finger at Julian. "You are the devil himself, but I'm glad to have you on my side."

The devil himself? Seemed a bit harsh to say, or rather, it wouldn't be if Fairport knew the true extent of it.

"I must dash. New coat for this evening's dinner. Must be on my best for my future bride."

Julian dipped his head, acknowledging Fairport's superior rank. "Then good luck to you."

"Yes, thanks. I shan't need it." Fairport disappeared around a corner.

No. A wealthy earl didn't need luck. He'd already been born with it, wedged between every tooth.

There was no way to atone for how awful he had made Ophelia's life. He should have never appeared at their house, so long ago. He should have never visited so regularly, or engaged in such welcome and stimulating conversation with her. And of course, he never should have opened his hotel room door that night. That wonderful night where he'd felt complete and whole for the first time. A night that he turned to in even the smallest of moments, not only for the eroticism, but for that feeling of acceptance. The peace she had given him when they had finally found their rhythm together.

Tomorrow then, hat in hand, he would go make the best apology he could muster. And break his own heart as he did so, for he was calling on the future Lady Fairport.

THE DRAWING ROOM was ablaze with candlelight. Lady Rascomb had never fully trusted the gas lines that were installed in the house and preferred the more forgiving light of actual fire. Ophelia didn't mind on cold, rainy nights like this evening, as the chill still seeped past the heavy tapestry of the winter curtains.

Lady Rascomb also maintained that Ophelia's flaxen hair—which was the same shade as her mother's and her siblings—looked best in candlelight, as it brought out the warm golden glow. But tonight, in this candlelight, she was not with her siblings or her mother. She was not even with a good friend. Good Lord, she missed Justine.

Lord Fairport was monologuing. Not that Ophelia minded all that much. She found it harder and harder to speak these days. The blow from earlier today had robbed her of it entirely. Dinner was agonizing. She did not want to hear others speak either. Words were too much, the noise of the silver forks clattering on the porcelain plates, the sound of chewing from every quarter—it was more than she could bear.

Had it been any other night, she would have excused herself. But she knew that tonight she could not. There was too much at stake. Instead, Ophelia tuned it all out. She heard not a word spoken, nor did she utter a word. It was the safest way to proceed, curled and tucked inside of herself for safety.

But now her family had conveniently left her in the drawing room alone with Lord Fairport. The opportunity for him to make his formal proposal, despite everyone acknowledging that marital contract negotiations had been dragging on for three months. Partly because during the holidays, the Rascombs absconded to a familial estate for most of a month, and while Arthur offered to return to London periodically to hasten the proceedings, Ophelia adamantly said she preferred to spend her last holiday as a Bridewell amongst other Bridewells.

But now it was nearly February. And it was cold and damp outside, and that same weather had made its home inside Ophelia's heart. All of her girlish hopes and dreams were dashed on cobblestones, evaporating in such an onslaught. She imagined the incorporeal on the trafficked streets of Holborn, dashed to pieces by horse hooves and carriage wheels. Disintegrating.

". . . and while I know that's not a reason to begin courting, I found that once I started dancing with you, I rather enjoyed myself." Lord Fairport looked at her expectantly.

Oh dear, she should have been paying attention. She made a noncommittal hum and nodded for him to go on.

"Many have told me this is foolish, but I say, dash it all. I said to myself, 'I quite like Miss Ophelia Bridewell, and so if she will have me, I shall have her.'"

Ophelia blinked. Was this the proposal part? She swallowed, hoping it would help her speak. Her lips parted, but no words came.

"I see you are overcome. Am I too bold?" Lord Fairport came closer to her.

He smelled of milk. How? There was no cream on the table at dinner. But still, he smelled like a child.

Instead, Ophelia shook her head. He was not too bold. Bold was arriving at a man's hotel room in the middle of the night. Bold was confessing her attraction—and her feelings—to a man a decade her senior. Bold was crying herself to sleep after his betrayal. It was awful. Bold hurt.

"Then Miss Ophelia Bridewell, would you consent to be my wife?" Lord Fairport asked, taking one of her hands.

She meant to speak—she honestly did. But no words could be spoken. Her body wouldn't allow it. Instead she nodded her head.

"Wonderful!" Lord Fairport said, standing, looking as pleased with himself as a boy who had just built himself a fort. "We shall inform your family straightaway."

Ophelia tried to be excited. Tried to speak again, but still nothing could escape her mouth. So she sat there as Fairport called her family in, as a round of champagne was opened, and congratulations were called. Eventually, after shoulder squeezes and hand holds, Fairport nudged himself into the settee beside her. His warm milk scent wafted over. It wasn't unpleasant. But then, it wasn't pleasant, either. It just was. And that's how she would be, too, as his wife. Merely existing, without purpose, without effort. A bit of flotsam set out in a warm sea, carried by the tide this way and that, until finally disintegrating and falling to the bottom.

Chapter Eleven

"I BEG YOUR pardon?" Julian stood on the freezing stoop of the Rascomb townhouse, only to be told that he would have to endure this agony all over again.

"They will not return before calling hours have ended. If you have a message to convey, however," Ferris, the butler, intoned.

Julian waved his hand. "No, no. That's quite all right. If you tell me where they've gone to, perhaps I might catch up with them." If he could muster the courage. He wasn't sure this was something that could be duplicated. It had taken a bit of brandy to walk out the door this afternoon.

"Bond Street, sir. Miss Bridewell has begun assembling her trousseau." Ferris looked at him sharply, as if he knew every stray thought Julien had ever had regarding Ophelia, and was now astonished that he would allow another man to enter her life. Well, that made two of them.

"Many thanks, Mr. Ferris. I'll see if I can track them down."

Ferris shut the door, and Julian turned back to the street. What was a man like him to do when his lover was shopping for her wedding trousseau for another man? No, that wasn't quite it, was it? Because if they were still lovers, he'd have talked to her at least once in the past two months.

Could Julian bear to track them down? That was the rub. He pointed himself in the direction of Bond Street and hoped he would come to a decision before he met up with them. He

146

perversely wished for a long engagement.

There was no part of him that believed Ophelia cared for the man. She was careful with her emotions and didn't trust easily, it seemed. Or at least not with men, anyway. A gust of wet wind swirled down the street as he crossed, causing Julian to hunch his shoulders even more.

No, this was the height of foolishness. In the meantime, he needed to worry about his own life, and his own plans. There had to be a grant of some kind lurking in this city for a surveyor like him. Some way to take him out of London, away from Europe.

Instead of Bond Street, he went to RGS, and on a blustery day like this, he walked in looking as trod upon as he felt. As he was drying in front of the fire, another man walked in, soaking wet.

"Quite the deluge out there," the other man said.

Julian made a noncommittal noise back, for politeness' sake.

"I don't mean to be too forward, but are you Sir Julian Dunstan? I read your recent article about climbing Ben Nevis. Brilliant work, there. You made it seem like I was on the mountain with you."

Julian gave a terse smile as the knife of guilt twisted into him further. "I am Sir Julian Dunstan, yes. But I'm afraid there was a mistake in the article, it wasn't mine. I was submitting for a friend."

"Oh? A bit of intrigue, how fascinating. Who was the explorer I should be complimenting then?" The man had an open and easy smile.

"They wished to stay anonymous."

"How disappointing. But I suppose if I could write like that, I'd be writing all kinds of salacious things for money."

Julian made his polite noncommittal noise again. They stood there in silence, drying. What was he thinking, charging off to find Ophelia and apologizing in public? That would ruin her reputation and provide gossips with enough ammunition to absolutely murder her in the papers.

The man had said it himself—salacious things make money.

And if he hunted Ophelia down like a spurned suitor, Lady Rascomb would never forgive him. Nor would he forgive himself.

※»»«««

THE SEAMSTRESS TOOK Ophelia's measurements while Lady Rascomb chose fabrics, and Portia second-guessed with a critical eye. Eleanor sat nearby on a plump round stool paging through a magazine of current styles. There was nothing about this that seemed fun to Ophelia, but the women in her life rallied to her in a way that seemed excessive, given the circumstances.

But her mother, sister, and sister-in-law were the women that would sustain her through the doldrums of her marriage. Life seemed so small all of a sudden. This would be what she was reduced to?

Prudence and Leo had already left Europe again, and Justine had returned to Augsburg after Paris. Justine had insisted that the winter celebrations were superior in Munich to London, and while she trusted Justine, Ophelia couldn't imagine missing out on the weeks they spent at the Berringbone property. Which of course, would change, for as a wife, she would be expected to stay with her husband and his family during a holiday season.

It seemed interminable. Like all of this drudgery.

Arthur had said he'd fought hard to keep her plans for the Matterhorn intact for this summer. Fairport had fought any future promises, but contractually, he had to allow her time to be at the Matterhorn this summer and he had no say in who might accompany her.

This meant Julian, of course. That despite a marriage to Fairport, she could still climb the Matterhorn with Julian, but only if it happened this summer, and not the next.

The contract, the clothing, the constant chatter regarding Fairport, it all suffocated her. The only fresh breath of air she could gulp was when she thought of the Alps. Those days two summers ago when they climbed so many peaks surrounding Zermatt. The way the cold and sludgy spring melted into the buttery fresh summer. It was the best Ophelia had ever felt. The freest, most expansive feeling.

And now she'd found its opposite: the small world of London and its decaying *ton*. But it was this cloying suffocation that she was supposed to want. The oppressive wet grayness that was her greatest achievement. It made her, frankly, want to wink out of existence. To take a step sideways into a shadow and go to sleep for a hundred years. Let her family continue on without her, oblivious to how she made herself smaller and smaller, until they didn't notice that she had disappeared.

The seamstress stopped taking measurements and scurried off. Eleanor shut the magazine and came over, taking hold of Ophelia's hand.

"How are you faring?" Eleanor asked, straining her neck to look up at Ophelia from where she stood on the center platform.

"As well as could be expected," Ophelia said, not wanting to lie.

"You don't seem . . ." Eleanor trailed off, examining Ophelia further. "You seem very unhappy."

"I am." Ophelia didn't feel there was any way around saying so.

"Ophelia, if you do not want to marry Lord Fairport, do not. There is no pressure."

Ophelia stared down at Eleanor and had the urge to laugh. But she didn't, as she knew Eleanor would not understand. Instead, Ophelia pointedly looked at her mother and sister holding court amongst bolts of fabric. "Is there not?"

Eleanor glanced over at them and set her mouth in a line. "If your family requires you to marry him, you may come live with us. There is no reason to sacrifice yourself for some ridiculous idea of family honor."

An angry chuckle moved as a wave in Ophelia's body. Was

there not? She was a Bridewell. She was the daughter of a viscountess. For nearly a thousand years, blood was spilled to elevate one family over another, and hers had survived. They survived by alliances, by blood pacts in the form of shared children. Her job, her very existence, was to be in service of this centuries-old tradition. And there wasn't pressure?

Ophelia opened her mouth to educate Eleanor on all the ways her family's title made their traditions different than those of a ship captain's family, but was rescued by Portia.

"I'm famished. Let's take a small break from this, shall we? A little tea and cake helps everything." Portia seemed to be getting thicker around the middle, and it could be tea and cake, or it could be another child on the way. Not that Ophelia minded any excuse for a respite from this tedium. A seamstress came back in and helped Ophelia back into her dress and adjusted her garments and clucked about her hair.

But Eleanor's offer stuck in Ophelia's mind. Arthur would be most unhappy if she did not carry through with this marriage to Fairport—after all, he had spent the time negotiating a contract. And he would be responsible for caring for Ophelia if she did not marry at all. She would be a burden on him. A burden to Lady Emily and their child when it came.

They bustled down the street to duck into the closest café. The weather was volatile, and not for being out in. But her mother had been insistent they do this today. Granted, the weather had not been this bad earlier.

As they were settled in at a table, and tea was brought, Ophelia saw a sliver of hope in the distance. She could not abandon her family and not marry. But she had remained unattached this far. Could she not ask to wait until after her Matterhorn ascent to marry? Yes, that was preferable. There would not have to be such a scuffle about merely a postponement.

Instead of spending her preparatory season buying a trousseau and setting up house, she could focus on the Matterhorn and outfitting herself and her company. She had Eleanor and Tristan,

Justine and Karl. Prudence had said she would go, but Ophelia wasn't certain Prudence would be back from her world travels in time. She would write to her and see.

She didn't know if Sir Julian was still amongst their party. He had not specifically said he would not go, which is what Ophelia waited to hear from him. Otherwise, could it all be just a misunderstanding?

She would plan for eight members, just in case. And that space in her accounting ledger where the money from the RGS was supposed to be . . . she wouldn't count it, just to be safe.

It made her feel better, just the thought of planning. Because if she could do the Matterhorn, nothing else in her life would matter. And if she stepped sideways into those shadows afterwards, no one would notice.

STEPPING INTO THE study made her stomach flip. This room had been her father's domain, and she hadn't wanted to see how it had changed now that Arthur had taken over. While they weren't a family that kept up with the royal set, there were still land and estates to be watched over and dealt with. A land steward met with Arthur a few times a year, and then there was a passel of officious men who paraded through as well. Money men and accountants and managers. Ophelia had always ignored them. It had come as a shock to find out that Prudence was marrying Mr. Leo Moon, after all, since he'd been one of those men that had paraded for so many years. It was odd to think of those men as having lives outside of their time sitting in her father's study.

It was late now, but the lamps were still blazing, so Ophelia didn't feel as if she were encroaching on any special time of Arthur's. They'd finished dinner hours ago, and their mother and Lady Emily had retired, too. Ophelia knocked at the door, even though it sat well ajar.

As she spied him, his head bent scribbling at the wide mahogany desk, it seemed so much like a scene from her childhood that her throat caught. How many times had she burst into this room demanding her father's attention? And how willingly he had given it. She would sit on his foot while his legs were crossed and he would bounce her while he balanced a ledger. Or she would chatter at him endlessly about whatever her latest hobby was while she sat on his desk and he sat back in his chair, his hands folded over his middle, listening.

And here was Arthur. Stepping into those same shoes. The idea was dizzying, the repetitive nature of it all, how the circle had turned and while her father was gone, Arthur was here, training himself to be the father to a new child that was blossoming in Lady Emily's womb. But where was she? Stuck in time. Frozen. Unable to be a part of the circle, because she didn't have the faintest idea where she would be happy if she were not the child.

"Come in," Arthur said without lifting his head. "I hear you lurking, Ophelia."

"How did you know it was me?" she asked, finally crossing over the threshold.

"I can hear that flicking thing you do with your nails."

She looked down at her hand, unaware that she had even been doing it. "I wanted to speak with you."

Finally he looked up, and the illusion that he was her father dissipated like fog blown off the Thames by a breeze. His wide-set eyes and pointed chin were an echo of a different relative, one that they did not know. His resemblance to their father was not as pronounced as Tristan's. Arthur motioned to the chair opposite. "Unless you'd rather sit more comfortably by the fire?"

Ophelia scooted across the room and sat in the chair he gestured towards. "This is fine."

There were dark circles under his eyes, and he looked tired, but he still gave her a kind smile. "What would you like to talk about?"

"The er—" Ophelia hoped he wouldn't be mad at her. "The marriage contract."

Arthur's eyebrows lifted as he clicked his tongue. "Would you like to see it?"

Ophelia folded her hands. "I was wondering if we could postpone it."

Arthur frowned. "The contract is signed. There is no postponing it."

"The wedding, I mean. The actual marriage part." Her fingers itched to start their clicking sequence, but she held them fast.

"Why? What has happened?"

"I wish to climb the Matterhorn unencumbered." That was the truth, but she knew that it might not sound real to anyone else. What would it matter if she had a husband at the bottom or not?

"If you're worried he would stop you, don't be. It's there, in the contract, that you will climb it and he has no power to keep you from it."

"I understand that those are the words on a piece of paper," Ophelia met his eye. She hoped he could understand how very different life was for people in a world where a contract might be broken. "But what does he forfeit if he does prevent me from going?"

"Oh, er, I'd have to check—" Arthur rummaged in the desk drawers.

"But it's more than that, Arthur. The wedding will happen, and then there will be a house to set up, and a staff to meet, and rounds, and what if I fall pregnant?"

Arthur blushed past his hairline at the mention of his own wife's condition. "Ophelia!"

"You needn't be so prudish," she admonished. "Honestly. Your wife is with child."

"Yes, but you are a *maiden*."

"An old maiden." Ophelia sagged. Her nerves fell away, replaced only with the deep and weighty sadness. "I have one thing in my life that I'd like to do, Arthur. One. I don't care about the rest of it. Let me climb the Matterhorn. Please."

Arthur contemplated her for a moment. "Is this because you do not like Lord Fairport?"

She sighed. "I don't *dislike* him."

"But do you like him enough to marry?" Arthur suddenly leaned forward. "Father was very clear with me, that no matter what, I was to allow you your choice of husband, and I intend to honor that. But if you don't tell me what you want, then I cannot know."

Her eyes welled up. "Oh, Arthur." They were the two that were least alike. She knew that he thought her strange and contrary. But what she wanted? She wanted something that never could be hers. To be the first woman up the Matterhorn. To wake up in the arms of a loving and honest Julian. To spend her years planning climbs and adventures with like-minded women— and men!—without the speculation and comments from a judgmental and curious society.

But those were as false as a golden slipper left on a staircase at midnight.

"Please. I'll marry him the second I return to London."

"He'll accuse me of trying to wriggle out of a contract," Arthur said. When she didn't say anything, he added, "But if you don't wish to marry him for any reason, anything at all, let's tear it up. You don't like how he holds a cricket bat."

A laugh burst out of her unexpectedly. "I haven't the faintest how he holds one."

"Perhaps he chews his food *too* thoroughly."

"Or he treats his mother *too* kindly." Ophelia relaxed, realizing that her brother was on her side. She had been so scared that he would make her go through with it before the summer. They could put off the trousseau, the clothes, all of it. What a relief.

"He is an absolute pushover for stray animals." Arthur mirrored her relieved posture. "It's going to be all right, Ophelia. And I know you think otherwise, but Emily and I have spoken, and we are fine if you and Mama stay here for years to come. Neither of you are a burden."

Ophelia nodded. It had been that word that chased her, *burden*. "Thank you, Arthur. You're a good brother. But I do try to keep my word, you know. I'll marry upon my return." She stood and crossed the study, noticing that it was the same and yet absolutely different in the room.

"Ophelia?" Arthur called.

She turned, expecting him to give her details on when he might call upon Lord Fairport.

"I'm proud of you, you know. I'm astonished at what you have already accomplished, and I support you as fully as I am able."

A breathy and tearful laugh came out this time. "You are going to make an excellent father, Arthur. As I would expect. You had the best teacher."

"The very best," Arthur agreed. "Good night."

Ophelia nodded again, blinking back the sudden tears in her eyes. At least she would no longer have to bear the expectation of Lord Fairport as she prepared herself for the Alps. That was a problem for September and no sooner.

ANYTHING TO KEEP thoughts of Ophelia at bay. Anything to keep him occupied so he wouldn't crash into her house, find her, and ruin her life because he could. More details had arrived about the South American venture from RGS, after all applicants were interviewed.

More assaying of mountains, though no desire for his experience with making topographical measurements. There would be some venture into the interior, but not much, thank goodness. That green hell was home to bugs that laid eggs under the skin. Julian had seen these hatch out of a man's elbow once, and that was enough to put him off the Amazon indefinitely.

RGS invited him to write an application essay, which occupied his days. Once he'd managed a decent draft, he went to the Society's building to write out the final copy. He didn't want any sort of chance that it could wind up wrinkled or smudged. After he had finished it and set it aside to dry, he turned to the provisions list. Any potential investor needed a reasonable estimate of what upfront costs were required to achieve this goal. In fact, his experience in this regard made him an excellent candidate.

Deep in concentration, he didn't hear the steps behind him.

"Did you do this?" Fairport barked at Julian.

Julian's head swiveled towards the doorway of the library. Fairport looked positively individualistic as he stood his ground. He seemed somehow taller than before, and if he were any other man, Julian might conclude he was perturbed by something. On Fairport, he seemed merely expressive.

"Do what?" Julian asked, sliding the papers covered in damp ink farther into the middle of the table to protect them.

"Miss Bridewell has postponed our wedding ceremony, and I ask you, is it at your bidding, sir?"

Julian stood, blocking line of sight to his papers, so no other intrepid adventurer might see his work and steal it for his own. He wanted this assignment. He *needed* this next assignment, for his sanity and his livelihood. Besides, there were only so many South American explorers who hadn't any interest in rubber or the Amazon.

"I have no knowledge of Miss Bridewell's motivations, nor have I spoken to her." Much to his shame. He had not been able to bring himself to her doorstep since that fateful day. Instead of finding her on Bond Street and begging her forgiveness for turning in an article that was attributed to him, he hid inside RGS.

If all went well, he would leave London for another decade, have another life in South American. He would return to England to meet the young progeny of his friends once again. Except this time, he would be a proper old man. Englishmen had a tendency to age exponentially in South America, and while Julian escaped that the first go-round, he likely wouldn't escape the second.

"All those months of negotiating," Fairport moaned, trudging into the room, as if Julian's innocence prompted a new conversation. "I thought it seemed odd, that she wanted to go with you. I understand you were her father's friend, and thus, Paris was you watching after her and all that—"

Julian's face almost flamed, but he kept a hold on himself. Paris had not been fatherly. His intent on meeting Ophelia there had nothing to do with keeping her safe, but rather with basking in her glow. In being unable to control the pull he felt towards her.

"So naturally I agreed to the terms of you accompanying her to Switzerland when I finally understood the dynamic." Fairport dropped into the chair next to Julian's, which obliged Julian to sit down as well.

Julian opened his mouth to protest that he wasn't going to Switzerland with Ophelia. They hadn't spoken in months now. There couldn't be any doubt in her mind that he would not go with her. Could there? But she was quite stubborn. She might see it as his word of honor, and not understand that while men would do insane things to uphold their honor, breaking their heart willingly was often a bridge too far.

"But now she is insisting on putting off the wedding until she returns from that venture." Fairport put his head in his hands. "It makes me think you aren't a father figure. Are you or are you not?"

Julian opened his mouth and closed it again, unsure of how to proceed. No matter what he said, he would end up looking like an utter arsehole. Instead, he reached behind him and grabbed the hopefully dry papers. "I intend to be on my way to Argentina this summer, friend. I won't be going to Switzerland."

Fairport's shoulders slumped in relief and he pushed the paperwork back in front of Julian, not bothering to look. "Oh, thank the Lord."

Julian stared at the papers he'd written. The dates expected, the money he asked for to upkeep himself while away. The numbers jumped out at him. His boat left two weeks before prime climbing season. She would be there in the grassy Alps, her blond hair pinned back in braids, and he would be on a boat, buffeted by the smells of other passengers below deck and then the open sea above.

He didn't like the emotion those images brought to the fore of his mind. But it couldn't be helped. His chest was hollowed out; the excision of Ophelia from his heart had taken the rest of him with it. "I had no idea you were so attached to her."

"Attached? I suppose I am," Fairport said, musing. "She is a rather odd bird, but intelligent, and very pretty."

Very pretty like the Matterhorn was *awfully tall.* "If you aren't in love with her, then why are you so anxious to secure this marriage?"

Fairport waved his hand. "Oh, you know how it is. Debts. Need a dowry and all that."

Julian felt as if he had been punched in the stomach. Hadn't part of Fairport's allure been that he didn't have any debts? Was that assumed because he was so excruciatingly boring that no one wanted to know his personal business? "Debts?"

"Mum has been on me to marry anyhow. Heirs and all that bit. Which is fine, I have no trouble there. Got one by accident some years back, but managed to keep that on the sly. Dear Mama has no idea about him."

Julian was about to choke. Ophelia was going to marry this wobbling piece of blanc mange? Who had already fathered a bastard? He didn't think Fairport had it in him, but apparently he was wrong. Did Ophelia know this? Did her brothers? Surely they wouldn't put her in such a position, or sell her to a man who needed her money?

"And if I marry some untitled heiress, then everyone will know I have money troubles. But I needed to know how hard to fight for this. If it's just her brother indulging her girlish fancies, then I've naught to worry. Say, I've a rather good tip on a horse. Whatever you've got, we can add to mine, and you can have a cut of the winnings."

But then, who was he to say? He listened to Fairport prattle on about horses and lineages, and which place was more secure to lay bets at. Was this what Ophelia would spend the rest of her evenings listening to? She was so much smarter than Fairport, so much more interesting. To pair such a flower with this drab shrubbery seemed inhumane.

Did her family know about the mistress and his bastard already? Did Ophelia? No, this was not his business. Not his at all. But surely, he should go visit her and feel it out, shouldn't he? A woman should not enter into such a situation without knowing she already had competition. Delphine had taught him that.

Chapter Twelve

OPHELIA DID NOT think about Fairport. His existence was of little use to her, especially now that she would not have to marry him for months yet. Instead, she threw herself into planning her second assault on the Matterhorn.

She had not heard from Julian, whose absence perplexed Lady Rascomb. In response to her mother's probing, Ophelia said, "He's probably met a woman."

It was something Ophelia had imagined with a punishing regularity. That being in the arms of a novice in Paris had made Julian yearn for the practiced attentions of Lady DeMarius. No doubt he'd been availing himself of her since his return. He hadn't even the time to clear up the debacle of her article being printed under his name. That slight would just go on unacknowledged. But Ophelia knew. The knife was still thrust in her, still bleeding.

Despite the pain, she still included him in all her mountaineering plans. He had never said he wasn't going. And he was the reason she was attempting the deadly mountain a second time. Technically, this was true. His interest is what gave her the excuse. She would go whether he went or not. At least, if they'd the money.

Yesterday she'd gotten a letter from Prudence, offering apologies and well-wishes, and explaining that she and Mr. Moon would not be able to reach Europe in time for climbing season.

Their boat was still well past India, and even if they were to get on a boat that very day, they still wouldn't be able to make the expedition.

It was disappointing to have one of the original members of The Ladies' Alpine Society unable to go, but Prudence offered a donation to the expenses of the trip. That helped make it sting less.

After all, the largest issue at this point was funding. Technically, her dowry wasn't hers, it was the estate's, so she couldn't use it without Arthur's permission, but he seemed possibly amenable. Currently, it was tied to the marriage contract with Fairport, but she wasn't sure if it was a monetary amount, or an account number listed, or lands. She had written out a request to use the dowry as her funding, but had not yet heard back from Arthur on the subject. She didn't dare ask for anything like this verbally, knowing there needed to be some kind of paper trail associated with it.

Ultimately, if the contract was not settled because she'd insisted on a delay, then it would mean the money was still available. Which could explain the subsequent amount of fretting from Fairport. He was like a child, whining about whether or not she loved him. She knew it was pretense, for she had no illusion that he loved her. But it could be that he loved the promise of her dowry. And she had better uses for it.

Eleanor arrived for an early morning call, which was fine, as Ophelia had not yet finished her letter writing for the morning. Once she started examining topography versus the numerous accounts of other successful ascents of the Matterhorn, she would not relish an interruption.

"I have to be home by eleven," Eleanor explained.

"I see," Ophelia said, but her eye was caught by a strange mark on her map of the Matterhorn. It stayed laid out all day now. There was no sense in tidying it away. And was that a new pathway? Could that bypass the columns that had injured her father? Oh, no. It was, in fact, a crumb.

"But I had to tell you, because I owe it to you. I'm afraid you'll be quite cross with me." Eleanor hadn't touched her tea. Ophelia looked at the tea, looked at Eleanor. She did look different. Almost, puffy somehow.

Ah. "You're pregnant," Ophelia said. The news struck her with a surprising disappointment. Another member off the team.

Eleanor gasped. "Who told you? I swear I only figured it out myself."

"No one, but it's the only thing that makes sense." Ophelia wanted to be excited for them, but she was selfish. So very selfish. It meant that Tristan and Eleanor would not be climbing with her this summer. It meant Eleanor was embarking on a life that Ophelia could not—would not?—follow.

"The timing is not ideal," Eleanor admitted.

Ophelia softened, reminding herself that Tristan and Eleanor had both been wanting a family. It wasn't right that she was making Eleanor feel bad because she'd gotten what she wanted. "The timing is fine." Ophelia leaned across the small table to put her hand on Eleanor's wrist.

"Tristan is over the moon about the baby, but he feels terrible about the trip."

"Don't worry. I have Justine and Karl to go with me. And Tristan can feel free to gift me the very best and latest equipment as recompense."

"I'm so glad you aren't angry with me." Eleanor stood.

Ophelia stood, shook her head, and stepped to embrace Eleanor. They'd been through so much together. "I couldn't be angry. I'll be an auntie."

Eleanor squeezed her back with a sudden ferocity. "But you get up there, Ophelia. Just because I can't be there doesn't mean I don't think you should go. I know there will be some who say you shouldn't go just because Tristan won't be there. But you go, Ophelia. Conquer that mountain. Do it for me."

Taken aback by Eleanor's outburst, Ophelia nodded in agreement. "I'll get there," she promised.

"Now, I have to get home, because I swell very badly if I'm out for too long."

Ophelia laughed and pushed her along. "Then go, go! I don't want Tristan to come yelling at me for making his wife puffy."

"He's a terror," Eleanor said with a wide grin. As if amiable Tristan could ever be one.

After her friend left, it was harder to return to her correspondence. She had news of Eleanor, which she would not share until Eleanor gave her permission. And it made her think again of her expedition. If Prudence, Tristan and Eleanor were out, who else was in the party? Justine, Karl, herself, and Julian.

But four was a good number. Enough to take care of problems that might arise, but not so many that the problem could scupper the entire expedition.

After Eleanor's departure, the afternoon passed slowly. Even Lady Emily lumbered down, now finally in what had to be her last weeks of pregnancy. Ophelia had thought it would have happened already, but apparently, the babe was comfortable where it was.

"Tea. Please." Lady Emily said, collapsing into a chair.

"I thought you were counselled—"

"Give me tea. The strong stuff. So dark it looks like tar." Lady Emily was normally genteel, even under these circumstances, but today she looked like a woman pushed too far.

"Of course," Ophelia said, pouring her a fresh cup and handing it to her because setting it on the table would render the cup inaccessible to Lady Emily. Her belly was nearly a third of her.

Lady Emily drank it down, no sweetener, no cream. She held out her cup. "Another."

Ophelia poured again, careful not to drip on the rug. Lady Emily drank it down again. "Again."

Ophelia stood by and poured yet again, until Lady Emily signaled she was ready to slow down. When she did, the teacup rested on top of her belly.

"Do you think it will be soon?" Ophelia asked, unsure of what to say in such a situation.

"I hope so," Lady Emily said, wincing as she pulled herself up. "I cannot take much more of this. I feel like an over-filled hot air balloon."

"Sounds dangerous." Ophelia watched her carefully, noting the puffiness that Eleanor sought to avoid settling in around all of Lady Emily's features.

"Arthur convinced me not to drink black tea, and now it is all I crave. Someone gave him a fool notion that it would hurt the baby, but if that makes this baby kick its way out, then I'll take all I can stomach!"

"Of course," Ophelia said, thinking they needed to more tea at this rate.

"Oh," Lady Emily said, opening her eyes wide.

"What is it?" Ophelia watched as Lady Emily held her belly and winced.

"It worked. Oh God, Ophelia, it worked. Give me more of that tea." Lady Emily rattled her teacup.

Ophelia sprang to her feet with the teapot and poured. "Is this a good idea? I'm not sure it's the best thing—"

"Pour the goddamn tea, Ophelia." Lady Emily's voice was low and feral.

Ophelia obliged, pouring down to the dregs. "I will call for some more." When Ferris arrived to wait on them, Lady Emily was visibly distressed. Ferris became visibly distressed at Lady Emily's visible distress, and Ophelia was in favor of not being in charge.

She sent Ferris down for more tea, called for her mother, dashed a note off to Arthur, and found some pillows to make Lady Emily more comfortable. The comfort didn't last long, and soon Lady Emily was up and pacing.

"The pacing is helping, but my goodness—" She bent over in pain.

Ophelia went to her, and Lady Emily squeezed her hand so hard that Ophelia wasn't sure there was an ounce of blood left in it. "So you need to get your mind off of it?"

Lady Emily stood back up, breathing hard. "I need to talk."

Ophelia nodded, and Lady Emily began speaking and didn't stop for a very long time. She covered every topic from dinner menus to her childhood friends.

It was more than Ophelia had heard Lady Emily speak in all the time she'd known her. By the time Arthur arrived home, many hours later, Lady Emily was ensconced in her room, in the thick of childbirth with a midwife in attendance and a physician on his way.

And it was some hours after that when the baby finished making its way into the world. Ophelia stood by Lady Emily every step of the way, breathing and sweating and fetching more bedding and swapping out food trays, and always tea, Lady Emily swore by the tea. Lady Rascomb stayed out with Arthur, and so Ophelia also gave swift updates, as she was the go-between for servants as well.

Somewhere in the clamor, in the intensity, Lady Emily had gripped her hand and said, "You are better than anyone I've ever met at—" and then the pain ripped through her, and Ophelia was left to wonder what she was better at.

But Ophelia didn't question it. She took care of everyone's needs, helped with the physician and the midwife, as both were called in, and neither of them wanted to share the patient. At one point, she was told she had a visitor, but Ophelia was too tired to accept the note or see anyone.

By the end of the process, she was elated and tired. Watching Lady Emily hold her baby was magical to see, and then witnessing Arthur do the same was heartbreaking. It was one thing to see Lady Emily or Portia hold her baby, and Ophelia had seen plenty of young mothers holding their children, but it wasn't the same kind of revelation to her as it was to watch her brother's face shift from shock to joy, as he fell in love with a tiny person in a fraction of a second. And soon, Tristan would also have the experience.

Ophelia smiled. And it was all thanks to a strong cup of tea.

IF JULIAN HAD not seen the birth announcement a day later, he might have thought he was being put off. Ophelia had not been available for his visit, and while a footman only said she was unavailable due to a family matter, the wide-eyed shuffling of him made it clear that something unusual was happening.

And now there was a baby girl to celebrate. Lady Agatha. Julian smiled. He liked babies. And mostly, he liked making faces at them and watching them gurgle applause. Their guileless trust in him was pure. Sometimes it was humbling, when he took in the wider ramifications of life: him being an Englishman, and many of the babies he held being several shades darker than he. His countrymen were tearing up the South American continent, and he didn't know how to stop it. So he climbed his mountains and held babies and gave medicines and gems he'd come across during his surveys. He did what he could do on the small scale.

Perhaps he could try again to visit Ophelia in a few days' time. Tell her what he knew about Fairport's money needs, and be firm about not going to Switzerland with her. He'd gotten a note back from the grant team. They liked his proposal and it was down to him and one other explorer.

In fact, they'd invited both of them to a dinner, which would help determine the fate of the expedition. Julian certainly didn't like the idea of breaking bread with his competitor, but it was likely one of those "gentlemanly" things that were expected of men in London, and so he would do it.

He wrote a letter in return, carefully accepting the dinner invitation and inquiring as to the date and time. And now he was obliged to wait. Wait for spring, wait for Ophelia, wait for his future. Which was dreadfully uncomfortable to him, and typically he walked when he was uncomfortable. So he donned his hat and muffler and went out. There was no mountain to climb, but there were steps, and that was a start.

OPHELIA SLEPT. SHE bathed late at night, after the baby was born. And then, given the luxurious nature of being a single woman with no responsibilities or debts, she kept on sleeping. There were a few moments where she awoke, a maid creeping in and out, but she turned over and closed her eyes and oblivion was once again there to meet her.

At one point, there was a tray at her bedside, but she ignored that, too. When she woke next, it was gone. Finally, it became too difficult to fall into that wonderfully safe velvet dreamscape, and she was awake. But it had been so cozy to be in her big bed, the world bustling about and giving her no reason to move about in it.

She rose from her bed and peeked out a curtain to find the world was still dark. The house sounded silent, so it must have been the early morning. Ophelia pulled on her dressing gown and padded downstairs. Rarely was this house entirely silent. The servants, her mother, Arthur, Lady Emily, someone was always about. Looking at the grandfather clock in the hall, she realized the maids would be up soon to light fires and begin breakfasts.

If she had been a child, all the immense dark quiet might have scared her. But now, it had a calming and soothing effect, especially after the birth of baby Agatha. Lady Emily had joked that her middle name ought to be "Ceylon" after the tea she drank to induce labor. Ophelia didn't think it was actually the tea. It was probably just time. She'd never been much for superstitions and seeing coincidences as causality. But she understood the impulse.

Sailing through these dark, exquisite rooms gave Ophelia a new appreciation for her life. The casual opulence that decorated every thought and opinion, regardless of if she wanted it to or not. And how that would change whenever she moved to a new household. At Lord Fairport's, she would live with the dowager countess Fairport, who would not appreciate any of Ophelia's desires to rearrange the house. Not that Ophelia had many opinions in the way of interior decorating.

She ran a hand over the smooth, well-polished surface of the walnut entry-table. A marble top had been added when she was a child, following an accident where she and Tristan had wrestled in this very room, knocking over a few lit candlesticks. Unable to properly get the burns out of the finish, a cut of marble was added as a surface. The solution to any problem here was to throw money at it.

Being a woman, once she married, she would lose all access to her money. She would not be in a position like her mother, she didn't think. While the Fairports seemed to have plenty, Ophelia would have to spend years ingratiating herself to her mother-in-law and husband for the kind of freedom Lady Rascomb had. And ingratiation was not something Ophelia was terribly good at.

No, she'd never wanted to be the fine lady, as Portia was, as Lady Emily was inherently. Ophelia could ape the moves easily, and had been primed for it, watching her mother. But where Ophelia was most happy was on an expedition. The planning, the anticipation, even the gathering of supplies and writing of confirmation letters, she adored it. Being in the location, the mountains or the hills below the peak, checking with local guides and seeing to proper nutrition for their health, it was invigorating.

But on the day of the climb, carrying the weight of the pack on her back, sleeping on the ground the night before, pushing herself to the very limits of what she thought she could endure, that was her favorite. The cold bite of mountain air on her cheeks, the wind threading icy fingers through her hair, the sweat that accumulated under her arms or in the crooks of her knees.

It was March now, the time they'd left for Zermatt two years ago. Karl said much had changed in the past two years—more hotels had cropped up, and more tourists wandered the hills, getting into trouble.

Suddenly, Ophelia knew what she would do. Instead of moping about London, waiting for time to pass, she would visit Justine in Augsburg, and then head to Switzerland early. She had letters to write this morning, warning ahead of her visits. And also to Herr and Frau Brunner, Karl's uncle and aunt who owned the inn they'd stayed in two years prior.

Of course, that meant writing to Julian. Her stomach sank at the feeling. Julian. She both wanted him with her at all times and recoiled from how desperate he made her feel. How unworthy and unwanted. She doubted that had been his intention, but he made her feel that way all the same. Still, she squared her shoulders. He had promised to climb the Matterhorn. The expedition included him, as he'd never formally backed out.

She could be professional and bring him along on an expedition without it causing undo pain. Probably. She could at least pretend it didn't cause pain, and that was enough.

Light crept through pulled curtains, and the tiptoes of maids sounded as loud as the slamming of books during daylight hours. Ophelia returned to her room to dress quickly, and then went to the drawing room to begin her letters. The room was cold, but Ophelia didn't care much. She had a thousand things to do, and she wanted to do all of them right now.

As she pulled her writing desk onto her lap, she noticed a note, folded over, with her name on it. She opened it, her heart stopping when she realized it was from Julian. He had stopped by to call upon her and her mother, but she'd been indisposed, helping to bring baby Agatha into the world.

It made her heart lighten, to know that he was still thinking of her, just as she thought of him. She wondered if he thought of her in the same ways. The times when she sighed next to a rainy window, but also the times at night, alone in her room, the ache between her legs pulsing in want.

She could not very well go traipsing over to his flat, but she wrote a note to him, asking him to please come again. It would be easier to update him and get all the details she needed for the Matterhorn trip in person.

The letter to Justine from several days prior was not finished, so she put a fresh date mid-letter and continued on with a recounting of baby Agatha's birth and her intentions to join her in Augsburg by the end of the month. From there, she would continue on to Zermatt as soon as she heard from Herr Brunner that the inn was opened.

As she folded her letters, a new calm overcame her. This was right. She inhaled a fresh breath, new as the day, new as a just-born babe.

❧

Chapter Thirteen

JULIAN WAS EXHAUSTED from horse racing. Not that he had anything to do with the horses. Or the racing, for that matter. But following two horse-crazy lords as they traipsed about Wales was more than he could handle. Fairport would have been in heaven. After three weeks of being at the beck and call of Lords Bordsterth and Costovin, with the hopes of obtaining that coveted commission for Argentinian silver mines, Julian would be happy to not look at a horse for at least a month.

He was hungover, which had been a perpetual state until he became slightly inebriated in the early afternoons. The men were drinkers of fine spirits, owners of horses, and gamblers of the first order. Which was likely why they were investing in developing more mining operations. More gemstones were arriving from various areas of the continent, and these men were betting on more. Silver was the money to be made, and accidental gemstone lodes were the ambition.

Which he could do for them. Surveys of the mountains were not for the sake of elevations, they were to determine composition, and likelihood of ore deposits. The boisterous lords made it seem like Julian had the job, now that he'd imbibed and gambled with them, but formal letters would be forthcoming. As of now, however, he was expected to be ready to depart London in June. He had two months left in the country of his birth.

He didn't know why it felt like he was never returning, but it

171

did. As if there was nothing for him to come home to. Without Ophelia, there really wasn't. These men were merely walking coin purses, not mentors in thought and exploration as the last Lord Rascomb had been. And he had no family, no land. Nothing. A bank account, and a meager one at that. His eyelids felt heavy. He'd slept on the train, but he wouldn't feel right until the brandy that had replaced his bloodstream had cycled through him.

"I thought coffee might be best, from the look of you," Nicholas said, coming into the flat.

"Nicholas," Julian said, grateful for the man's clairvoyance. He snatched the cup up as soon as the valet placed the tray on the table. "You are saving my life."

"Looked a bit worse for wear when you came in." Nicholas stood back, his hands folded, giving Julian a look of sympathy.

The dark bitter liquid went down his throat, coursing into his system in welcome relief. It wasn't a fine roast like he drank in Ecuador, but it was coffee when he'd had nothing but brandy and whisky. "I never want to see another horse race for as long as I live."

"Did you not enjoy yourself?" Nicholas asked, taking it upon himself to open Julian's one meager trunk to unpack.

"One day, maybe two, would have been enjoyable. Three weeks of talking about horses, breeding schedules, lineages . . ." Julian trailed off, his brain still foggy. He sighed. "And drinking. Always a spirit in one hand, a cigar in the other. I won't breathe right ever again."

Nicholas tutted sympathetically. "I've put your post there on the tray. Something from Miss Ophelia Bridewell, if I may be so bold as to bring your attention to it."

Julian shot a look to the valet, to see if the man was teasing him or in some way meddling, but Nicholas went about his business, inspecting Julian's clothes for stains. Before he could read anything, he finished his coffee. His stomach roiled under the weight of non-alcoholic liquid. The pile of post seemed unusually tall.

"A good slice of mutton ought to clear that right up," Nicholas said. "Old cure that my da' swore by."

"Unless you have some in your pockets, that is not going to happen any time soon." Julian pawed through the stack, noting that it was in chronological order, with the oldest on top, for ease of sorting. The top one was from Ophelia.

He opened the missive, a short thing, really, that invited him to call on her again, since she'd missed his visit due to the arrival of baby Agatha. He had a letter from a friend in Ecuador, which he put to the side to linger and read later. And then, near the bottom, another letter from Ophelia, thicker than the last.

Curious, he unfolded the letter to find that it was two pages long. She made no mention of Paris, nor emotions of any kind. Rather, this was a letter from an expedition leader to one of the mission's members. It contained a packing list, train schedules, rendezvous points, addresses, and weather expectations. "What on earth?"

Ophelia really did believe he was meeting her in Switzerland. But it had been months since they'd spoken! How could she not know? Julian went to swing his jacket back on, but then, after re-examining the dates, realized she'd already left London. He winced. This was terrible. He felt like an utter cad. She would be so disappointed. According to her letter, her brother and sister-in-law were no longer joining, and neither were Mr. and Mrs. Moon, taking the expedition number down to only four of them: Mr. and Mrs. Vogel, Ophelia, and himself.

He preferred climbing in a smaller group than a bigger one. Less could go wrong. Fewer chances were taken. And in a dynamic of two obvious couples, it made the unspoken decisions all that much easier.

He shook his head. The weight of the past months crumbled on his head, covering him in an ash of shame. "I'm a terrible person."

She was so naïve and he'd been a coward. At nearly forty, he ought to have learned how to gracefully back out of an invitation.

The idea had been his, an impulse in a wild moment of wanting to see pleasure on a beautiful woman's face. No, not any beautiful woman. Ophelia's.

And then he'd fallen in love with her—well, metaphorically speaking. Because he couldn't actually be in love with her. She was barely more than a child, and he was a disgusting wretch for wanting her so badly. He felt old—incredibly old compared to her—and hated himself for ignoring the voice that kept him from taking her to bed.

But he'd done so. Willingly. Happily. And being with her had been better than he ever could have imagined. No virginal tears— that wasn't Ophelia. Just a complete giving over of herself. She had trusted him so completely with her body and her heart.

Yet, when she'd asked for a story of his past, he had shut that door as fast as he could. He could see now that they'd made love, and she'd wanted to become closer to him, only, Julian couldn't, because he didn't want to talk about his failures. He didn't want to show her whatever nameless part of him that wasn't good enough for Maria. The part that caused Delphine to be jealous and rude. Could she not just accept him as he was? With his smattering of gray chest hairs and salt-and-pepper beard?

But she didn't understand that because she didn't have a past. At least, not then. Now he was her past. And Lord Fairport, that limpid liar, was her future. A man who wanted her for her money, and not for her unusual, incredible self. Ophelia hadn't mentioned a wedding date in her letter, so perhaps Fairport had let her postpone the ceremony?

Julian would write to her—it looked as if she'd still be in Augsburg. He could post a letter to both Augsburg and Zermatt to catch her. Which should be enough. This wasn't something he needed to go in person to explain, was it? No. That was foolishness. No one travelled across Europe just to say he was not pursuing further contact. Height of absurdity.

While he stayed at his flat the rest of that day, berating himself for his willingness to hurt a perfectly lovely girl, the next morning he found himself drawn to Tristan Bridewell's outfitter as soon as it opened.

"Sir Julian!" Tristan announced, his eyes lighting up when they found him.

Julian bowed and greeted his friend. He was glad to see he received a warm salutation. After his abandonment of the Bridewell family for so many months, he wasn't sure how he would be received.

From a curtained-off area, a woman's head appeared. "Sir Julian?"

Julian peered around the corner of a four-staked tent that would absolutely not work in Alpine conditions, to see Mrs. Bridewell's face. She looked odd, somehow not like herself, but he couldn't place it. As he stepped further into the shop, she emerged with an expression that was not as welcoming as her husband's.

She folded her arms in front of her and stood next to Tristan. "Good to finally see you," she said, the invitation to explain himself laying in every clipped syllable.

"Yes, and you as well." Julian clasped his hands behind his back, unsure of himself under the scrutiny of Ophelia's sister-in-law. "I, er, I was wanting to, of course, offer felicitations on Lord Rascomb's new arrival." He felt warmth creep up his throat and into his cheeks.

Tristan nodded happily, but Mrs. Bridewell showed no emotion.

"And, I've been so busy this winter, interviewing a, well, ah, that's not important, is it?" Julian's throat was dry. "What I would like to say is that I only yesterday received Miss Bridewell's letters."

"Did you?" Mrs. Bridewell said, her expression clearly waiting for more explanation or apology or something. Oh drat, had he cocked this up so badly? Yes. Yes, he had.

He licked his lips, wincing as he tried to prepare his next verbal volley. "I have written to her, in duplicate of course, one letter to Augsburg, one to Zermatt, just in case the post doesn't catch her in time."

"Catch her in time for what?" Tristan frowned.

"To tell her to not expect me for the Matterhorn ascent, of course." Julian scanned their faces. Both of them looked properly shocked. That was not a good sign.

Mrs. Bridewell recovered first. A frown would be an understatement. Her face creased into an anger he had only seen in the most extreme situations. "You are abandoning her again?"

Tristan heard the spitting tones of his wife and immediately popped his hands up as if he were refereeing between them. "Now, let's hear him out. Not everyone is suited for such an endeavor."

"I'm perfectly fit," Julian asserted, his hackles rising in response to Mrs. Bridewell's volley. "But I am not obligated to go on her expedition."

The slow turn of Mrs. Bridewell's head reminded Julian of a raptor focusing on its newfound prey in the grasses. "Obligated? To go on an expedition *you* proposed? That she has spent months planning to make it easy *for you*? And when no funds that you promised from the RGS came in, she renegotiated her dowry to facilitate this, *for you*. But *you* aren't obligated?"

Thoughts and emotions tumbled through Julian's mind. Her dowry? He shook his head. "Lord Fairport is marrying her without a dowry?" That made no sense. The man had been salivating after it.

"My brother convinced him to stay the wedding until after the Matterhorn expedition." Tristan tried to bodily move his wife towards a chair that sat in the corner, but she would not be budged. She glared with her full force at Julian.

A crystal bubble formed in his heart. This tiny, iridescent precious pearl of information began to bump around in his chest. He recognized it: hope.

"Get your hands off me, Tristan. I swear to the Lord Almighty if you touch me again, I will take one of those blasted tent stakes and absolutely wreck this shop," Mrs. Bridewell spat.

Tristan snatched his hands away, but continued a soft-faced pleading. "My love, the baby, though. You are very emotional right now, and it's not something—"

The look of pure hatred that flashed on the woman's face combined with Tristan's whisperings about a baby made it instantly clear why they would not be on the expedition. And also explained why his presence was so hated. Mrs. Bridewell had clearly wanted to go; when else would an opportunity come for her?

And now here was Julian throwing that opportunity away. Her points of inconveniencing Ophelia also hit the mark. He'd spent the past months wishing he could bury his head in the sand . . . of another country entirely.

He'd put all of this squarely on Ophelia's shoulders, for wanting more of him. But this was his fault. Spending so much time alone had given him the privilege of absolute privacy at all times. As soon as someone asked for more than his surface level, he ran. Literally booked the next train home. Shit.

But there was no way to change it now. If he suddenly turned down the offer to survey silver mines, then what kind of career did he have? Was he really willing to turn down a decade worth of work to chase after a girl who was far too young for him anyway?

What a terrible time to have such an epiphany.

"Will you please just sit down? Eleanor." Tristan pleaded with his wife as all these revelations fell around Julian's head.

"Letters are the very least you could do. Even though we all know you should do more," Mrs. Bridewell shot at him as she allowed herself to be herded into the back corner's chair.

Julian fiddled with his hat, realizing he was clutching it tight enough to ruin the brim. He had obligations before Ophelia, of course. His career. His monetary solvency. These had to be priorities first. He had to think of his future. But what was his future when he was entirely alone?

"I have another appointment," Julian called to the back of the small shop, trying to leg it out of there as fast as he could. Because, when was he not? But the other appointment was true. "I still have a matter to discuss with you, Mr. Bridewell, but perhaps another time."

Tristan waved him off, still herding his angry wife.

"Yes, good to see you! I'll be off!" Julian said, escaping the store. His actual real appointment that was not at all made up was at the RGS printers. There was much groveling to be done, promises from Mr. Bates to extract, and likely a bribe to be paid to Mr. Murray.

Later, after the sun had set, he plodded home in the twilight, where Nicholas accosted him with his post.

"This one seems to be important," Nicholas said, turning as if he might peer over Julian's shoulder to read it as well.

Julian thanked him for the prompt notification and headed up to his rooms to read it in private. It was the formal, expected offer from Lords Bordsterth and Costovin for the Argentinian silver expedition. They included a ticket for the ship sailing on June 15th, and information on lodging arrangements upon arrival.

It was all set. His life could continue on, as if there had been no bump. No change. As if the man who'd returned from South America and the one that existed now were the same.

He wished for his mentor again. The only man he would have been able to speak with about such a difficulty. Who could he turn to now? None of his acquaintances here would be discreet enough, and there was no one who could be discreet enough that wouldn't immediately side with Ophelia out of principle.

But he was nearly forty. It was time for him to grow up, think for himself. He didn't need a sounding board to do what was right. For months he had dodged the responsibilities of an honorable man. He would start with what he could fix.

"THIS IS SO pretty!" Ophelia said, again, and again, and again, as Justine walked her around Augsburg's squares. There were fountains in almost every single one, and it made the burgeoning spring weather all the more pleasant. There were many people sitting on benches reading, which seemed to be an excellent way to spend an afternoon. The sunshine on one's face, a good book, the sound of a burbling fountain to add to the pastoral yet urban scene.

Justine's expression was almost dreamy. "The only thing missing in Augsburg is you."

Ophelia pulled her elbow tighter, which pressed Justine in close. "London is lost without you."

Justine snorted. "You mean bored. What do they talk about now that they can't talk about me?"

"They are bereft," Ophelia said with mock mourning.

"They are vultures. But no matter. I am having my revenge—perfectly married and perfectly respectable as a merchant's wife."

It was Ophelia's turn to snort. *Merchant* was technically true, but it didn't encompass her friend's large house with intricate architectural details that she was still noticing upon third and fourth looks. While nothing they wore or displayed was opulent, Ophelia knew well the difference between average cloth and exceptional craftsmanship. Justine's dresses were modest, as befitting her status as a married woman, but there were of the best quality. Seams so small they were invisible.

Inside her home, everything was polished and tidy. There was not a fraying cushion or deflated pillow. The art was nicely framed and not too crowded on the walls, giving the entire house a bigger feel. Not that it needed to feel bigger when it was already more than ample. Their dinners were excellent, and the pastries were to Justine's exacting palate: not too sweet. Ophelia could eat apfelkuchen every meal and be happy.

"Karl is too busy for us this evening. The big market is happening next month and he and his father are frenzied," Justine said, moving them along past the Augustus fountain.

"I hadn't noticed," Ophelia said. She'd met Karl's father, a lovely man who looked very much like his son, only not quite as tall, and half as broad. While Karl looked like a mountain guide, which he'd been when they'd met him, his father looked precisely like what he was: a prosperous merchant.

She wondered what Julian would think of Augsburg. Would he have insights about the fountains or the architecture? Would he know of the mythologies of Mercury and Hercules? Ophelia pushed the idea away. In front of her and Justine walked a man and a woman, arm in arm. They were easy and familiar in their movements, comfortable in a way that made Ophelia believe they were married.

That sucking sensation in her chest started again. The hollowed-out feeling that she had fought so hard against, that only helping Lady Emily through her labors had cured. That the primal arrival of life made insignificant. The only thing that could keep her feelings at bay was that balance.

The need to walk up a mountain sang through her blood. She needed the Matterhorn to fix her broken heart. Even if the man who had broken it was right alongside her, matching her step for step, it didn't matter. So much of mountaineering was pushing until there was nothing left but one's own pulse of life against the uncaring monolith of stone.

She'd sent a footman with her missive to his place of residence, hoping to receive a note in return, but when her man returned, he said that Sir Julian was gone to Wales for an extended venture with no forwarding address. So she waited to reach him, hoping for a note, or for him to show up during calling hours. But that didn't happen. She put off leaving as long as she could, still stupidly waiting, believing that he would come.

But he didn't. The hope that had buoyed her for those weeks popped, as insubstantial as a soap bubble. So she'd written the most professional letter she could manage, because she was beginning to suspect he didn't want to climb the Matterhorn with her.

She didn't doubt his willingness or desire to climb the mountain. The part that was making the trip untenable for him was her. And that hurt so much. Much more than she believed possible. The hurt generated that sucking maw in her chest. The one that whispered how unlovable she was along with every beat of her heart.

Ophelia clung to Justine, pushing those whispers down and away. Justine loved her. And that would have to be enough. But could it sustain her from now until eternity? She shuddered.

Justine glanced over with concern and pulled her close. "I'm always here. I will kick Karl out of his own house if that will make you happy."

Tears clouded Ophelia's eyes. Why did it hurt more to have someone love her? "No need. But thank you."

"You're first. He's second." They walked together, skirts swaying in time. "A distant second."

Ophelia laughed, and it allowed her to pretend the tear escaping was from joy.

⇥⟫⟨⟨⇤

JULIAN KEPT HIMSELF as busy as he could. Planning, writing a new article, taking in all of London because he planned on never returning. He went to the opera, to plays, to chamber music. He walked along the Serpentine, and visited the British Museum. It was on one of his walks in Hyde Park that he ran into Delphine.

She was on horseback, a groom on a horse behind her. Julian raised his hand in greeting, using the movement to sweep his hat off in a gallant bow. The smile that spread across her face was genuine. Julian returned his hat to its perch on his head and waited for her to halt her horse.

She dismounted and handed the reins to her groom, informing him to meet her at the edge of the park. Julian was surprised by the order, giving him far more time to converse than he thought she would want.

"You look well," he said, careful to not be so formal as to use her title, but not so impertinent to use her given name.

"As do you." She smiled and swung her riding crop. "Will you walk me to the entrance?"

"Of course," he said, and they fell into step. He could feel her examination of him, the smile that played upon her lips as she did so.

"I lied," she said.

"Oh?" Julian turned to meet her gaze, which was nothing short of triumphant.

"You don't look well. You look simply awful."

He nodded, aware that he'd lost weight in the past few weeks, as he spent the hours he couldn't sleep walking the length of London. Perhaps it was dangerous to make himself a target of the underbelly of London, but while he felt watched at times, he also felt that those pickpockets and cutthroats pitied him. As if they could sense his moral turmoil and his—if he dared say it— heartbreak.

Because he had finally come to realize that he had been ready to pitch himself head over heels into Ophelia's world. He had loved being in Paris with her and her friends. The group of them had fit, even though he was new. The other men were doting sorts, proud of their accomplished and unusual wives. None of them required the chest pounding that often occurred when meeting a group of men. They were all so happy. Content. And he wanted to be among them.

Paris made it seem as if he could step into her world, her family, this bosom of warmth and support. The kind he'd never had. And at the center of it all was this charismatic, driven, intelligent, beautiful woman. She was a culmination and epicenter of an incredible group of people, and she led them.

The biggest miracle of all was that she wanted *him*. Broke, broken, and old. But she wanted to hear his stories, learn his perspectives. As if she wanted to live his life vicariously through him. And when she'd wanted one small, private bit, he'd shunned her for no other reason than he was appalled someone might ask for it. She had wanted to know him. To see him without all of the "adventurer" labels slapped all over his life. She'd wanted to know what love had looked like to him, and he couldn't bring himself to tell her. Or even defend himself. His denial ate at him, gnawing like a mouse worrying a burlap sack, waiting for its contents to spill out.

"Do I look so tragic?" Julian asked, looking at Delphine.

She examined him again after her teasing, and her expression shifted from glee to cynicism. "You do. But I'm guessing it's not caused by our parting."

Julian licked his lips, hoping to come up with a happy turn of phrase that would soften the blow. "Ah. No."

"Thought not," Delphine murmured.

They walked in silence for a moment.

"I did miss your company," Julian said, wanting to offer her something.

Delphine laughed, a brittle, almost sarcastic sound. "I'm sure you did."

"Your friendship. Your eye for art, your appreciation of music." Julian watched her as he clarified.

Her lips thinned. "We were better as friends, weren't we?"

"I think so."

She listed away from him, swinging her horse crop in her hand.

"What is it?" A leftover ember of affection smoldered in him. An echo of what she had wanted from him.

"It's a pity. I rather liked you. More than friendship. At least, for a while." She gave him a whisper of a smile.

"You would have tired of me in no time."

"That's probably true."

June was almost upon them, and the park was crowded, even though it was not quite the fashionable hour yet. Julian didn't like the crowds that came with the fashionable hour.

"It's Miss Bridewell, isn't it?"

Denying the claim flashed through his mind. But it was pointless. Delphine was an astute reader of people. "Yes."

"But she was to marry Lord Fairport."

Julian suppressed a shudder. "Yes."

Even Delphine made a face. "If he was still wealthy, I could understand."

Julian frowned. He knew from Fairport's own mouth that he was in need financially, but was it that bad? "That bad?"

Delphine laughed. "After your girl postponed the engagement, Mama Fairport sent letters inviting all the age-appropriate heiresses from New York to Boston to visit her this summer. Expect a deluge of Americans in the ballrooms."

Julian laughed at her tone of distaste. "I won't be around much longer, so that isn't a threat to me."

"Yes, still pursing the lofty summit of the Matterhorn?"

"No. I took a contract in Argentina."

Delphine stopped short and put her hand on his arm. "But why? You were so excited about the Alps."

Julian shook his head, frowning. "It's not right. I can't, I mean, it's hard to—" He stopped babbling and took a breath. Before he could start his thought anew, Delphine looped her arm through his.

"Heartbreak," she said simply.

Julian nodded his head, feeling that burlap sack gnawed completely open, and his guts spilling out everywhere. "I can't be that close to her and not confess my feelings. The last months have been agony. It's better if I just stay away."

Delphine nodded as they slowed to a stately amble. The entrance to the park was getting closer. The groom and her horses were at the ready for her. "Why should you not tell her? Why should you not be with her?"

Julian scoffed. "I'm old. I'm poor. My career takes me to the other side of the world for decades at a time."

Delphine considered his options. "Age is relative. She's rich.

And why could she not go with you? Miss Bridewell strikes me as the sort of person who rather likes adventure."

Julian blinked. It had never occurred to him that Ophelia would want to go with him. Or that staying in London and having a family might not be what she wanted for a future. He honestly didn't know what she wanted. He felt like a complete dunce. Why had he never asked what she had wanted? Why had he assumed she would be like the conventional women of the *ton*, when she was organizing mountain expeditions instead of charity drives? "Oh."

Delphine patted his shoulder as she extricated her arm from his. "Not that I meddle in other people's personal affairs. However, I think you taking that contract is a mistake. You'll find another one when the time is right. But if you never confess your feelings, if you never ask Miss Bridewell what she wants, you will shrivel. Take a chance, Julian. Give her that opportunity to be with you. The one you couldn't give to me." She gave him a wistful smile before turning to hail her groom.

Julian watched her mount and ride away. Pulling away from his present course seemed too difficult. If he broke his contract, would he ever be trusted by another company again? The clatter of other horses pulled him from his reverie. His walk home took longer than usual, his thoughts heavy and churning.

Chapter Fourteen

Z ERMATT WAS EVEN lovelier than Ophelia remembered. June was warm and sweet-smelling. The donkey ride from the Zurich train station was far more pleasant this time, given the superior weather. Entering the village proper, with its close cobbled streets and small shops, felt like entering a party already in progress.

Both the citizens and tourists from all over Europe sat in chairs lining the walls of hotels and at cafes with tables outside. They smoked and laughed, drank beer and extended their legs, clad in calf-hugging gators and ending in heavy, hobnailed boots.

Ophelia's heart felt lighter to be amongst them. With Karl's presence, they would be able to enter those groups and discuss routes and tell stories, if they wanted. This was a consolation. She didn't have to be a lady here, where she had to keep her ankles crossed, keep her voice soft and look up through her lashes. Here she could obsess about everyone's climbing innovations, everyone proudly unloading their packs to show off how they had modified an ice ax, or pack, or harnesses.

They discussed rope fibers and dimensions. Disputes over how to shed weight on an ascent often erupted. By the time the long summer sunset finally faded, they would settle in to listen to the harrowing stories told by seasoned guides and climbers.

It was not the first time that Ophelia envied the ease with which men were allowed to move in the world. She would give everything up if she could enter a tavern without the entire place coming to a halt to stare at her.

Justine tried to convince her this happened because of her beauty. Perhaps this was true, but Ophelia thought it was something else entirely. They sensed her aloofness. They could feel her snobbish manners that were so engrained in her from an early age. There was no possibility of fitting in anywhere. But if she surrounded herself with friends, it didn't matter if she stuck out or not. Because they were all extraordinary.

On the lead donkey, Karl called out to friends on every street corner. He waved and shouted, and they shouted back at him. Being a mountain guide was a good life. At least, it seemed so to Ophelia.

Arriving at the inn, located further up on the hillside, above town, was another joyous reunion. Herr and Frau Brunner came out, practically pulling them off their donkeys to embrace them. A gangly young man appeared to take their trunks up to their rooms. A new cast of faces were there to help the couple since Karl had moved back to Augsburg. Frau Brunner cupped Justine's face in her hands and spoke affection and pleasure in German. Justine cackled in laughter and responded in kind.

Ophelia's German had been decent their first time in Zermatt, but it had certainly atrophied. The words no longer flowed in understanding. Rather, she had to translate it in her head, word for word.

During her stay in Augsburg, everyone had spoken English around her—no doubt as a signal of welcome. They settled into the hotel and Ophelia bathed to wash the donkey scent off of her. Dinner was as good as she'd remembered. Unlike two years ago, now the dining room of the inn was crowded, full of tourists from all over. The table next to them were speaking a dialect of Italian she didn't recognize. And as they entered, she heard a mix of French and Spanish and Swedish from various groups.

This inn was no longer their secret. Clearly, Herr and Frau Brunner prospered. Meals came out on time, whisked into place by an efficient young woman only a few years younger than Ophelia. The young porter they'd encountered earlier was taking finished plates and refilling glasses with beer or wine around the various tables.

Their hosts reappeared during the last course, delivering dessert and small etched liqueur glasses around the tables. At their table, the young woman brought apfelkuchen for Ophelia and Karl, with a cheese plate for Justine, knowing she preferred it. Here, Herr Brunner sat down to chat and pat Karl on the shoulder. This time, the conversation flowed in German. Ophelia was tired enough that she didn't bother to try to follow along.

When they settled in for the night, Justine and Karl retiring to their room, and Ophelia to hers alone, she felt that sucking vacuum in her chest again. It felt cold in her room, which was the same sparsely decorated one from two years ago. But it felt more bare than before. Perhaps because last time she had Justine in the bed next to her, while this time she was alone.

And she realized finally what everyone else had known for months: that Julian wasn't coming. He would not be here. As soon as the idea formed, the last months of waiting for him made her feel all the more ridiculous. Any normal person would have known he wasn't coming. But she couldn't let herself give up the hope that he might care about her. She had, after all, given over to animal desires with him, how much clearer could she have been?

But then came his painful dismissal of her attempts to get closer. His easy teasing and mockery, as if what had passed between them was nothing more than a brush of a hand. Oh, she had humiliated herself in so many ways. How stupid could she be?

She'd gone to him in Paris, caught up in a beautiful city, full of wine and success. Of course he hadn't stopped her, because what man would turn away a willing woman? Hadn't she been taught that from her earliest years? A woman had to safeguard herself at every age, for there was always a man wanting to take something from her. Then like a wanton idiot, she gave herself to Julian, only for him to put up the wall between them. An impenetrable one, that even time could not crumble.

He'd abandoned her at every turn. He had not wanted to climb the Matterhorn. No, he said that to gain her trust and her favor, likely in hopes that he could seduce her. She was such a fool for falling for every single one of his charming conversations. And when he got her published, even that was for his own gain! His name was right there, in print, on *her* work.

Oh, such a trifle that her work would now be credited to him, erasing her adventure, her competence, her daring. Women don't *do* that sort of thing, obviously. So why should anyone believe it if she protested? At least he could have come to her in person to apologize and explain. But no.

She cried in earnest now, an unusual event. But she couldn't stop it. The tears came, and the sucking feeling encompassed every part of her. What a fool she was to think she could do any of this. Redeem herself at the mountain that killed her father and injured her friends. Make the summit. Find a person who would love her for her, and not her dowry.

Removing the pins from her hair and brushing it helped bring the wracking sobs to merely tears. She stepped out of her dress and corset and pantaloons and stockings. She changed her shift into a night gown and laid in the cool, hard bed. It wasn't enough. So she took the blankets and pillow from the other bed and put them on her own, the weight soothing her. Even still, she curled herself around the other pillow and cried herself to sleep.

OPHELIA SLEPT THROUGH breakfast. Her stomach churned, and her eyelids felt the size of the blanket draping her body. She didn't dare look in a mirror.

The sucking sensation had shrunk back down into just her

chest, but she felt tired and listless for the first time in her life. The ache in her joints and the weight of her bones made it impossible to move.

A quick knock on the door broke Ophelia from her misery. But she didn't bother moving yet. "Who is it?" she called, her voice scratchy and weak.

"It's Justine." There was a pause and a murmur behind the door. "And, well, Karl. He's here too. Checking on you, darling. You weren't at breakfast."

Ophelia would have responded, but her mouth felt glued together. Besides, what else was there to say? After the pause stretched long enough for Justine to realize Ophelia would not be answering, she knocked again.

"I'd like to come in, please." Justine said through the door. "This isn't like you."

What was she like then? Over-opiniated? Full of herself? Confident for no reason? Overambitious? Ridiculous? She'd been called all of those things. "No, thank you," Ophelia answered.

The doorknob rattled. Through the pale wood Justine said, "Karl, go away. Amuse yourself somewhere else. Ophelia?" She raised her voice when she called Ophelia's name. "It's just me now, and I'm coming in. If you don't open it for me, I'm breaking down the door. Herr Brunner is going to be very upset with me, but I don't care. It's better than trying to scale the wall outside your window."

That at least made her smile. Because Justine really would do something absolutely outlandish and absurd to get in. Ophelia pulled herself up out of the blanket layers.

"I hear you moving in there," Justine called.

Ophelia slung on her dressing gown.

"I hear you walking." Then, quieter, Justine said, "Karl. Dear Lord, get on with you. Go chop some wood or carry a sheep or whatever you did here for fun."

There was a murmur of a low voice and then footsteps. Ophelia smiled to herself at her friend's antics. And how understanding Karl was. Ophelia could stand Justine seeing her like this, but not Karl.

Finally, she opened the door, and Justine seemed almost surprised, crouched down like she was whispering. She straightened. "Oh. Right."

"Come in," Ophelia said, holding the heavy wooden door open.

But Justine looked her square in the face first, no doubt seeing her red, puffy eyes, her red nose, and general dishevelment. "Oh, darling."

"Get in here before I start crying again. You know I can't stand it when someone is nice to me."

Justine entered. "Do I know that?"

Ophelia leaned against the door to help it close. "Well, it's true, anyway."

Justine took in the room, which was uncharacteristically messy. Ophelia's dress was a pile on the floor; when she got back to London, her maid was going to have a fit.

"Let's start here," Justine said, picking up her stockings and draping them over the chair.

"You? Tidying up?" Ophelia teased her.

"Shocking, I know. But for you, I will walk through fire." Justine smiled and picked up the pantaloons and corset.

The sentiment felt like a stab through the heart. Justine really would do anything for her, which was not the case for anyone else. Julian was certainly not inspired to feel such. As for the rest of her family, they were paired off, with new families to nurture. And her mother was still in the deep pool of grief.

In an impulsive moment, Ophelia stepped forward and flung her arms around Justine. "Thank you for being here," she murmured into Justine's lavender-scented hair. "I couldn't press on without you."

Justine turned and took Ophelia's head in her hands. "I know Karl exists and is my legal husband and everything, but you are most important to me. You need me, I will drop everything and come to you. No matter what. Understand?"

Ophelia nodded, some of the pain retreating a bit farther. Justine hugged her back into an embrace.

"Now, I'm going to just enjoy this snuggle a little longer, because you hardly ever give random outbursts of affection."

Ophelia chuckled. "Fine."

They spent the day in Ophelia's room, ordering up pots of chocolate. When Frau Brunner caught wind of Ophelia's state, she sent up a cold ointment for her swollen eyes.

"I have for cucumber sandwich. But now, use for the face," she said, delivering a tray of hot tea and cucumber sandwiches to accompany the ointment that smelled precisely of cucumber pulp and milk. "I bring the apfelkuchen and the käse next."

The pampering was lovely. And by the end of the day, she felt far less sorry for herself, and far less unlovable. Was there still a massive Julian-induced hole in her heart? Yes, but it didn't hurt quite so much.

She still missed her father and wished she could speak to him, but in a way, it felt as if he were there with her. That while his body left Zermatt, his spirit never really had. For the first time since the accident, she felt like he was just in the other room, reading a climbing journal. He was accessible, available to her, waiting for her questions. It was almost as if she could reach out her hand and expect to feel his grasping hers in return.

She fell asleep with the lamps still blazing and Justine by her side.

IT MIGHT HAVE been June, but Zurich at night was still cold. Julian's train was delayed for hours due to a rampant sheep herd on the French border and a cow herd on the Swiss border. He would have to wait until morning to find a donkey up to Zermatt.

He was jumpy and nervous and dedicated, all at once. The force he felt driving him to Ophelia was unlike anything he'd experienced before. As if every minute away from her had squeezed his ribcage smaller and smaller, and then when he finally could make his way to her, he had no more breath left.

What had seemed like a grand romantic impulse when boarding the train in France suddenly seemed very poorly planned now that it was cold and dark. Still, the drive to find Ophelia pushed him onward, despite his bones crying out for rest.

He couldn't see the moon, but there were still street lamps lit. If he could only find a place to stay. Sleep would be nice. He could still feel the jostle and vibration of the train in his bones.

There was a figure walking quickly down the street. All the other passengers dispersed already, knowing precisely where they would be for the night.

"Excuse me?" he called. Oh, his German was rusty. French or Spanish, that he could handle. His brain churned, trying to come up with the words. "Pardón?"

The figure ignored him and breezed past without looking up. So Julian continued on his way into the city. He spotted a group carrying luggage, so he followed them to a small guesthouse, but there were no more rooms available. While the hostess was apologetic, she helped direct him to other possibilities and assured him that speaking French was acceptable there.

Julian tried the first suggestion, only to find no vacancy. The second was closed for renovation. The third had already locked their doors and refused to answer. The hour grew later and later, and the prospects seemed dimmer. Julian wasn't sure what to do. He was tired and cold, and his pack felt heavier and heavier. But he might as well walk. It was what he was good at.

In the dark, he figured the direction he needed to go to eventually find Zermatt, and started. Soon, he found the water, Lake Zürich, and walked its shores. He spotted the moon, reflected in the water, and it gave him a light to walk by. It wasn't unpleasant, even though he had been tired. As ever, the movement invigorated him in a way sleep could not.

He passed by a small hamlet and kept on. The path was clear and obvious, which made it easier for Julian to continue. In daylight, this must be a beautiful and tranquil place to live. And after some time, an hour or two, he began to smell sugar in the air.

It wasn't the smell of bread or pastries, but confection. Like a moth to a flame, Julian floated until he pinpointed the building from which the heavenly smell arrived. It was chocolate. The kind of chocolate that he missed from South America. Deep and rich, roasted and dark.

The sky lightened. Julian hadn't noticed. The train had arrived so late, and he'd spent so much time trying to find a place to sleep that he ended up walking all night. The path forked, and Julian followed the road away from the lake. A man sat on a tree stump next to a very large building, a mug steaming in one hand, a cigarette in another.

"Hallo there," Julian called out, raising a hand. He knew this man's tranquil solitude and didn't wish to scare him.

The man turned, surprise clear enough, even in the dim morning light. "Grüß Gott," he greeted, his voice jagged and rough, perhaps from sleep, perhaps from the tobacco.

"Sprechen Sie Englisch, oder Französisch oder Spanisch?" Julian hoped he wouldn't have to rely on his German.

"Französisch und Englisch, ja," the man said, stubbing out his cigarette and standing.

"English, please," Julian said, wondering if his sleep-deprived brain would do well in French. "Good morning."

"And to you also. What has you walking at this hour?"

Julian could smell the coffee wafting from the man's mug, and he found himself suddenly hungry. "My train arrived in Zurich very late last night, and there was no place to stay, so I've been walking."

"You walked from Zurich?" the man asked. "Friend, you must come in and rest. Where are you going to?" He ushered

Julian to follow and led him into the building behind him.

"I need to make it to Zermatt as quickly as possible." Julian staggered when the man opened the door and the smell of chocolate enveloped him. What was this place?

"Ah. A mountain climber, you must be. I know many."

"Sort of. My, er, the woman I am rather fond of has plans to climb the Matterhorn. I am supposed to go with her, but I am afraid I'll miss her departure."

The room was spare and small. A table and four chairs dominated the space, and a small kitchen was installed on the opposite end. "Please." The man gestured to a chair.

Julian wondered if he sat down, would he fall asleep? "Thank you."

"I am Markus. And you?"

"Julian," he said, feeling strange about sharing his first name and not his last. But the informality seemed to suit the strangeness of the moment.

Markus gave a curt nod in acknowledgement and poured a mug of coffee. "Here you are. I normally have two cups in the morning, but today I will share."

Julian could weep for how hot the coffee was. It was bitter and dark and absolutely what he needed.

"So your lady will climb this Matterhorn? That is no small thing."

"No, but she's going to make it this time, I am positive."

Markus nodded. "The women now. Instead of the children, they will do the climbing. Instead of the cooking, they do the working."

Julian hadn't thought about that before. How the world was changing once again. How sometimes women gained opportunities and then lost them. Science was moving at a rapid pace, education was expanding in all directions, so did it not make sense that people expanded too?

"Do you think it is acceptable for them to do so?" Julian asked, curious, for he had no idea how he felt about such things.

But at first thought, it seemed perfectly reasonable.

"Of course, yes. I have a wife. She goes for her long walk up a mountain, she comes back feeling much better. I prefer it."

Julian smiled.

"You are hoping this lady to make your wife?" he asked.

The question knocked the wind out of Julian's chest. Was that what he was truly after? He had, after all, cancelled his assaying assignment with his profound apologies. The lords weren't even that put out, since they had another explorer waiting in the wings. Still, he'd travelled across Europe. Why would he do this if he thought his love would be unrequited? And certainly, if she did return his sentiments, he would want to marry her. Have her forever. "Yes. I think so."

Markus smiled. "Ja, so." They clinked coffee mugs. "Then we get you to Zermatt."

"Thank you. But I am so tired from the night's walk, I need a nap before I go." Even the coffee was not enough. It helped, yes, so that if he had a long walk to the next inn, he could make that journey.

"Sleep outside," Markus said. "It is very pleasant out there, under the trees. I will keep watch on your belongings."

Julian had no trouble sleeping outside. In some ways, he preferred it. But he shifted in his chair, unsure.

"You sleep," Markus insisted, gesturing again outside. "I will arrange you a way to Zermatt. Many people go in that direction. We will get you there. Climb the mountain, get famous, say something nice about our town and our chocolate. Yes?"

Gratitude welled in Julian's chest. "That would be very wonderful."

"Good. When you wake up, I'll give you more coffee, and also a chocolate."

Julian nodded, swallowing back the dry bitter taste of the coffee. "I am so tired."

"Then sleep, my friend! I will do this for you." Markus stood, taking Julian's cup from him.

"Why are you doing this for me?" Julian stood as well, happy to stow his pack under the table.

"Working in a factory is very boring," Markus whispered conspiratorially. "It will give me and a few others something to do. And besides! Maybe you like the chocolate, and that is advertising!"

Julian chuckled. "I will happily crow about your chocolate."

"Good. Go!" Markus ushered him out the door.

Julian padded down to the grove of a few trees near the doorway, finding a spot that clearly was used for napping. Gentle morning light was flooding the cityscape, but from Julian's perspective, he had a forest with dappled sun. The ground was damp, but the ground was soft, and Julian's oilcloth travelling coat would keep him warm and dry. It took little time for his eyes to close and drop off into sleep.

JUSTINE AND KARL kept Ophelia busy climbing all the mountains in the range. They were adjusting to the higher altitude, testing equipment, and improving their fitness with each day. At night, Karl joined Ophelia to tinker with gear while Justine regaled them with funny stories. Frau Brunner tutted over Ophelia's breakfasts and made sure she ate her meals.

If they returned from hikes soon enough, Frau Brunner would have a lovely afternoon tea at the ready, each day becoming more elaborate as Frau Brunner learned some new "English custom" from another guest in town.

And a few times she and the Vogels went down to talk and meet with other climbers from around the world, who were staying in Zermatt with their same goals. They discussed snow conditions, melt patterns, routes, ropes, gear. The other climbers didn't seem to care that she and Justine were women, and openly told ribald jokes and vulgar stories about pissing off mountain-tops.

Ophelia knew she should be shocked, but she giggled along with everyone else, letting the liquor or the beer color her cheeks. The daily hikes were causing her dresses to loosen, but Ophelia was an adept hand with her needle, and didn't mind taking things in as a lady's maid would do.

It was in those discussions that she learned most about Alpine climbing. The rawness of it, not just in her own experience, but in others' as well. The loss of friends, of toes, of fingers. But they all returned, just as she had, regardless of what they came without. It made Ophelia feel less alone in her single-mindedness to summit.

She could see in their faces some doubt as to whether or not they believed she could, but once they compared times up other peaks surrounding Zermatt, they nodded approval. She didn't need their respect or their approval to climb the Matterhorn, but it helped nonetheless. That intangible agreement that she belonged with them, and they belonged with her.

Those pilgrimages down to the Mount Rosa hotel and its surrounding taverns helped keep her mind occupied. She was absorbed in her body and its performance, that she was able to keep herself blank on the inside, unable to grieve, but also unable to feel the rush of accomplishment after each successful summit.

But it did not matter, for they were close to leaving for the Matterhorn. The weather was improving, and it was almost prime snow conditions up at altitude. The time when the snow slides from early summer would no longer threaten them and before the cold regained its foothold at ten thousand feet and above.

Each night after dinner and before bed, Ophelia would march herself outside and stare at the mountain. "I'm coming," she whispered. It could have been a warning or a promise. The mountain didn't care, and neither did Ophelia. It was a fact, all the same.

Chapter Fifteen

Markus had been a godsend. Fueled by his rewarmed coffee, a slice of bread, and some very delicious chocolate, Julian was right as rain by noon. True to his word, Markus arranged a carriage as far as Bern, a horse as far as the mountains, and then a donkey into Zermatt.

Each transfer had been easy and swift, each of them expecting him. Whatever magic Markus wrought, he was second to none. Before night fell, Julian was in Zermatt, and the view did not disappoint.

The white-capped mountains surrounded the bowl of the village with breathtaking clarity. He left his donkey with a Swiss man who seemed to know all about Julian, though he didn't speak a word of English. Instead, the man motioned over to the Mount Rosa hotel, where men of all ages lined the exterior wall, lounging while enjoying coffee and tea, wine and beer, cordials and liquors. They were all in Zermatt for climbing, as evidenced by their ruched gaiters over their calves, sunburnt chins, and wind-chapped cheeks.

The name of the hotel didn't ring a bell in his memory, but Julian approached to chat with the array of adventurers. He had Ophelia's instruction letter in his pack, stowed away carefully. He would have to unpack the whole thing to get them out.

They greeted him and he waved his hand in greeting as well, asking if anyone spoke English, Spanish, or French. The answer was a robust yes from all of them, but the oldest man there spoke French the best, so Julian's Spanish-accented French was how they conversed.

It turned out that two English ladies were enough of an anomaly that every gentleman knew where they were staying, which was at the inn up the hill. Many of them eyed him with distrust after the inquiry, clearly protective of her and her privacy.

"I'm her climbing partner," he insisted. That earned him some modicum of respect, but it didn't matter. Ophelia would have to vouch for him in person before they would trust him. Which was oddly heartwarming.

None of them offered him a seat next to them, so Julian didn't have to navigate international decorum in declining. He set off for the inn at the edge of town.

Instead of enjoying the quaint shops, the adorable flower boxes, and tidy houses, Julian's sweaty hands betrayed his nerves. By the time he arrived at the small inn, which sat nestled into the hillside, smelling of fresh hay and fresh-cut lumber, he was nearly shaking from nerves.

Steady breaths while he thought through the topics he wished to bring up to Ophelia, namely his inability to share his inner person, helped calm him. He'd never been this nervous over anything. Not being caught on a peak in a lightning storm, nor having to talk down an angry Spaniard intent on impaling him, nor even a close encounter with an anaconda (which was why he chose to explore the mountains of South America and not its waterways).

But as he was collecting himself, someone called his name. Julian looked up, relieved to see the amiable broad form of Karl Vogel walking towards him. "A messenger came to tell me you were wandering about Zermatt looking for us."

"Mr. Vogel," Julian said with utter gratitude. "I cannot tell you how happy I am to see you."

"Call me Karl, please. It is simpler. And I am surprised to see you. Does Ophelia know you are coming?" The German man folded his forearms in front of him, likely out of comfort, but it was a powerful display of strength, nonetheless. It reminded Julian of the animals that intentionally made themselves bigger when a rival male entered their territory.

"I don't believe so, no." Julian cheeks heated despite the Alpine breeze.

Karl clicked his tongue. "I do not wish to meddle."

"Good."

"—But."

Julian winced and waited.

"She is very upset with you." Karl looked at him with narrowed eyes. "You have some very big apologies to make."

"I know I do," Julian said. "And I am more than prepared to make them. I've traveled a long way thinking about nothing but that."

"Probably you will need to do some begging."

"No doubt about that," Julian agreed.

"Also, are you going up the Matterhorn with us?" Karl asked.

It took a moment for Julian to change gears from thinking of Ophelia and his shame to thinking about the ambitious trek. He hoped any residual fitness he had wasn't completely shorn away by his London months. "Ah, yes. I am planning on that, actually. As part of my begging for forgiveness."

Karl grinned and clapped him on the bicep. "Excellent. Four is better than three, in my opinion."

"Any update on when that climb might take place?" Julian asked, wondering how much time he had to make amends enough that Ophelia might put her life in his hands, and his in hers.

The man's gaze shifted to the mountain tops, as if he could evaluate the snow from where he stood. "Soon, I think. Perhaps five days? The weather seems to be shifting already. It is early for the season, but I think if we wait too long, we will miss our window."

So Julian had only a few days to put things right. Hopefully all he would need was an afternoon, but he had a feeling it would take much more than that. "I don't suppose you know if there is a room vacant here?"

Karl grinned. "If you don't mind sleeping with the goats."

"Better than where I slept last night." Julian was too anxious to be tired yet, but he knew it was only a matter of time before his exhaustion took over and he was useless.

"I am teasing. I'll find you something. Ophelia is with Justine on a trail that direction." He pointed. "You can leave your things with me, if you like. Or you can wait for their return here."

Julian was ready to dump his pack and dash down the trail, but then doubt assailed him. "What do you think is the best thing to do?"

Karl frowned as he thought. "I am not certain. They have banished me from all conversation for several days, so I do not know how she is feeling."

"I don't want her to feel like I'm ambushing her," Julian said.

"No, no. Perhaps I find them, tell them she can meet you at a tavern and discuss?"

Julian sighed. He did not want to go sit in a tavern for an undetermined amount of time. "I don't think I am able to, I didn't sleep last night."

Karl gave him a strange look.

"I would need a nap first." Indeed, this entire conversation had him quickly deflating. "Perhaps you could point me in the direction of the goat shed?"

"Come," Karl said, wrapping his thick arm around Julian's shoulders. "Let's get you to a room, a nap, and perhaps a wash-up. I'll tell Ophelia that you have arrived, and she can figure out if and where she would like to speak with you."

"Brilliant," Julian said, suddenly barely more than staggering on his feet. It turned out that Karl's uncle ran the inn, and Julian got an excellent rate and a good room. When he opened his pack to get his shaving kit, he saw a small unfamiliar box packed on top. He plucked it out and examined it, finding a note scrawled across a piece of paper tucked in the string that held it closed.

Forgiveness is easier with chocolate.

Julian smiled and set it aside. Another gift for Ophelia, then. He bathed, shaved, made himself presentable, and then fell asleep on top of the covers in his spartan bachelor room.

※

A KNOCK ON the door woke him from a dead slumber. Julian glanced at the window, noting that night had already fallen. He'd slept through dinner, which had not been his intention. He sat up, thinking it might be Karl, to tell him to come down and speak to Ophelia, or perhaps the uncle, Herr Brunner, who seemed a very nice fellow.

"Coming," he croaked. A wave of dizziness hit him but passed quickly. His mouth was dry, and his eyes felt scratchy. He hadn't gotten enough rest, but that was no matter. It wouldn't be the first time he'd had to press on with little physical strength. He was determined that Ophelia understand him, that at least if she couldn't forgive him, there could be that.

When he opened the door, his jaw dropped open because it wasn't Karl.

Ophelia stood there, in her evening dress, a light blue chiffon-like drape around her shoulders. She was stunning, and his mouth didn't seem to work any longer. He'd forgotten how truly beautiful she was. The more fool him.

"I didn't think you were coming," she said.

"I did," he said, which was possibly the most idiotic thing he could have said. They stared at each other. "Would you like to come in?"

Ophelia shook her head. Which made sense. He was inviting her into his room, after all, and that did signal an intent that he was well aware was not appropriate.

"A walk perhaps?" he asked.

She gave a slight nod, and that beautiful golden hair caught the low light, shining like a beacon of old. He should be grateful she would bother to even give him five minutes, let alone a walk.

"I'll grab my coat," he said, stepping back into his room and letting the door slowly swing closed. He took a deep breath and gathered his jacket and hat. This was his chance. If everything blew up in his face, it was his only chance.

He saw her gifts sitting on the small dressing table. Should he explain first, and give gifts later? Yes, that was best. Otherwise, she would be carrying them on the walk, and that was cumbersome.

He stepped outside, catching a glance at her unguarded face as she gazed down the passage. Before she registered his presence, Julian saw despair. She was thinner, making her face appear narrower. He didn't know if her emotions were tied to the place, and she was experiencing grief over the loss of her father, or if it was fear regarding the Matterhorn, or worse—it was because of him.

"Shall we?" he asked, gesturing down the hall, towards the stair, and ultimately, the front entrance.

She gave him a tight smile and set off down the hall. Her steps were short, measured. The evening dress wasn't restrictive, so it didn't require such a small gait. But she held herself tightly, taut like rope stretched so thin it begins to fray.

They walked out into the warm night. Julian offered his arm, but Ophelia didn't move toward him. She kept the distance so large between them that he was afraid he might have to shout.

"If we walk toward the village, there will be light to see by," Ophelia said.

"Of course," Julian said, following her lead. The tension between them was full of ache and sodden hopes. Julian didn't know where to even start. What could he say to her to make up for what had happened in the last months? When he was able to finally pull himself together enough to speak, she spoke at the same time.

"I apologize, go ahead," she said.

"No, please, I don't intend to talk over you."

She gave him a devastating look and asked lightly, "Don't you?"

It landed like buckshot, humiliation scattering inside him. "I don't. I'm here to apologize to you at the very least."

She considered it, and he was desperate to hear her next words. "And at the very most?"

He swallowed hard, not wanting to open his entire chest for her evisceration. "To summit the Matterhorn with you."

She nodded, and it was obvious that this was an inadequate answer, but he didn't know why. His brain shook like a gold panner.

"I know I have several things to apologize for," Julian said, not sure where to start. "And the first is for leaving you in Paris, without saying goodbye."

"Is that the first chronologically, or the first you're saying?" Her tone was light and delicate, and it panicked him.

Whatever his answer was, he knew it was wrong. "The first I'm listing. In a long list."

She stared at him, unblinking and expressionless.

"Very long list," he assured her. He cleared his throat. "Ophelia. I want to tell you—er, if you want to know, that is. I want to answer the question you asked me, back in Paris. The question that I couldn't answer because I didn't know that you were really asking to share myself. I didn't understand that it wasn't a question rooted in jealousy, but rooted in a desire to know me. I pushed you away, and that hurt you. I see that now."

"Then why did you leave Paris?" Ophelia asked.

"Because I knew I had disappointed you. Your coldness unnerved me. And I knew that I had done something wrong, but I thought that I had dishonored your father's memory by going to bed with you. It was silly to think more about a dead man than you, who were right beside me. It didn't occur to me that in fact, the connection between *us* should have been honored. And I didn't do that."

Ophelia eyed him, and he could see her skepticism floating between them, despite the fact that moonlight was the only illumination. Finally, she looked down, as if she had taken his measure completely. "What would you say now if I asked that question again? If I asked you about your past lovers?"

Julian cleared his throat. "I would remind you that I am a decade your senior. That the ten years in which I lived outside of Europe were spent as young men are wont to spend their unattached times."

"Which means you cavorted with actresses?"

Julian cringed. Even hearing the words out of her mouth felt awful. "No, because those kinds of women were . . . unhappy?" He finished. How to explain to a lady the state of some of these women? Taken from their people, or their lands already flattened from disease and clear-cutting? He shook his head. "No, I took a lover. A woman I thought I would marry."

"Oh," Ophelia whisper, the surprise evident in her voice.

"I realize now how naïve I was. She was the daughter of an indigenous woman and a Spanish man and spent time in the village where I based many of my surveys. I kept rooms there, and offered her a place to live while I was away. Which was frequent. And when I would return, we would live together. She'd made the place her own in my absence, and it made my scant rooms feel like a home. I was foolish enough to believe she felt something bigger about me, and not that she had a very nice place to stay where I was rarely there to bother her."

"What happened next?" Ophelia's voice was soft. She clasped her hands together, letting them bounce off her legs as she walked.

"She left."

"I bet it still hurt."

"It hurt my pride, yes," Julian admitted. "And I thought I loved her. It took falling in love with you to understand that it was different." The words were out of his mouth, *falling in love with you*, but she didn't seem to notice. Did she understand how difficult it was for him to offer up his past like this? To be open and vulnerable to her derision or worse: disinterest.

Ophelia looked at him, her expression serious and thoughtful. "You wanted a home."

Julian nodded. "My parents died when I was young, and I kept on living at school. I didn't really have a home."

"Is that still the same now? You want a home?"

Her question was like a rock thrown into a pond. His mind had his immediate answer, but then everything fell into place as the ripples cast outward. "No."

She frowned. "Then what do you want?"

Julian smiled because he felt his chest expanding, as if he'd been wearing a too-tight waistcoat for a decade, not knowing how to take a full breath. "I want you, Ophelia. I want your friendship, I want your respect. It may be too much to ask, but I also want your love. I haven't loved since my parents died. I've been alone. And I'd forgotten how big a person can feel when one loves someone."

Ophelia caught her breath and stopped walking, so he did as well. "Those are quite the demands."

"They aren't demands. They are offers. Ones you aren't obligated to take." Julian held out his hands, hoping she might put hers into them. She didn't, but he kept his outstretched, just in case. "I wronged you, Ophelia. I hurt you, yes, by the way I treated you in Paris, and by leaving. But I also wronged you professionally. You know that I would never purposefully take credit for someone else's work."

Ophelia's features smoothed into cool detachment.

"So I have, in my room, the reprinted edition of the latest RGS journal. They retracted my name, and credited your last name, Bridewell. Someday, perhaps you can take full ownership of that work. If not, everyone will think it was Tristan. But people who know you, even a little bit, will understand that you wrote that article. Your achievements are wondrous, and belong to you."

She slid her hands into his, but didn't meet his eye. But that was fine—he could wait. He would wait until eternity dawned for Ophelia Bridewell.

◦

Chapter Sixteen

OPHELIA STARED AT Julian's hands. His thumbs now rubbed gently over her knuckles, but the lump in her throat made it impossible to talk. She felt beyond surprised. This was so far past any expectation she'd had of him, and it made her realize that she had gravely misjudged him.

He cared about her. He had used the word "love," even. This wasn't some passing fancy, or him taking advantage of her naïvete. Did she love him in return? How would a person know such a thing?

There was a tiny voice in her mind, one she'd never heard before, that squeaked, *You already love him.*

But listening to voices was for the abjectly insane, and not a very practical person like herself. She realized that she was beginning to tremble.

Worse, Julian noticed. "Are you not feeling well?"

Her first impulse was to snap, *I feel fine!* But she didn't. Far from it—she felt hot and cold all over at the same time. Her mind was whirling like a too-fast carousel. "I'd like to go back, please."

"Of course," he said, and this time when he offered his arm, she took it.

Was it because she felt ill? No, she didn't feel that ill. But perhaps it was that he melted her. That all she wanted was to fall into him, weep about how much she missed him, how lonely it had been planning this trip without him. But experience had taught her to be wary, so she kept herself apart as much as she could.

Leaning on him as she was meant she could smell him, and remember how achingly perfect everything had felt with him. From laughing in the drawing room in London, to the group dinners and his hotel room in Paris. Being with him felt right. Sort of like being home. Was that love? She'd have to think on it.

They walked on in silence, Ophelia's head unspooling thread after thread of possibilities behind them. Once they returned to the inn, Ophelia expected to be descended upon by Justine or someone. But even the front desk was vacant. Julian reached over the desk to retrieve her key, and escorted her upstairs.

At her door, she turned to him, wondering if he would request a kiss or explicit forgiveness. To her surprise, he requested nothing.

"Do you need me to fetch someone to help you?" he asked. "Or perhaps I can have some tea sent up?"

She looked into his pitch-black eyes and saw the warmth there, human and open and willing. It was so different than how he had seemed those months ago in Paris.

"I think I'm fine."

He unlocked her door and handed her the key, opening it so she could step through. "If you aren't too poorly, I would like to bring you something before you retire for the night. It's in my room, if you'll allow me to fetch it."

"Of course," she said. "I'll wait."

He gave her this crooked half-smile that made her heart flip over. As if she needed reminding that he was attractive. He'd developed a white streak of hair in one eyebrow that she liked. It made him seem unusual, or perhaps a bit mysterious. She stripped off her hat, gloves, and overcoat, then poured herself some water from the dressing table ewer to steady herself.

She needed to be honest. She had forgiven him for not telling her about this woman back in Paris. He was correct, that she'd asked the question out of a desire to connect, but if he had been truthful in that moment, who was to say that she wouldn't have gotten jealous? Perhaps she would have. But then it would have been her decision. Her choice. And she could even forgive him for leaving so abruptly. She'd been so mad at him that next morning.

The knock on her door came quickly, and when she answered it, his hair was a bit askew, as if he'd taken the stairs three at a time. He was even a bit out of breath.

"Here you are." Julian handed her a white box tied with string and a blue book. The RGS journal, embossed with gold. She opened the book and its spine creaked, the binding tight and unused.

There, in the index, the reprint of her article, with her last name next to it, and an italicized apology for printing it under the wrong name. The lump in her throat appeared. There it was. Her life's work. Tears welled in her eyes and she had to look up so they didn't fall and damage the table of contents. She let out an embarrassed huff. "Thank you," she whispered.

"I know how much it meant to you." Julian looked down. "I had been careless with your feelings. I didn't understand. But I'd like to think I do, now."

Ophelia smiled and looked down at the box. "And these?" She fumbled with the string.

"Those," Julian said, swaying with an emotion she couldn't place. Mischievousness? Embarrassment? "Those are a gift from my new friend Markus, who helped me when I tried to walk through the night from Zurich to Zermatt."

Ophelia gasped. "It's much too far to walk!"

Julian nodded. "As I found out when I encountered Markus, who works at—" He waited for her to finish untying the string and opened the box, revealing beautiful square chocolates. "Markus works at a chocolate factory. In Hörgen."

"They smell divine." Indeed, her mouth was watering.

"You should have been at the factory," Julian said.

"May I?" Ophelia felt like she was committing some kind of

trespass by eating one. As if each confection held secrets, and biting into one would let the whole world know the truth.

"They are yours Ophelia. You could throw them out the window. Though, I would hope not."

She dipped into the one at the corner, for one did not just pick from the center. It wasn't orderly. The chocolate shell was hard and perfectly bitter and dark, and the middle soft and almost warm. "These are exquisite. Have you had one?"

Julian nodded, his eyes taking in her every feature. His attitude should have alarmed her, but instead, it made her feel loved. Seen. Cherished.

"These kinds of treats are all the more delicious when shared." And she meant that. But she meant more than that too, she just didn't know how to say it. All she could do was talk about the chocolate.

"If you'd like to share, I certainly won't say no," Julian said, taking one from the opposite corner, and not from the middle because that was the only proper way. Ophelia relaxed her shoulders, not realizing until that moment how upset she would have been if he had taken from the middle.

The bite of chocolate was the only thing that pried his gaze from her. "Oh, my, that is exceptional, isn't it?" He stared down at it, rolling the chocolate in his mouth, just as she had.

Ophelia put the lid on the box, and shifted her weight, causing the door to bump her hip. Julian finished his chocolate. She didn't know how to say all the things she felt, nor did she know if she was even ready to say them, let alone feel them.

"Tomorrow morning we're having a meeting after breakfast to discuss our route and the weather conditions on the Matterhorn, if you'd like to come," she said, instead of thanking him for the chocolates, the apology, and travelling across Europe. "Though, you'd have to prove you can acclimate quickly since you haven't been with us these months, training."

But his smile was wide, as if he understood that she was saying all of that during that invitation. That it was a gentle teasing.

That she was forgiving him, shepherding him back into her life. "I might be out of shape for myself, but I think I could manage to not be desperately behind. I would love to attend the meeting, and perhaps verify my fitness with Karl tomorrow afternoon."

Ophelia nodded, suddenly feeling shy and nervous and not at all like herself. Forcing herself to look up at him, she realized that she felt almost desperate to kiss him. Heat seeped into her cheeks instantly. "Thank you—er, see you tomorrow."

She was already closing the door, when his low, gentle, "Goodnight, Ophelia," rumbled across the threshold. Not recognizing her fumbling self, she leaned on the back of the door, listening to his footsteps down the passage and then to the stairs. It was then that she realized she was crushing the chocolate box against her. Her journal. Her chocolates. And possibly? Her hope.

Her first impulse was to find Justine and tell her everything. But then, her cooler, rational mind took over, and she realized she wanted to keep this to herself for a little longer. Because though he had not yet asked, it dawned on her that Julian would be the man she would marry. And she was Ophelia Bridewell, and once she made her mind up, there was no force on earth that could prevent her from doing what she thought was right.

"ARE YOU GLOWING?" Justine said as Ophelia sat down for breakfast.

Ophelia touched her cheek. "Am I?"

Justine elbowed Karl. "What do you think? Is that a glow?"

Karl looked up from the meat and cheese layered in slices on his plate to his wife first, then to Ophelia. He chewed quickly, swallowed and nodded once. "Glow." Then he went back to his breakfast.

Ophelia shrugged, a smile creeping onto her face that she couldn't stop. There was a pot of tea on the table, and a buffet of traditional Alpine breakfast foods on one end of the room. While she couldn't stomach the amount of food that Karl ate in a single sitting, she appreciated the sheer variety of sliced meats and cheeses, types of bread, honey, oats, berries, and fresh yogurts.

Here, there was no luncheon, as one was expected to be out on the mountains. It made Ophelia want to fill her lungs with the crisp and clean Alpine air. She loved this place. It felt as familiar and home-like as her brother's Berringbone estate or the townhome in London.

Julian entered the dining room, and the feeling expanded. There was no place she'd rather be, and no one she'd rather be with.

"Ohhhhh," Justine said softly.

Ophelia meant to shoot her a look of stern crossness, but instead, her residual smile stayed as she glanced at her friend. Even Karl glanced over his shoulder as Julian approached.

He looked handsome this morning. His frock coat flared out from his waist, the length brushing his knees. The buttons were polished and he looked well-rested and fresh-shaven. His dark hair was brushed so it shone like a raven's wing. And when he looked at her, she could see the same joy and contentment in his heart that matched hers. "May I?"

Ophelia gestured to the seat next to hers. "Please." She knew that across the table, the couple shared a look, and she didn't care. In fact, she was glad. Because their joy was hers, and vice versa.

"You look like you finally got some sleep," Karl said to Julian.

"Yes. And not in the shadow of a chocolate factory," Julian quipped, looking over to her.

She was caught in his gaze, unable to speak or move. Then Justine cleared her throat.

"Will you be climbing the mountain with us?" Karl asked.

Julian tore his eyes from hers, and she blinked. The room suddenly felt hot. She poured herself a cup of tea, offering Julian one as well. He declined.

"Yes, I will. What an achievement, to be someone who has

stood on that summit." One of the servers came over when Julian signaled and poured coffee into his teacup. "And Ophelia, as expedition leader, has made it clear that I must pass a fitness test."

Karl grunted. "Today is an off-day for a few guides. I plan to go down to Mont Rose and see what conditions are on the mountain. I heard Anderegg was attempting it yesterday with a party of Americans. I'd like to see if they were successful. You can prove to me your abilities this afternoon."

"And if they were successful?" Ophelia asked.

"Then I'll ask about snow pack, and we will make our attempt in the next few days. The weather has been good. I don't want to miss the window." Karl settled back into his plate.

"There's a possibility we could be climbing the Matterhorn in a day or two." Ophelia felt the spark she'd always had when discussing mountains. To be on top of the Matterhorn would be incredible. She wondered how far she might see. What it would look like up there.

→»»»«««←

JULIAN FELT MORE awake than he'd ever been, and it wasn't the imported coffee. After his quick—literally quick—hike with Karl as they'd run up steep trails, his body felt lighter, the air was cleaner, and the snow-capped mountains brighter. Julian had acquitted himself better than he would have thought, but he'd never struggled with altitude changes as others did. And ten years of doing nothing but mountaineering apparently took more than a year to wipe away.

But it wasn't that which kept him basking in the Swiss sunshine. The way Ophelia looked at him this morning gave him hope more than any words she could have spoken.

Sitting outside was a pleasure here. The faint clanking of bells around the necks of cows and goats reached him from up in the hills. Hillsides surrounding the valley were awash in yellow flowers. The smell of the grass, currently being scythed in organized swaths, filled his nose. Peace had never so forcefully presented itself to him, not even when hiking alone in South America. There he'd had an objective and a goal.

Here, this was leisure at its most opulent. Joy was a flower that he could pluck daily. Julian laid down and let his eyes float shut. After the Matterhorn, he would ask Ophelia to marry him. Perhaps he ought to ask her brother first, as she was the daughter of a viscount. Sister of one now. He could wait.

Still, he imagined her golden hair flung across the white pillow in Paris. Her blue eyes widening as he had told her about her article publishing. His mind remained fuzzy and drifting until he heard his name being called. Julian sat up, propping himself on his hands, trying to pinpoint the sound.

Karl came striding up the mountain like a Valois goat. "Julian, let's go."

Julian raised his eyebrows. "Why?"

"Conditions are good. We leave tomorrow. The ladies are sorting gear. We need to get our packs prepared."

Julian was on his feet, bounding down after Karl, happy and content. Ophelia was about to get her dream, and he would get to be a part of it.

Chapter Seventeen

THEY DEPARTED THE inn mid-morning to no fanfare. Not at all like the expedition from two years ago, which had mules and a cart. There were only four of them this time, and Karl and Julian carried the heavy tent poles, and Ophelia and Justine split the canvas walls and food.

A gnawing foreboding gripped Ophelia, and no matter what she thought about it, the feeling wouldn't pass. Even as the bluebird-cloudless sky insisted on optimism, her mind couldn't forget what happened at their last attempt on the Matterhorn.

The descent down the mountain in the dark had been the worst moment of her life, and it had lasted thirteen hours. Helping secure her injured father in a rope-lattice cot, strung between her brother and Karl, had been surreal. But now that fever-dream came back to her mind's eye, more real with every step.

She shoved the uncertainty away. They'd learned from their mistakes. They had a smaller group and better equipment this time. The weather was good. Julian was not her father.

Yet, her mind kept treading over the same thought, that she had killed her father with her ambition, and she was about to kill Julian with it this time. That Justine and Karl might be seriously hurt, just as Prudence and Eleanor had been. And if Julian was hurt like her father, were they strong enough to carry him down? Or would they have to leave him to go get help? Would he die there?

The fear was overwhelming.

But then they got to Schwarzsee, where the whitewashed walls of the simple church gleamed in the sun. They stopped for water and had fruit from their packs. Julian stared at the Matterhorn, so elegantly framed by the grassy hills there. He sat on the warm rock, and while Ophelia wanted to sit with him, she couldn't bear it. The idea that any of them might be harmed was making it difficult to speak.

Justine noticed, her gaze sliding Ophelia's way frequently. She whispered something to Karl, and he summoned Julian. Justine shouldered her pack and came to where Ophelia stood.

"Tell me what's wrong," she said, gesturing to Ophelia's pack. "It's easier to talk when you're walking."

Ophelia shouldered her pack and obediently matched Justine's shorter stride. The sun was still out; afternoon clouds had not yet appeared. The Matterhorn sat aloof and heavy in front of them. Just like last time, they would camp at the Hörnli Ridge and wake up to begin climbing in the pre-dawn light. Because it wasn't necessarily the ascent where accidents happened. The vast majority of expeditions were injured on the way down. They needed the light for the descent.

When Ophelia didn't respond, still unable to bring voice to the gnawing anxiety, afraid to give it voice, Justine supplied it.

"Is it because of what happened last time?" she asked.

Ophelia nodded. A lump formed in her throat. Of all the ridiculous bodily responses. The lump made it hard for her to breathe. She gulped for air. Justine stopped and pulled at her arm, to ensure she stopped as well. The two men were well ahead, seemingly unbothered by the extra weight of the tent poles.

Justine gripped both of her arms. "Everything is going to be fine, Ophelia."

Pushing the lump away with all her might, Ophelia nodded. She closed her eyes, wishing away the terrible thoughts.

"We have Karl, a literal guide. Then you, who have a lot of experience. Then Julian, who is even more experienced. He told

Karl he was out on mountains almost every day of the last ten years. Some of them with higher altitudes than this one. He knows what he's doing."

Ophelia nodded, gobbling up her affirming words as if they were tender morsels and she no better than a dog.

"If anything, I'm the weakest of everyone. And you know that I'm not falling. I can't. I'm too close to the ground."

Ophelia's laugh came out suddenly, surprising her. Justine was right, of course. She was upset over imaginary things, not real events. "Perspective," she said, meaning she needed to have some.

"Perspective," Justine echoed back to her. "Shall we catch up to them?"

Ophelia smiled, feeling that lump in her throat receding, and the air all the more tolerable. "Let's go."

Justine's conversation was constant, which Ophelia found enjoyable. Others, she knew, found Justine to be too talkative, but at moments like these, Ophelia doubly appreciated Justine being exactly the way she was.

The stretch from Schwarzsee to the Hörnli Ridge was pleasant and not at all difficult. The men were there constructing the tent frame when they arrived. The mountain loomed behind them, huge and imposing. The afternoon clouds gathered at the top, and Ophelia wondered what it would be like to look at them from the top down instead of the bottom up. She got out the tent's canvas and handed it over to Julian. Between the two men, they had it set up in no time.

"Tristan is especially proud of this tent," Ophelia added, given both Karl and Julian were looking at it with suspicion.

"It feels like it's going to blow away in the wind," Julian said.

"I've never successfully had a tent on this ridge," Karl added.

Ophelia picked the biggest rock she could find and hauled it into the tent. The flapping of the canvas was loud from inside. And she wasn't certain they would all fit. She scrambled out. "I'm beginning to have my doubts as well."

"Why was he so proud of it?" Justine asked.

"The canvas is supposed to be wind-proof, and the tent poles are supposed to be lighter than the previous style's."

"Wind-proof?" Julian asked, raising one eyebrow. He ducked inside for a moment, but when he emerged, he shook his head. "I can't feel the wind, that's true. But it's like being in a rock grinder."

"Can't be all that bad." Justine ducked in, followed by Karl.

Karl's head peeked out from between the flaps. "I don't think we would all fit in here."

Justine pushed past him and emerged back out into the fresh air. "There is no way I could sleep in there. The sound is deafening."

"Should we take it down?" Julian asked. All three of them looked to her.

Because she was expedition lead. Giddiness flooded her. Any of them were strong, capable personalities. It would be reasonable to defer to Karl as an expert in alpine climbing, or Julian, with his ten years' worth of experience. But she was the declared leader, and this was her expedition.

"We should take it down lest it blow away," Ophelia said. The men nodded their assent, agreeing with her choice, and began to dismantle it. Pride welled in her. This would be the adventure she'd longed for, she was sure of it. The gnawing sensation evaporated, carried away by the whipping wind.

They settled in against the embankment of rocks that had grown since the last time they were there. Still, it was cold, and her ears ached from both the chill and constant whine of the wind. They set up their blanket bags, ate their cold dinner of cheese, apples, and nuts, and settled in. They would rise at three in the morning to begin their trek.

Justine and Karl snuggled in together, sharing body heat, and Ophelia shivered. Julian gazed across the hard rocky ground and pulled his arm out of his blanket bag, offering her a place next to him.

Ophelia frowned. Propriety dictated . . .

"Oh, go ahead," Justine said. "It's freezing, and there's two blankets between you. I won't tell."

Karl snorted, pulling his wife closer. Julian chuckled, nodding his head to reiterate the invitation. So Ophelia scooted over like an inchworm, awkwardly sliding over the protrusions of rock to settle in Julian's embrace.

Warmth and peace blossomed and in minutes, Ophelia was deep in sleep.

IT WAS DARK out, but Julian's eyes popped open. Ophelia still lay sprawled across his chest, and he did not wish to move her. Still. He glanced over at the other slumbering couple, and spied Karl striking a match to check his watch.

"Is it time?" Julian asked, breaking the ice-thin silence.

"It is." Karl shook out the match and pulled on his sweater and heavy woolen coat before exiting his blanket bag.

Julian was loath to move Ophelia, but he reminded himself that there would be opportunities to revel in her proximity later. He had just gained her forgiveness, and he was not about to disappoint her by not waking her. He touched her gently and murmured her name until she stirred.

Everyone dressed quickly, drinking water and pulling on their hobnailed boots. They took turns sewing the gaiters to their trousers at both the knee and to their boots, to protect their legs from snow. While the women still wore skirts, the thick woolen stockings might as well have been trousers. Though Julian still had to focus his mind as he sewed the gaiter flap to the inner lining of Ophelia's boot. She had a very shapely leg, and he remembered what it had felt like to wrap his hand around her bare ankle.

With the moon already setting and the only light a bit of

stardust, they left what they could at camp and started across the shoulder-wide stretch of the Hörnli Ridge.

They were roped together at the waist, with Ophelia at the front, Julian second, Justine third, and Karl last. She set a commanding pace, but not an uncomfortable one. Indeed, as they picked across the dark ridge, skirted a bulbous formation and began a scramble up the face of the Matterhorn, Julian found himself enjoying the exertion. It was . . . fun.

Rarely had he found compatriots for such a climb, and here he was exchanging grins with each of them as loose rocks rolled down, or one of them peered across a glacier. Words weren't needed. Stories weren't told. They all took turns letting out whoops of joy after jumping off a boulder, or when a fresh, cold breeze whipped past them.

They stopped and turned as the sun rose, sitting on a stone ledge wide enough for all four of them. From midway up the mountain, they swung their legs out over the expanse beneath them passing around slices of Frau Brunner's day-old buttered bread and sour apples.

"This couldn't be more perfect," Ophelia whispered.

Julian found her hand and was happy when she squeezed his back. Justine put her head on her husband's shoulder and sighed as the orangey-pink newness painted across all their faces.

They were at one of the edges of the world, a place that felt as if very few would ever trespass its exact stones. Their toil and sweat granted them the precious dispensation to see the sun rise in such a spectacular manner.

Once the sun had climbed into view, Ophelia stood. "Climbing?" she asked.

"Climb on," Karl said.

They continued up, stopping only when they arrived at the chimneys—a place heavily discussed the day before en route to Schwarzsee. Ophelia's face went ashen. This was where Rascomb had his fatal injury. It had turned the previous party around, as it had many other expeditions. They unroped while Karl pulled a belt with a metal loop from his pack. And before Julian unlooped his climbing ax, he took Ophelia's gloved hand again. It took her a moment to blink and turn to him, squeezing his hand, an expression of determination on her face. Once he had that assurance, he adjusted his clothing until the rope was snugly fit around his waist and the ax dangled from his wrist by its fabric loop.

"Ready?" Ophelia prompted, and they all nodded, performing the same actions with gear from their own packs. Armed with far more equipment than last time, Julian knew she was overcompensating for the previous failure. But it made sense. And he would happily carry safety gear. Ophelia nodded to Karl, who had successfully climbed this chimney formation dozens of times.

He spidered up the ice and stone wall faster than Julian could trace. While Julian had been nicknamed the goat, Karl was far more capable. His prowess was impressive, and a goat nickname was not near apt enough.

At the top, Karl fastened the rope and threw it down for them. Ophelia glanced at both him and Justine before taking the rope and threading it through the metal loop on her belt. Her ax dangled from her wrist, easy to use should she need the grip. But she didn't. She deliberated upon each move of her hand and her foot, which meant that her climb took ten times longer than Karl's had, but she reached the top without a single slip. Justine went next, and like Ophelia, she pondered each move. But with her short stature, she was unable to use the holds that both Ophelia and Karl had. Still, she scrambled her way to the top.

Julian was last, and while it was cold business to press his body against a sheet of icy rock, he had been through worse. He didn't dare say so, but it was not the ordeal he'd worried it might be.

At the top, Ophelia stared off into the distance as they stowed their gear.

"Are you well?" he asked.

She turned to him, her eyes startlingly blue in the midmorning light. "We've already made it farther in a few hours than we did that entire day."

He heard the sadness in her voice, tinged with astonishment. As if she hadn't believed it could be such a smooth endeavor.

"Karl. It's time for you to lead the way." Ophelia sighed and tied in, now taking the second position. Justine came third, and Julian was in the back.

They hadn't but stepped around a rock when they discovered the beginnings of a small hut.

"I didn't expect that," Justine muttered.

But then, there had been many deaths, and this chimney had been the crux of the route for many expeditions. It made sense that if a shelter were to exist anywhere on the mountain, it would be there.

"I'd heard about this," Karl called from in front.

They peered in, only to find one small room with no furnishings. It was purely meant for shelter. This would save more than one climber's life, that much was certain. Thankfully, they didn't need use of it.

They skirted around the rock and began another ascent, full of boulders. They were tiring, yes, a staircase made for a giant. None of the distances were large enough for each climber to require assistance, but each step required a great deal of effort. Their pace slowed as they neared the next change in rock texture.

Scree fields. Julian hated scree fields. Some loved them—the scramble was part of the fun. But he'd a fear of them suddenly, for no real reason. It was the inability to make certain purchase. But one couldn't effectively climb a mountain without entering scree fields on a regular basis.

They stopped on the top of the last boulder, breathing heavily, staring at each other, nodding in silent agreement that they were accomplishing their goal well. Crusty snow coated the far side of the scree field, giving them ample views of how the icy side closest to the mountain was pulling away, ready to come crashing down. It was reminder of how lucky they'd been with the weather so far, but the warmer part of the day was still ahead of them. Snow and rockslides remained pending disasters.

"Climbing?" Ophelia prompted.

They all nodded and Karl set off, leading them in a diagonal across the scree field. It was a longer route, but it kept them from a steep angle that would make it more likely for them to slip. It was drudgery, Julian's feet sinking into the small mounds of pebbles. The rhythmic crush of them trudging up the hillside put them into a trance. He was grateful for the gaiters, as they kept out the smallest of them. He could feel the snow-tinged air coming off the other side of the mountain, and he knew they were close. This would be the push right here.

He heard it before he felt it. The too-low sound of a foot sinking deeper than it ought, then the yelp as Karl slipped. Ophelia must have looked up too quickly, because she too was sliding down the mountain on her belly.

Justine cried out in alarm, still standing. Julian rushed up to her, grabbed the ax from her pack loop, and slammed it as hard as he could into the rock. If there had been more time, he would have instructed Justine to grab his, as the only way to access the tool was to take the pack off entirely.

He hoped Karl and Ophelia would stop sliding of their own accord, but they were too far to the left of the mountain face, which cut off in a sheer drop. If they fell there, it would be fatal.

Julian threw himself to the ground, gripping the handle of the ax, hoping he had enough purchase to keep them all on the mountainside. "Get down!" he screamed at Justine.

Justine obeyed, and they both watched, terrified as the people they loved slid further away. She was murmuring *No* over and over. His mind wouldn't work. It was as if even his lungs wouldn't work without Ophelia in the world.

His body ached in abject and impotent fury as he watched. Ophelia ducked her golden head. Her shoulders strained as she dug in, pebbles flying as she pushed her feet out wide. Karl did the same, but Julian couldn't watch the man. His heart was shooting away from his chest, tucked safely inside Ophelia's woolen layers. *Please*, he begged over and over again. *Please*. He couldn't be left alone again. Not now.

The ropes grew taut as the span widened between Julian and Justine and Ophelia and Karl. But they were slowing! Julian caught his breath. They might make it. The sound stopped. Julian refocused out of his terror. All he could hear was his own ragged breath.

"Fee?" Justine called out. "Karl?"

Ophelia was dug in, her golden head down in the scree. But at least she wasn't falling.

The guide lifted his hand and gave a curt wave. He clawed his way over to Ophelia, and Julian watched with desperation. But she lifted her head and waved. Julian heaved in relief, eyes welling up. What would he have done if he'd lost her?

The two heads were close together, then Karl shifted and Ophelia took out his ax from his loop, and then she turned and he retrieved hers.

"Don't move," Karl called.

"Hang on," Julian told Justine.

None of them spoke as Karl and Ophelia pulled themselves back over to them on their bellies, breaths heaving and the puff of steam from their mouths a joy. When they got close enough, Justine pulled Karl into her arms, and Julian did the same—hauling Ophelia the last foot and rolling over onto his back.

"I'm so glad you're safe," he breathed, his eyes closing for the first time since the horrific sound of their slide. He opened his them and inspected her. Smudges of dirt streaked her face, and a small cut on her forehead oozed bright red. "Are you hurt?"

She shook her head. "Only scared. But that was temporary. My mittens are a bit scuffed."

Which was an understatement. The drab brown things had an open flap, displaying the innards of undyed wool. He held her close.

"We're nearly there," she said, calm and unflappable.

"I thought you were scared," he said, thinking she might need longer to steady herself.

"I was scared. When I was sliding. But now I'm not sliding, so I'm no longer scared. We should get to the top." Ophelia rolled off him and pushed to her feet, pulling the rope line clear of the others. "Let's get to it."

Julian shook his head in amazement. He thought he was good at keeping his feelings at bay.

They got to their feet, restored axes to pack loops, and carried on. For they couldn't exactly stop there on the scree field, could they? He admired her. More than he'd ever thought possible. Her bravery. Her skill. Any person—male or female—would not be thought a fool if they sank into a babbling wreck after such a slide. But Ophelia lifted her head and told them to climb.

⇥⟫⟫⟨⟨⇤

NEARLY THERE. OPHELIA was sweating beneath her dress, and the accordion bunching had failed early on. She no longer had the luxury of hands-free skirt hiking. It was her damned skirt that caused her to slip and lose her footing, and she might never forgive dresses for nearly killing her. Karl had turned to see what the issue was and misstepped, which had startled her in turn, and down they both went.

She appreciated Julian's concern, but they needed to focus. Past the scree field was one last climb, and then they would be at the top. Head down and eyes open. The air was cold in her lungs, but her icy veins only invigorated her.

Fog enveloped them, misting around them and obscuring everything but the rock in front of her. It was difficult to see Karl ahead or even Justine and Julian behind, their outlines obscured, the edges of the mountain a mystery. But then they trudged clear of the fog, and she felt the sun strong and warm on her back. The sweat dripped from her temples and she wanted to tear the woolen cap from her head, but she didn't.

Suddenly, Karl stopped and ushered her forward. "This is it. Ophelia. You first."

They'd done it. They were here. She took the final steps up the ridge. And there was the top. She summited.

This was no peak, but a flat stage, small and mighty. Her eyes welled up. This was what it was for. All around her was a lake of clouds. She stood in the sky.

Julian was beside her. She smiled, no doubt like a lunatic, but she didn't care. This was it. They were here. She gripped his hand hard. How she'd wished her father could have seen this: the stretch of clouds, the incalculable blue of the sky, the yellow sun hot and bright. But he would have been proud of her. After all, she was Ophelia Bridewell, and when she got an idea into her head, it was going to happen. And she'd gotten that from him.

"This is incredible," he whispered.

She stifled a sob. "Welcome to the sky."

Chapter Eighteen

"J USTINE!" OPHELIA CALLED.

"I believe that is my cue," Julian murmured, his hand slipping around Ophelia's waist for a brief moment.

She looked him in the eye, in love with him, the mountain, the world. And his dark eyes mirrored her emotions, understanding what it was for her to stand here, and why she needed Justine at her side, too.

He stepped off the summit, ushering Justine to join her.

Justine immediately turned in a circle, while Ophelia guarded her with her arms, hoping she wouldn't step off the edge. But then Justine threw her arms around Ophelia. "We did it," she whispered. "Oh, Fee, this is amazing."

Ophelia wrapped her arms around her friend in return. "We did it," she repeated, the years of work and effort, the fundraising, the excursions, the hardship. It culminated here. They were at the top.

"I wish Prudence and Eleanor were here," Justine sniffed.

"Me too," Ophelia said, happy to let the sun blind her eyes for longer. It would have been quite a triumph for all four of them to be up here, but she understood. Prudence had never had the bug the way the rest of them did. And Eleanor was starting her family—something she hadn't believed she would ever do. They had priorities that came before this mountain, while Ophelia didn't.

After a few more minutes of embracing Justine at the summit of the Matterhorn, wishing for her mother, her brother, her friends, and her father most of all, Ophelia was ready to face the next challenge. Justine wanted a few more moments at the top, so Ophelia stepped away carefully to let Karl join her.

Ophelia stepped down and into Julian's arms. She felt as if she could die right then and be content with her accomplishments. Not that she wanted to, but her goals had been achieved. She had published an article in a prestigious journal, and she had summited the lethal Matterhorn. To add to the incredibility of it all, she was in love.

Since Justine and Karl's backs were turned, Ophelia dared to lift her face to Julian's. She studied his dark eyes, suddenly certain that his love was no false play, no vanity, no push for money or status. "Would you kiss me?" she whispered.

He grinned and leaned down, stopping his mouth mere millimeters from hers. "Are you certain?"

She gave him a look of utter impatience and made up the distance herself. Both of their faces were cold, while the sensation was pleasant, there was not enough feeling in her lips to kiss him properly. "I think we should marry."

⋙✦⋘

JULIAN COUGHED IN surprise. Right then, Karl and Justine stepped off the summit, cutting short their conversation. But Ophelia didn't seem to care if they knew, so she looked at Julian expectantly.

"Do we need to, er," Julian coughed again. "Isn't there someone we have to talk to?"

She looked around, and seeing only their four-person expedition, she asked, "Who would we talk to?"

Julian's eyes widened. "Your brother? A lawyer? The Queen? You are a viscount's daughter. I don't know what the protocol is."

Ophelia waved her hand. "I'm sure it's fine. We'll figure it out."

"But—Lord Fairport—" Julian couldn't believe he was actually saying the man's name. That awful, money-grubbing liar.

Ophelia made a face that made it clear she felt the same way. "Never liked him very much. Shall we start down?"

Julian blinked. Was the matter settled? His protests were merely ones of protocol. He didn't want to entangle her in a family squabble that could have been avoided if they'd exercised patience.

The others were already picking their way down as he stood there, thinking.

"Coming?" Justine called back over her shoulder.

Julian obeyed the summons and started down as well. Down climbing was clearly far more difficult and exhausting than the ascent. They made it through the fog of clouds, as if they were descending back down to earth. It was easy to see how deaths occurred as they skidded down the scree fields and bands of snow. Julian held his breath watching Ophelia take the large steps that sunk into the soft scree pebbles. He didn't understand how she wasn't terrified.

The ground stretched out below them for miles, and the sense of gravity was far more intense, pulling and gripping them. He'd never had these thoughts before—something about his feelings for Ophelia had awakened him to the dangers of the mountains. But she acquitted herself nimbly.

They came around boulders, the snowy expanse that had taken the lives of the four men on the Whymper expedition. Julian's left foot slipped.

Perhaps he was too busy looking over the cliff. Perhaps the noon sun had gotten in his eyes. Or melted the snow.

He scrambled to regain balance, leaning back only to land hard on his arse. Before he could even register the pain of the landing, he had already slid past Ophelia, whose eyes widened as she saw him falling.

"Hold on!" Ophelia screamed.

But soon he was past her, and then past Justine, who exclaimed, "Scheisse!" And while he didn't have time to ponder what language to swear in, it struck him as oddly funny.

Oddly funny for a man who was about to fly off a cliff onto a glacier far below. He tried to sink his feet into the snow, but it was crusted over with ice. He couldn't get purchase. He flipped onto his stomach, digging the spikes they'd nailed onto the front of their boots into the ice. A mitten slid off and he sank his nails into the ice, feeling them give way against the superior force of Mother Nature.

Ice shards cut across his face, stinging his skin. *What a terrible waste*, he thought. *I just fell in love.*

And then the rope around his waist yanked him hard to a stop. His intestines squeezed like they were being pressed into jelly, but he was grateful. The coolness of his emotions evaporated. His heart pounded hard as nausea flooded him. He laid his cheek on the freezing icy crust of the ground.

"Julian!" Ophelia shouted.

He steadied his breath and got to his hands and knees, testing the traction of his location. "I'm all right," he called back.

The rest of them let out a collective sigh. He looked up to see them all sitting on the side of the mountain. Ophelia had run uphill to the nearest boulder, effectively looping the rope that connected them all around the rock, which was then used to anchor him.

His hands shook. Not far away was his mitten. His fingers throbbed, and when he inspected his bright pink hand, he saw blood from where his nails had almost been torn off. Slowly, he inched over to his mitten. And then back to the trail where his friends waited for him. Time, for once, was on his side, and they could take longer here if they needed.

Ophelia unwrapped her rope and joined him, touching his cheek, her finger coming away with a sliver of blood painted across her pad.

"Let's get off this fucking mountain," Justine said, breaking their trance.

"Ready?" Ophelia asked him in a whisper.

Julian nodded and straightened. More than she knew. He was ready for all of it. Marriage, London, writing, perhaps taking up teaching, or if Ophelia wanted to keep exploring, he would do that. He didn't care anymore. His life was meaningless without her. Had it ended there, and he was merely another life claimed by the Matterhorn, every breath he'd ever taken would have been wasted.

His triumphs had been empty. Another man would have come along and made the same measurements, the same survey, done the same calculations to discover the topography. But going forward, he would be a man who loved Ophelia Bridewell, a man who would be the companion of a fearless lady explorer. A woman who blazed trails and uplifted other women. He could help her credibility in the wider world. He could help her publish. And that would be how his legacy could be remembered. A man who did not take, but rather a man who gave.

And if she would let him, he would give it all to her.

The rest of the mountain passed in a daze for him. At one point, Justine slipped and twisted her ankle—surprisingly difficult to do in the hobnailed boots. Karl fussed at her, and she fussed back until Ophelia prodded them on.

As Justine claimed, her limp evened out as they continued. The wind chilled them as they passed back over the long, thin Hörnli Ridge, until they dipped low enough to escape it. By late afternoon, they arrived back at their camp.

Julian stared at the tent poles and blanket bags they left there. They were all exhausted and hungry and cold. Even the exultation of summiting had faded. They all wanted to be back at the inn, tucking into a large, hot dinner.

Without much conversation, they packed up their remaining items and trudged on. Another few hours to the inn. They walked quickly now that they were on a relatively flat trail. No more ice or scree or lethal cliffs. The dirt on the trail made him feel almost weightless, considering the difficulty he'd already subjected himself to. He glanced over at Ophelia, who seemed tired, but happy.

She flashed him a smile that energized him. Her lifelong goal was accomplished. A sense of pride bubbled up inside of him as well. This was not the most elevation he'd ever scaled, but it had been technically more challenging.

They passed the white-walled church, knowing there were only a few more miles left until dinner. The timing would be perfect, though Julian wished they weren't conforming to European standards of being dressed for the evening meal. He wanted to drop into his seat as he was, needing the energy to bathe.

As they passed through the trees, still not talking, Julian had to marvel. The difference a year had made for him. A confirmed bachelor, dead set on returning to South America. Now, a man who intended to marry the woman marching next to him, ready to take his next cues from her.

There was clamor in the back of his head about money and work and setting up a life for them. But his heart was clear and true. He would make this work in whatever way he could. They would, as Ophelia said, figure it out.

"Almost there," Karl called over his shoulder.

Ophelia glanced at him, this time a mischievous grin replacing her wide smile. Her pace quickened. He grinned back; food, clean clothing, a warm bath, those were all waiting for them. He matched her pace. When he caught up, she quickened more, and he matched. Soon, they were all-out running, leaving Karl and Justine behind them. Their packs shook awkwardly on their backs, but it didn't matter. He carried more weight, and Ophelia was quick. They matched pace until they collapsed in front of the inn, gasping for breath.

"I'm telling your mother how uncouth you are," Justine called to Ophelia as she and Karl made their way to the inn at a regular pace.

Ophelia let out a peal of laughter that Julian had never heard before. It sounded like bells. He wanted to hear that sound every day for the rest of his life.

THEY ALL DROPPED their packs in Justine and Karl's larger double room. One by one, they all surreptitiously rolled their shoulders, the ache of heavy packs finally easing. She caught Justine's eye. "We did it," Ophelia whispered.

"I knew we would," Justine whispered back, and then threw herself into Ophelia's embrace. Over Ophelia's shoulder, Justine added, "Your father would be so proud of you."

Which of course, made Ophelia cry. Tears that had been pent up and waiting for over a year spilled over out of her control. A tension that she had been holding shuddered and released and she sagged against Justine.

Justine shushed and rocked her from side to side. Ophelia wept with relief, with pride, with grief. Finally, she pulled away, wiping her eyes as she did. Justine was prepared, already handing her a handkerchief. Obediently, Ophelia wiped her nose and straightened, realizing suddenly that the men were no longer in the room.

"They went down to see if dinner could be extended for us."

"Oh. That's—" Ophelia had no more energy left to converse or move or anything. "—that's a really good idea."

"Here," Justine guided her over to the dressing table and poured some water in the bowl. "Splash some water on your face. Freshen things up."

Ophelia obeyed, and as she was wiping the grit of her sweat from her hairline, the door opened.

"Come down, no need to change clothes," Karl said, beckoning. "The dining room is cleared out, so it will just be us. My

Tante will serve us herself."

Karl held out his arm, dusty and dirty as it was. But none of them were any better. Julian appeared behind him and waited for the other couple to pass before he lifted his arm to her. Ophelia could have fallen into him just as easily as taking his arm.

"Are you well?" he asked, his dark eyebrows knitting together in concern. "Your lips are blue."

Ophelia glanced down at her fingernails, which showed them to be purple. She shivered, unable to tell how she was feeling. Lightheaded from exhaustion, fatigue, and hunger. "I need food."

"Frau Brunner is serving up the soup course as we speak."

They descended down to the dining room, and Ophelia was so grateful to sit. Frau Brunner set the bowls of dumpling soup with large slabs of dark bread slathered thick with fresh butter on the side in front of each of them.

There was no time to stand on ceremony when one was this hungry. Ophelia could feel each mouthful of broth slide down her throat, warming her from the inside out. The dumpling was delicious and salty and soft, and the bread and butter tasted of anise and nuts. As they were finishing, Frau Brunner brought them four aperitif glasses, filled with an amber-colored liqueur.

Ophelia didn't want to pause her eating but was disappointed to see she'd finished her soup. Herr Brunner came out of the kitchen, holding two more of the amber-filled glasses. He handed one to his wife and raised his to give a toast.

He spoke in German, but even through her haze, Ophelia understood the overall message of celebration and accomplishment. They toasted and Ophelia watched as they all tipped back their glasses. So she did the same, and the sweet amber liquid burned all the way down. Her head swam as her body warmed.

Soon, Frau Brunner returned with more plates, this time of meat and carrots and parsnips and yams and potatoes. Ophelia devoured it all, wishing there was more bread to clean the plate of its sauces.

Herr Brunner brought out a bottle of port and filled their

small glasses again. Then he disappeared with the four empty plates, and Frau Brunner returned with thick slabs of apfelkuchen, cheese, and walnuts.

This time, Herr Brunner left them after pouring the libation. Ophelia sat back, enjoying the fullness of her belly and the fuzzy warmth of her feet.

Julian raised his glass of port as Justine folded a slice of hard cheese into her mouth.

"We sit with two of the four women to have ever summited the Matterhorn," he said. "Impressive company indeed."

Karl raised his glass. "The most fearless of climbers, and women without peer."

Ophelia allowed the laughter to bubble out of her, but the two men kept their glasses raised until she and Justine scrambled to meet their gesture. "And to the men who help."

They clinked their glasses together and she sipped at the port. It was a flavor full of dark cherries and molasses and tobacco. Quite a difference from the bright sweetness of the first drink. She dug into the apfelkuchen as Justine set herself to the cheese.

Frau Brunner brought out small cups of coffee. "For digestion," she said as she rubbed her stomach.

Considering how much Ophelia had already eaten, the coffee was probably a good idea. It wasn't as if it would keep her up. The early morning and the unconquerable fatigue of climbing almost 15,000 feet into the sky would see to that.

The coffee enlivened all of them, and they recounted the day to each other, comparing perceptions. Karl confessed to having nerves at the chimneys, even though he climbed without hesitation. They compared and measured the small scratches on their faces from the scree and ice sprays, discussed bruises that might appear overnight, and laughed at the hilarity of success. She didn't want the night to be over, but they were all exhausted, and didn't want to make more work for Frau and Herr Brunner, who had been so solicitous.

When Ophelia finally stood up, her feet felt twice the size of the boots they were squeezed into. "I don't think I can bathe tonight," she said. "I'm too tired."

"Tomorrow," Justine agreed. "Tomorrow, I will be very clean. Tonight, I just want my bed. Karl, can you carry me?"

Ophelia knew that Justine had said the last part as a joke, but Karl swooped in and hoisted her across his shoulders like some kind of livestock.

"I didn't mean like this," Justine wailed, but she didn't fight it. Ophelia laughed at her friends, her heart full. At the first floor, Julian peeled off from their troupe.

"Goodnight all. Thank you for this incredible journey." He bowed slightly at the waist, and Ophelia felt a pang of longing for him. She wished he were joining her.

"Goodnight," they all said in their own time without pausing their upward trajectory. To stop might mean to never start again. On the next floor, Ophelia went to her room, and the Vogels went to theirs.

In her room, Ophelia looked longingly at the bed, but then collapsed onto her chair to dislodge her boots. She had to pick the stitches from the gaiters and her stockings before she could untie the bootlaces. Once those were off, she felt almost energized, as if that was the refresh she needed to keep undressing. The thick woolen stockings were next, and it felt somewhat strange to not have anything between her outer dress and her legs. They'd not worn chemises because of the need for free movement of their legs.

After disrobing completely, she poured water into the bowl on her dressing table and used the rag to clean herself. Dirt and salt had mixed at her elbows and neckline. Once she'd scrubbed as well as she was going to without having a proper bath, she stepped into a fresh chemise, and it was like stepping into a brand-new life. Her bed was going to feel so good.

But there was a scratching at her door. Was it Justine, coming to check on her? She pulled on her robe but didn't bother belting it as she opened the door.

It wasn't Justine.

Julian stood there in his shirt sleeves. His dark hair was rumpled as if he'd been running his hands through it. He looked almost wild but for the singular focus as he gazed at her.

"Is everything all right?" Ophelia asked, drawing her robed closed.

"We should get married."

It took her a moment to sort what he had said. "What about your concerns? My brother and Lord Fairport?"

"I don't want to marry them." He shook his head, looking very firm about that.

Ophelia laughed. "I don't want to, either."

"Good. So we are agreed?"

"Agreed." She stuck her hand out, and they shook hands like the Americans. But Julian didn't let her hand go.

"I need you, Ophelia. Today proved it to me."

His broad palm was calloused and firm, and she remembered how it had felt all over her body back in Paris. How she wanted to arch into him. "I was terrified that I was going to lose you when you slipped."

He nodded. "You caught me. And I'll catch you. We can keep each other safe better than anyone else."

She knew he meant more than just the mountain. He meant the whole world. There were people who could be shelters in the storm of humanity, and as Justine had always been one, Julian could be another. And she could be one for him. "What about—"

"I don't care, Ophelia. Whatever it is, we can figure it out."

And that was all she needed. She yanked on his hand, pulling him inside her room. She pushed the door closed, and him up against it. Pressed against the expanse of his chest, she looked into his coal-dark eyes. "This is forever."

"At the minimum," he said, his hands coming to cradle her jaw.

His mouth was at hers, and the communion she'd longed for was finally here. After so many months aching for him, he was hers.

"How do you smell of lavender?" He panted as he kissed along her cheek and neck.

"I washed—I didn't want to go to bed feeling all that grit on my skin." She managed to get the sentence out, even as her senses were filled with Julian's smell and touch and feel.

He half-groaned, half-growled. "I shouldn't be the one to bring dirt into your bed."

Her vision swam more than it had after the port at dinner. "Then let me wash you," she gasped as one of his hands palmed her arse, pulling her against him, the length of his manhood evident.

He released her, and she backed up to the dressing table. Indicating the chair, she said, "Sit."

It took him a moment of looking at her, so long that she became self-conscious at how the dressing gown must be gaping open, letting him see her through the flimsy material of her clean chemise.

But then he sauntered over and sat, looking at her, never breaking the singular eye contact that connected them. She knelt and picked the stitches of the gaiters against his trouser legs. He toyed with her hair, and she couldn't help but notice the shallow breaths he took as he wove the strands around his fingers. She helped remove his boots, as dirty and mud-encrusted as hers had been. Then she stood between his legs and unbuttoned his shirt until it was loose enough to pull over his head. She pushed the braces off one shoulder, then the other, enjoying brushing her hands over his capable arms.

He pulled the shirt off himself, and she dipped and rung out the rag from her washbasin. She ran it over his face first, cleaning his hairline and then around his ears. He closed his eyes as she cleaned his neck and shoulders. She rewet and rung out the rag again, sweeping over his pectoral muscles, and under his arms. Attending to each arm with care, after his right arm was done, he began caressing her in turn.

She turned her attention to his fingernails, where dried blood outlined the nail beds. His fall on the mountain had clearly hurt him worse than he'd wanted to mention. "Does this hurt?" she asked, running the rag gently into the crevices. Julian shook his head. After she finished one hand, she laid it against her cheek, reveling in the wide palms and calloused fingers.

He stroked her face with his thumb, and when she turned to his other hand, he let that one fall, tracing along her neck, her clavicle, her shoulder. His palm grazed her breast, and they both sucked in air at the contact, but he skimmed his hand back up to her hair, as if he wasn't ready to go further.

But she was ready to go further. After she cleaned the other hand, she kissed the nail of his middle finger. His dark eyebrow went up, a spark evident in his eye. Slowly, experimentally, he pressed the finger on her bottom lip. She didn't know how she knew what to do, only that he was asking for something, and she wanted to give it. She opened her mouth, and he slid his finger inside. The rough callous of his finger was a harsh texture against her tongue, and Julian exhaled sharply as she licked.

He withdrew his finger, and she rewet and rung the rag again, now with both of his hands roaming. Between her legs, her own pulse had quickened, and she felt a longing for what she had felt before. Starting at his neck, she drew lower, descending down towards his waistline. He groaned and one hand palmed her arse, while the other reached up to cup her breast.

Her eyes fluttered shut at his touch. So welcome. So wanted. "I'm never going to finish washing you at this rate."

He chuckled and reached up to slip her dressing gown off her shoulders. It fell to the floor in a heap. Ophelia kicked it away. Julian pulled her down to take her nipple into his mouth through the sheer chemise fabric. After the physical abuse of the day, the sensation felt decadent. He kneaded her arse as he sucked, only making her feel drowsy with desire.

"I will have to clean you before you get into my bed," she whispered, barely able to form words.

He grunted. "But you taste so good." He took her other nipple into his mouth.

She let him go longer until she could barely stand it, wanting his fingers between her legs, wanting to have a turn enjoying his body as he enjoyed hers. "You must stand."

With a frustrated groan, he pulled away, leaving two wet spots on her chemise and her nipples hard and aching. He stood, and there was a moment of delight for her to see how much taller he was. Broader. Different. She unbuttoned his trousers and let them fall.

She picked up the rag absently, staring at his cock jutting up out of the thick thatch of dark hair.

"Please don't make me wait, Ophelia."

She dragged her attention back up to his eyes, where she could see barely restrained desire. It matched hers. And she liked hearing him beg. She took the rag to his hips, and he gasped at the cool water combined with her hot touch. His thighs were corded with muscle, defined from hours spent in the mountains. She cleaned front and back, taking a moment to cup his firm arse as he had hers. The thought of him thrusting into her while she dug her fingers into his firm buttock was intoxicating.

Begrudgingly, she continued down to his shapely calves and then to his foot. And then she rewet the rag and started the process on the other side, lingering again on his thigh and his arse. A drop of liquid formed on his cock, which waved and pulsed of its own accord. "Do you not have control of it?" she asked as it bobbed.

He laughed hoarsely. "Not right now."

After the other leg was clean, she rinsed the rag and set about cleaning the last spot. Gently, she brought it between his legs, cupping him there, and suddenly his hands gripped her wrist. He sucked in a breath and closed his eyes.

"Careful there. I want to be inside you, and I can't if I climax too soon."

"Guide me," she said. Covering her hand with his, he pulled her slowly over his testicles and along the solid length of his cock.

She couldn't decide where to watch, the fascinating ways his cock changed with her hand, or the expression of pleasure on Julian's beautiful face.

"I can't last much longer, Ophelia, I'm sorry."

"Don't ever be sorry, Julian," she said, taking the rag and dropping it back in the washbasin. She pulled him over to the narrow bed, and then took her chemise off. His rough hand skimmed the side of her body, his touch so light that her flesh prickled.

"Do you know how much I love you?" he asked, pulling at her hair, running his fingers down her neck. Every single one of his touches both more than she ever could have asked for, and yet, still not enough.

"You've never told me." Her heart pounded harder, waiting to hear this one confirmation: that he did love her.

"I couldn't sleep when we were apart. I thought of you constantly. I was so ashamed to think that I had hurt you, or belittled you, or ruined you."

"The idea that I could be ruined is—"

He captured her mouth, thumbing her nipple and pulling her thigh around his. Her wetness caught the cool air of the room. "No politics. No world. Just us."

"Just us," she repeated and laid back onto the bed, pulling him on top of her. She liked the weight of him, the pressure of his body on hers, even though he braced himself on his elbows.

One hand drifted down her body and in between her legs. He stroked there, slow and full. She was exhausted and needy, straining and relaxed, and the opposing feelings quieted all her thoughts and stoked her desire more and more. She forced her eyes open, her muscles tensing.

"Are you almost there?" he asked.

"Yes," she panted.

He stopped stroking with his hand, and instead gripped himself, using the head of his cock to run the length of her. "I'm glad you're wet. I want us to be together when we climax."

"Just . . . like . . ." Ophelia gritted her teeth, her desire growing stronger and stronger, threatening to spill over. Then he pushed his cock into her slowly. "The summit."

She pulled up her legs so he could get closer, go deeper, and gripped his arse to pull him in. He thrust deep and hard, and she came apart, dismantling all sense of self as she cried out.

He thrust twice more, and then pulled out, spilling all over her belly. He groaned and rolled to his side, barely fitting on the bed. She felt the loss of his heat, even as she was barely aware of herself apart from him.

"Don't go far," she mumbled.

"Can't," he panted.

Ophelia peeled one eye open. His head hung down, eyes closed, features slack. She was about to express concern, when he shook his head.

"I thought I wasn't going to make it. That I would be like one of those animals that dispensed so much seed that it sapped my life force."

Ophelia laughed, pleased with herself. She looked down at the sticky pool on her belly, pointing. "Is this not normal?"

"Not for any man over the age of thirty." Julian hoisted himself to his feet and retrieved the infamous rag. He cleaned her gently and threw it back in the washbasin.

"I don't want you to leave yet," she said, hoping he would join her back in the narrow bed.

"Surely you jest. Karl would have to bring in four more built just like him to drag me away from your bed." He slid back into the bed, one arm under her, embracing her.

She was going to say more. There was supposed to be more conversation. "I love you," she whispered, settling into his shoulder, and that was the last she remembered. Surrounded by his scent, his solid presence, there was nowhere on the earth she'd rather be. At least, for the foreseeable future.

Epilogue

"WHAT ABOUT THIS route?" Tristan pointed over her shoulder.

Ophelia swatted his hand. "Don't touch my maps with your dirty fingers."

"My fingers aren't dirty," Tristan protested.

"Are you not changing the nappies as you ought?" Justine teased him from across the room.

"I could," Tristan said. "But I'm rather bad at it, so I don't."

Justine rolled her eyes.

"Then do better," Ophelia said. "Learn."

"I'd rather he not," Eleanor said from the corner. She held the babe in question, little Prudence, who was sleeping contentedly. "I have a system."

Tristan raised his eyebrows. "Not my fault."

"If only there were decent topographical maps," Julian said.

"I thought—" Karl said.

"I'm being facetious," Julian said.

"After all, the Royal Geographical Society is paying for the excursion," Tristan said with exaggerated snobbishness.

"Not exactly," Ophelia said, finally lifting her gaze from her maps. "It is being paid for by Lord Fairport."

Karl choked on a currant. "The man you were once going to marry?"

"That's the one," Julian chirped.

"His wife, the American, has developed a keen interest in mountaineering and wants to have an outfit she designed tested in real conditions," Ophelia said.

In the background, baby Prudence gurgled.

"Probably because you've been publishing all of your fascinating articles," Justine said. Even Ophelia could hear the pride in her voice. If she were among anyone but her good friends, she might blush.

The butler, a young man who was still training, Nicholas Michaels, appeared in the doorway. "Mr. and Mrs. Moon," he announced, trying very hard to sound official.

"Prudence!" Justine tried to jump up, but her overripe belly kept her from moving quickly. She hugged the taller woman as best she could, which only made Ophelia laugh. She laughed so much these days.

"Nicholas, can you please fetch young Arthur from the nursery? He's going to want to see his auntie and uncle," Tristan said.

"And the nurse can take little Prudence to nap afterwards," Eleanor said, getting to her feet smoothly.

Ophelia didn't say anything, rather just stepped into Prudence's waiting arms. The four of them were together again, The Ladies' Alpine Society, complete as they were. They would grow next year when Justine's first was born, and perhaps Prudence would have children.

She and Julian had discussed growing a family, but instead they opted for adventure. A lifetime of exploration, surveying, mapping, and writing. There was so much to innovate in their world—clothing, gear, ropes, tents. And with Tristan's outfitters' shop, Ophelia's articles, and Julian's maps, they were a nexus on the forefront of Alpinism.

The only part of her life that stung was that her father had not lived long enough to see it. But Ophelia counted herself lucky that she'd had a father as supportive as hers. That she lived a life able to climb, able to find a freedom that so many women didn't. But, as Julian said, by cutting the trail, other women could follow behind her, and have an easier path.

Other people were better suited for charity work and motherhood. Others were better at campaigning for women's suffrage and more freedom under the laws. But what Ophelia could do was prove what women could *be*. That there was not only a mind and a body, but a will and a strength that could not be defeated. And that inside every person beat that same pulse, man or woman.

For, as Julian liked to say, "Climbing a mountain is an exercise in suffering." And as Ophelia always countered, "But reaching the summit is an exercise in triumph."

The End.

Historical Note

I hope you have enjoyed reading the Ladies' Alpine Society. While these four women are fictional, the world in which they inhabit is not. British climber Lucy Walker was indeed the first woman to summit the Matterhorn in 1871, followed shortly by American Meta Brevoort. Both women were in the midst of men climbers, and both had climbed and stayed in Zermatt at the Monte Rose hotel every summer for years, waiting to find the best window to attempt the Matterhorn.

These women climbed in long woolen skirts, and the innovation Eleanor discovered in the third book in the series, *Into the Breach with You*, with the accordion-style pleating of the skirts was real. Later, towards the end of the century, women climbed in trousers and changed into skirts to pose for sketches and even photographs.

But Alpine climbing was an evolving sport, and as more women climbed, more men complained, eventually spurring A.F. Mummery, a renowned male climber of the late 19th century, to quip, "all mountains pass through three stages—An inaccessible peak—The hardest climb in the Alps—an easy day for a lady." He was climbing with Lily Bristow at the time, who often led her expeditions, as she was a superior climber in the steep rocks. He did give her praise for her technique, but while Lily Bristow climbed in the 1890s, it wasn't until the 1940s that her posthumous letters were printed by the *Alpine Journal*.

For the writing of this series, I used a number of resources, but mainly Edward Whymper's account of his climb in *Scrambles in the Alps*, and the first-person accounts of women climbers collected in *Mountaineering Women* edited by David Mazel. The account of Meta Brevoort climbing a mountain called the Bietschhorn (12,970 feet elevation) was published in 1872 in the *Alpine Journal*, and written with clever pronoun games to disguise the author's gender, as the *Alpine Journal* was a men-only publication at the time. This tidbit, of course, inspired Ophelia's arc for publishing in The Royal Geographical Society.

As for The Royal Geographical Society, it was a highly prestigious organization in the 19th century. While the men who ran the organization were largely commoners, aristocrats who fancied adventure were recruited to be the "face" of the group. They sponsored many explorers and adventurers, and while they initially believed in science above all else, this later, disgustingly, became the basis of a Eugenics movement at the end of the 19th century.

I didn't want to overly complicate the plot by having both The Royal Geographical Society and the Alpine Club, so I combined them into one entity for the purposes of these novels. However, it is interesting to note that during the time period I write about, noted mountaineer Leslie Stephens was president of the Alpine Club (1865-1868) and editor of the *Alpine Journal* (1868-1872). The reason why this is interesting, aside from his numerous first ascents in the Alps, was that he was the father of noted lady scribbler Virginia Woolf.

Over the century to come, many women climbed, made first ascents, and contributed to the sport (including inventing the first climbing harness). However, like many sports where the early presence of women was deemed distasteful, they were ignored, or at best, used initials and pronouns to hide their gender. The twentieth century improved upon that state, but I still hope that the contributions of women can be remembered by modern public.

Women athletes are not abnormal or new.

About the Author

Edie Cay writes steamy feminist historical romance. Her debut, A LADY'S REVENGE won the Golden Leaf Best First Book (2020), as well as the Indie Next Generation Book Award (2020). The second in her series, THE BOXER AND THE BLACKSMITH won the Hearts Through History Legends Award, A Man for All Reason in 2019 as an unpublished manuscript, and then went on to win the Best Indie Book Award (2021). The third book, A LADY'S FINDER was a finalist for a Lambda Award, the most prestigious LGBTQ+ literary award in the world. A VISCOUNT'S VENGEANCE garnered the Best Indie Book Award for Regency Romance as well in 2023.

Previously, she published short stories, poems, and non-fiction in small presses. She co-wrote and starred in several short films and documentaries from MadLaw Media, including "Big 5 Dive" about scuba diving in the Great Lakes, and "How to Be Sexy," a fictional short about confidence and self-worth.

She obtained dual BAs in Creative Writing and in Music from Cal State East Bay, and her MFA in Creative Writing from University of Alaska Anchorage. She has been a professional musician, bookstore employee, and a healthcare worker.

She has participated in several anthologies, including Unlocked, The Grand Mistletoe Assembly, and the upcoming Beneath the Midwinter Moon.

Her next series will be about Victorian women alpinists, out in August 2024 from Dragonblade Publishing.

She is a founding member of the historical fiction collective The Paper Lantern Writers, and helps edit and publish their anthologies. She gives presentations at conferences around the world on the history of women's boxing and other aspects of Regency culture and writing.

In addition to fiction, Edie writes and reviews for the Historical Novel Society. You can keep up with her on her website, www.ediecay.com, or follow her on Instagram or Facebook @authorEdieCay.